The Best Worst Mistake

ALSO BY LILY PARKER

OFF-LIMITS SERIES
Book 1: The Best Wrong Move
Book 2: The Best Worst Mistake
Book 3: The Best Wild Idea

The Best Worst Mistake

LILY PARKER

Choc Lit
A JOFFE BOOKS COMPANY

Choc Lit, London
A Joffe Books company
www.choc-lit.com

First published in Great Britain in 2025

© Lily Parker

This book is a work of fiction. Names, characters, businesses, organizations, places and events are either the product of the author's imagination or are used fictitiously. Any resemblance to actual persons, living or dead, events or locales is entirely coincidental. The spelling used is American English except where fidelity to the author's rendering of accent or dialect supersedes this. The right of Lily Parker to be identified as author of this work has been asserted in accordance with the Copyright, Designs and Patents Act 1988.

No part of this book may be used or reproduced in any manner for the purpose of training artificial intelligence technologies or systems. In accordance with Article 4(3) of the Digital Single Market Directive 2019/790, Joffe Books expressly reserves this work from the text and data mining exception.

Cover art by Rachel Lawston at Lawston Design

ISBN: 978-1781898567

*For your best friend who deserves everything,
but doesn't know it yet.*

CHAPTER 1

Abby

Anyone here could be the cup's rightful owner, I think, glancing through the swarm of people crowded into Carrie's coffee shop. I dab the back of my hand across my lips, trying to get rid of the evidence that I've just hijacked someone else's drink, but a few green speckles circle the lid already — right where my berry-pink lipstick stain has just marked the whole thing as stolen.

Shit.

I sniff the to-go cup. "What was that?" I mutter. *And who orders grass-colored, seaweed-flavored muck when macchiatos and lattes are on the menu?*

I squint at the cup in my hand. A name scribbled across the middle is illegible except for a rather large D at the start — *oh, hello there, old friend. A sign that I need more of you, perhaps?* I snort to myself, thinking I must ignore the subtle nudge from the universe that I need more capital D in my life (especially if it tastes like that).

I stick the cup back on the counter and step away. Probably should have caught that *before* stealing a swig and upsetting my taste buds.

"Please tell me this is just a fun prank you've pulled and that's not someone's actual order?" I ask, pointing to it.

Carrie, the owner of the shop, swipes a bead of sweat from her brow and eyes the pink O wrapped around the mouth hole.

"A far cry from your usual." She nods toward it. "But maybe that'll teach you not to swipe other people's orders."

"Sorry." I scrunch my nose. "I'll Venmo you for that."

"Don't be silly," she says, shooing the offer away with a swipe of her hand. "I'll just make another for that guy, wherever he went." She glances around the shop. "A little vanilla or honey usually helps the flavor on those matcha lattes, but we can forgive him for not adding it. He was hot."

I follow her eyes, looking for the missing owner but no one seems to be rushing to grab it.

"I do feel like I might have just saved some poor health nut from a very unfortunate situation this morning. Death by green froth," I tell her. "Your new guy must have made that one."

She nods and gets to work on the next drink, looking happy to have a momentary distraction from the growing line behind the register.

I scan the crowd again, mentally preparing an apology for the moment some healthier-than-average customer makes their way over and points to the lipstick I accidentally left behind on their cup.

"Maybe I'll buy him a donut to make up for it," I tell her, over the whirring vibration of the espresso machine to my right.

Carrie snorts and shakes her head.

Ha. Can't imagine how well that would go over. I've been coming to this coffee shop long enough to know that you don't get between a New Yorker and their morning caffeine if you value your life.

"By the way, is there any caffeine in that?" I ask.

"Not compared to your triple shot," she says. *Damn.* I'm going to need the extra caffeine if I'm going to get through the latest merger Brett plopped on my desk over the weekend.

Carrie's hands fly through routine, making another order, not missing a beat of the careful concocting going on behind the counter. Steaming milk, pouring espresso over ice, wiping up a spot with the corner of her apron, dunking little silver pitchers under a soapy stream of water. She once told me that manning the counter here is like a meditation practice since she hardly has to think about what she's doing anymore. At least that's the case *most* mornings. Today isn't counting toward her meditation practice from what I can tell. In fact, the last two weeks have been more stressful than most, ever since her new hire came on board.

"So, you're saying it has less caffeine than a mocha, tastes like it was made from boiled seaweed, and people still pay money for it?" I push the cup a few inches further away from me, like it might jump back into my hand if I allow it to sit too close.

"It's supposedly healthy," she says, cracking a smile. "I think the green color sways people." Carrie looks unfazed, like she's heard this assessment of the matcha a few times.

After hearing a small crash, she plants her feet to watch her new hire, who just so happens to be her nephew, which, in most instances, would be amazing, I think. Except, in this case, her nephew also happens to be an imbecile.

"I'll get to your order in a sec, Abby. As long as I can keep the customers from rioting," she adds, narrowing her eyes at the people lined up behind the register.

There's more than one person tapping their foot, but most of them are silently staring toward the front like maybe if they glare hard enough, the queue will start moving faster.

"I wish I could help but I would only make this worse, so, really, no rush," I tell her, brushing a few crumbs off the counter. "I'd rather be here than heading into the office anyway. People-watching in here during rush hour is like watching Bravo TV. Intense, a bit over the top, full of drama, and yet, oddly satisfying."

"Right?" She finally grins, looking around at the New Yorkers lining the walls. "Mornings in this city rarely disappoint.

Although, I think I've said the word *sorry* so many times in the last two weeks that half-hearted apologies are the only language I speak now."

She grabs another cup then writes my name across it, even though I'm standing right here. Probably for the best, considering I just stole someone else's.

"You could just have him unload boxes in the back. Or tell him the shop burned down later this evening and you regret to inform him that he no longer has a job?" I offer.

She shrugs absentmindedly while he attempts to froth a little pitcher of milk, but the silver wand is screaming in a very not-frothy way. Even with my very limited coffee-making knowledge, I can tell he didn't shove it down far enough.

"I could. I *should*," she admits. "But he's *family*, you know?"

No, I don't know, I want to tell her. Instead, I nod and say, "Right," like I know what that type of familial bond feels like. A bond made with blood instead of broken promises. One that exists only because you're supposed to look out for each other. Like it's written in the stars, or the laws of nature, or something — a universal connection based solely on shared DNA.

"What does *skim* mean?" her nephew calls out.

I bite my thumbnail while Carrie's chest rises and falls. She barks at him to stop making drinks and go handle the cash register since the line is nearly out the door — a risk, for sure, since it's one more task the kid's not yet mastered.

I start to ask if putting him behind the register right now is the best idea, but the look in Carrie's eyes brings my lips to a tight close.

"You're right, I'm sure he'll catch on by the end of the day," I say, nodding enthusiastically. "Maybe make some flash cards for him to study. Start with all the different types of milk."

Even after a few weeks of Carrie training him around the clock, the kid still looks hopeless — he has finally managed to turn the cash register on but is now struggling to put a guy's order in.

The customer's angular, bird-like face is growing increasingly red while her nephew starts relying on his good looks and charm to get him through the complicated order. This only deepens the bird guy's anger — since there's nothing cute or charming about a lack of coffee.

Bird Man is now nearly yelling his order in a thick Brooklyn accent, which somehow makes the whole interaction even more intimidating.

Carrie pauses the steam wand she's dug into a pitcher (correctly, I might add), but her breath picks up speed and she manically chews her bottom lip while she watches the two men.

We simultaneously suck in a breath when her nephew gives up and starts writing the guy's order on a little pad of paper beside the machine.

I want to cover my eyes.

This kid even writes slowly.

I strangle a smile just as Carrie shoots me the type of expression she might dole out if her dog was suffering from a painfully slow-moving porcupine attack.

Three groans rise up from the growing line behind Bird Man from Brooklyn, whose distinctive features have taken on an aggressively crimson hue.

I steal a glance at my watch, knowing my boss is going to have a conniption fit when he arrives at the office and I'm not sitting at my desk. My response will be, *"Brett, I slept on the iron platform you call a futon in my office again last night, and was up working before sunrise for the twelfth day in a row. So if you could just let this one longer-than-usual caffeine break slide..."*

"He's not going to last, is he?" I squeeze the words out the side of my mouth, wishing I had my mocha to sip on while watching the train wreck unfold.

She tosses a little pastry bag at me from the pile of yesterday's spoils before shuffling toward her nephew. I catch it and find a crisp mini almond croissant inside, which Carrie knows to be my favorite. My stomach rumbles at the smell.

"Godspeed!" I call out watching her approach her nephew who's started reading a dusty collection of old papers stapled together. Probably the original handbook for the register.

Carrie's going to eat him for breakfast.

My stomach growls again.

I lean back to watch the drama play out, reaching into the waxy bag, tearing little bits of pastry off before popping them into my mouth, thankful to have something to snack on for the show.

"Mmm," I groan, ripping off another bite.

"Those any good?" a man's voice pipes up beside me. I hardly hear him over the noise of the steaming wand the new guy is operating incorrectly, again.

"Very." I don't look over. Not when Bird Man is pointing a long, skinny finger at both of them, while Carrie does her best to defuse the situation with a giant smile plastered across her face. If I didn't know her so well, I'd think that smile was genuine, but I can tell she's well past the end of her rope.

I chew slowly, thinking back to my own first job. I'd accidentally spilled thirty-two ounces of root beer across the lap of some poor dad on my second day waitressing tables at Pizza Hut. His wife had sat beside him, silently opening and shutting her mouth like a guppy when, without thinking, I'd placed an entire stack of napkins across his wet crotch — just doing my best to be helpful. I'm pretty sure I'm blushing at the memory of trying to take the stack of napkins back off her husband's soaking wet lap upon realizing what I'd just done. She'd smacked my hands away, saying my assistance was no longer needed.

I tuck away the memory.

First jobs are brutal.

"You've hired an imbecile!" Bird Man yells, pointing his beak at Carrie.

"New Yorkers, eh?" The same baritone voice beside me barely cuts through the noise of the bustling shop. There's something about his voice that strikes a familiar chord. "Real passionate bunch."

"Mmm," I mumble, tearing off a long strip. It's covered in sliced almonds and the powdered sugar dusted across the top melts in my mouth.

"I'll have that right out for you, and it's *on the house*," Carrie says, announcing those three magical words that every customer loves to hear. It's definitely the right move since the customer's veins have started protruding from both sides of his scrawny neck. Finally, the guy tips back on his heels, relenting with a tight line for a mouth.

"Alright," he grumbles. "Make it a big one then."

"The biggest," Carrie assures him, her smile growing wider and more unhinged by the moment. "Next!"

Bird Man steps aside and I fight the urge to clap.

"That owner is unshakable," the persistent guy beside me adds. "I might have decked that guy if I were her."

"Mmm, K," I reply, doing my best not to encourage the man by engaging in any small talk.

New Yorkers don't do polite chit-chat with strangers. Especially at this time of day, and especially if it can be avoided. So whoever is talking to the side of my head right now must be from out of town.

Carrie murmurs something to Bird Man that's apparently charming enough to make him bust out a genuine, real-deal laugh. *Nice touch*. Then she comes around the side of the counter a moment later to pat him around the back while handing him the biggest Americano I've ever seen.

He slips a ten-dollar bill into the tip jar beside her.

"That's for you," he tells her. "Not your dimwit at the register."

"Sorry 'bout that, Joel," she says, apologetically.

"See you tomorrow," he tells her.

She leads him to the door as if she's ending a dinner party with her closest friend in tow.

I beam at her, throwing out a thumbs-up.

"Is this my matcha order?" the out-of-towner beside me asks. Something in me might be able to place that voice if I got a look at him.

Out of the corner of my eye, I catch his hand reaching to grab the drink off the counter — the one I've already taken a sip of and nearly spit back into the cup.

Shit.

"I'm sorry, I thought it was mine and already drank—" I start to say, ready to steal it back out of his hands, but when I turn, I'm met with two prominent pec muscles beneath a sturdy black shirt.

I follow the trail of buttons up to a pair of deep-set hazel eyes. I gasp.

My jaw falls open.

I blink up at him.

The man grins, his perfect lips stretching wide like Brad Pitt in his younger years. A perfect professional cut of wavy, sun-streaked hair falls just above his brows before he brushes it back with a quick pass of his hand, bringing my attention to the very same hazel eyes I've stared into a thousand times before — usually from some unnatural angle while he's making me scream out his name at least once, if not two or three times in a row.

CHAPTER 2

My stomach flips end over end while Dax and I grin at each other like a couple of school-age kids about to cause some serious mischief. His face is six years older, but his eyes are the exact same, crinkling up at the edges, as if not a single day has passed since we stood a few inches apart. Playful, intense, leaving me with nowhere to hide — even if I wanted to.

As if driven by muscle-memory, my feet rise up to the tips of my toes and I launch myself against his chest, wrapping him into a hug so tight that I manage to surprise myself. Pressing my cheek into the wide ribcage surrounding his heart — I can tell it's beating fast, just as fast as mine. Maybe even faster.

He feels warm. Familiar. *Safe*.

My hug throws him off balance and he takes half a step back before holding me firmly like an anchor, returning an embrace that's somehow, someway, even tighter than mine. He laughs into my hair and I close my eyes to soak in the sound — the vibration of it, deliciously intimate, even in a crowded room.

When was the last time I was pressed into someone like this?

It must have been the last time I was hugged by him.

Six whole years ago and yet my body is responding as if it's been only a few hours instead of two thousand and ninety-something days.

Dax Harper. My whole world slows down. Sights and sounds and smells all fading away until it's just the beat of our hearts and four arms overlapping, a feeling I haven't had since he — since we — well, since the day I ghosted him six years ago.

I release him suddenly and take a step back, fully aware of how eager that must have looked, considering I was the one to put all the time and space between us.

"Dax?" I clear my throat. Okay, that came out way too high-pitched and borderline squeaky to get away with being cool, calm, or collected right now.

Rein it in, girl.

I suck in two lungs' worth of air and exhale as slowly as I can manage without choking on the oxygen leaving my body, doing whatever I can to sound more casual the next time words emerge from me.

"Abby," he says through a slow smile — all gravelly and smooth and deeply baritone, yet a bit clipped and breathy, somehow all at the same time. It's only one word but now that I'm looking at him, it takes me back to the dozens of nights we spent talking in hushed tones about nothing in particular. Lying in his bed, the world would stop spinning just long enough for me to close my eyes and listen to him deliver the happenings of his day as our pulses quietly slowed back to normal.

We'd lie there while he gave me a humorous rundown of what his plans were once our law school cleared out for Christmas break, or Easter back at home with his parents in L.A. So many nights I'd promise myself just five more minutes beside him as he dragged his fingertips up and down the softness of my wrist and I listened to his heartbeat. And then I'd leave, closing the door behind me, never allowing myself to stay long enough to see the sunrise through his cheap university blinds because we weren't those types of people. We were the types of people that made ourselves wave goodbye before we could ever be considered more than two humans who simply liked to get lost in each other's bodies. Anything more than that was something I couldn't imagine having, or sticking around for.

But that was so long ago.

Besides, what are the odds?

We grin at each other, playing an old, familiar game with our eyes until we both laugh in disbelief. He drags me back in for a second embrace, but we both pull away faster this time.

"I thought you were in L.A. What are you doing here?" I ask, proud of myself for sounding downright chill this time instead of like a breathy, high-pitched school girl nursing an ancient crush.

"Apparently getting my drink order stolen by the most gorgeous woman at the only coffee shop in the city to be taken over by an angry mob this morning," he says, nodding toward the crowd of customers.

"Oh, I highly doubt that last part," I tell him, grinning. "This *is* New York, after all."

"You mean there are other mobs storming coffee shops?"

"Are you kidding me?" I lower my voice, as if sharing a secret. The scent of his cologne makes me even more hungry for him. "At this very moment, I can guarantee that at least fourteen other coffee shops are getting stormed by under-caffeinated mobs. If you close your eyes and listen hard enough, you can usually hear them chanting."

The edges of his mouth curve up like a bow — like a present meant only for me.

"Is that right?" he asks.

"Mmm, it is," I manage to say, stealing a glance at his lips. "I'm rarely wrong."

"Except for when you chose this coast over the one I'm on," he says, arching one of his thick brows.

I scoff. "Rookie move."

He suddenly leans closer, with a smile filling his whole face, sending my heart racing all over again. In my wildest imagination he's about to kiss me, but it's only to let someone reach behind him for their order.

I exhale slowly.

"It's been, what, at least five years?" I ask, taking a step back to put a little more space between us. "Maybe six?"

He looks up to the ceiling, searching his memory for the last time we saw each other, and I take it as my opportunity to soak in his every detail.

The sturdy length of his hands.

The razor-sharp cut of his jaw, clean shaven and smooth.

The taste of his—

No.

His eyes zip back to mine as if he's just heard my thoughts, and I snap back to the present, blinking innocently.

No, I'm not standing here conjuring up memories of what those hands — your hands — are capable of doing to my body, Dax. Don't be silly.

"I haven't seen you since graduation," he confirms.

We both graduated magna cum laude from Northwestern Pritzker School of Law. Wore matching sashes and everything, although there's only one photo in existence of Dax and I together. It's of us standing awkwardly, not touching, in graduation gowns, right outside the university's enormous auditorium doors. My best friend Olivia had suggested we take the photo when we crossed paths with Dax after the ceremony was done, insisting — no, hissing into my ear — that I would want photographic evidence of the years we spent together. More than together, in the most *together* way possible, while never actually putting a label on it. He towered above me in that photo, even though I was wearing my first set of sky-high stilettos, the pair Olivia had let me borrow that day. She had shown up as my only plus-one during the ceremony. In the photo, Dax is beaming at the camera, his hair longer than it is now and streaked by the midwestern sun that'd started shining earlier than usual that spring. His hazel eyes squint out toward the cotton-candy-pink sunset behind Olivia and her phone, making us look as though we are both bathed in gold, his eyes more translucent than they'd ever appeared in the dim light of his bedroom.

The only thing that's changed about him now is his hair. It's shorter, styled into a more professional cut, but everything else about him could have been clipped straight out of that photograph and pasted into the coffee shop right in front of me.

"So, six years, and some change," he says.

I shrug, as if I didn't know the exact count in my head.

"You're still living on the west coast?" I ask.

"You mean the *best* coast?" he corrects. *His voice just dropped an octave.*

"You can't call it that until you've spent some real time on this side of the country," I tell him, squeezing him gently on that boulder attached to his arm. We'll call it a shoulder. The same shoulder I used to cling to when he'd be pushing into me from—

No, girl, no.

Stay focused.

I clear my throat, calling upon the skills I've perfected to keep my cool after a few years' worth of experience commanding the attention of a courtroom, conference room, or any room really that needs a top-tier attorney to do an important job. Even when I'm short of breath and my knees are buckling.

I straighten my spine when another customer reaches around me to grab their order off the counter, bringing us closer together.

"I'm not sure I need to spend more time here to know that my coast is the clear winner," he says, nodding toward the unruly line.

His eyes dart toward the people piled behind the register, the ones starting to rebel angrily again since Carrie allowed her nephew to return to taking orders while she catches up on a growing number of drinks still needing to be made. The shop around us has grown more packed and we're getting crunched together like sardines, which isn't necessarily a bad thing.

His eyes fall back to mine, as if daring me to object.

"In defense of New York's commuter crowd, caffeine withdrawal is real," I say, tilting my chin defiantly. "Overpowering, I hear."

"Evidently," he answers grimly, rubbing his jaw. This conversation is getting so ridiculous that I'm not even sure we're talking about coffee anymore.

He pulls a stray hair from my shoulder and for the smallest fraction of a second, I feel the heat of his fingers push through the fabric and onto my skin.

Lord help me.

"So, then what are you here for?" I ask. "Your mom's firm isn't forcing you to move across the country now, are they?"

I blink away any possible excitement at Dax and I being in the same city again for any substantial length of time. Successfully controlling everything about my expression — at least until Dax's face curls up into a smirk. Then heat rushes down my spine and I can tell his thoughts are right there with me.

"You'd hate that, wouldn't you?" he asks.

A teacup of anticipation tips over in my stomach, sending fizzy bubbles of hope swirling around like that science model of a tornado that my fourth-grade teacher had us make using a couple of two-liter soda bottles.

Before I can get too ahead of myself, he adds, "I'm just here for a quick work trip. I fly back to L.A. in the morning."

The faint note of relief I hear in his voice is enough for me to mentally pop each bubble of hope I'd felt rising in my chest with an imaginary pushpin.

Without even thinking, I glance down at his ring finger.

Empty.

So blissfully empty.

But when my eyes meander back up to his, Dax is barely holding in a laugh.

Caught.

So clearly caught.

He holds up his ring finger.

"All you had to do was ask if I was single, Abs." He wiggles it back and forth.

I roll my eyes and scoff, not once but twice, hoping to distract us both from the thin veil of pink I can feel creeping across my cheeks.

"Don't act like you're not equally checking out my status," I say, holding up my empty left hand, wagging my finger around so he doesn't have to hide his own curious attempt to look. Although, I wouldn't mind watching him squirm while he tried.

"I don't need to look," he says. "I already saw your profile pop up on Rumble right after we landed."

"Ah." I force a tight smile. "How serendipitous."

He leans his back against the counter, watching me turn red while his lips turn up into the most wicked grin.

"So, unless you're hiding on the dating apps out of pure disdain for your current boyfriend, then I'd assume you're single for now, too."

That cute little flutter inside me grows into a full-blown rabble of butterflies, threatening to beat their wings right out of me.

He's single.

And sexy and sharp and incredibly handsome.

Fuck.

"Here's your triple, hon," Carrie says, passing the to-go cup over the counter ledge between us.

I take it and shoot her a silent look that says we have much to discuss.

"Thanks," I say, coolly. "I need this more than usual. Brett has been riding my ass like you wouldn't believe."

"Mmm, lucky Brett," Dax mutters, almost too quietly for me to hear, tipping his cup up toward mine in a silent *cheers*.

I watch him draw the cup up to his lips in slow motion, still stuck on that little quip of his, before it dawns on me that he's about to drink that nasty green thing I sampled earlier.

I nearly push it out of his hands.

"You don't have to drink that," I say, pointing to the rim where my lipstick outlines the hole in the top. "I already had a sip of that before I realized it wasn't mine. My bad."

He looks down at the smudge of pink, then brings it back up to his lips and takes a long drag anyway, keeping his eyes fixed on mine before tucking his lips inside his mouth to lick them clean. He finishes by dragging his bottom lip across his teeth, almost as if he's scraping off any transferred lipstick. As if that's not enough, he tops things off with the most stupidly attractive little smirk, dropping his free hand into the pocket of his trousers to watch me react.

I bite down on my own lip — a poor defense, but the only option I have to keep myself from drooling on the floor after watching that little . . . what was that?

Did he just lick my lipstick off his cup on purpose?

A flash of his tongue swipes across his bottom lip before he breaks into an even wider grin, as if to erase any doubt from my mind.

Um, yes, yes, he really did.

A shade of pink (most likely darker than the lipstick Dax just *licked off his cup*) creeps across my skin and I force myself to look away before my reaction gets any more obvious.

"I've missed that," he says, swiping the back of his finger across my cheek, so lightly that I'm not sure if he actually made contact with my skin or I imagined it. "The way you go pink like that."

Unable to form words, I turn to Carrie for help. She's still watching us from behind the counter with an amused look on her face.

I widen my eyes at her and, on cue, she springs back to life.

"I, uh, here, let me make you another one of those," Carrie stumbles through her offer, looking guilt-ridden, like she shouldn't be watching whatever is unfolding between me and the unbelievably hot guy who ordered the healthy green thing. She passes off another subtle look that says *you're going to spill all the tea on this later* before attempting to grab the old cup out of Dax's hand.

But he pulls it into his chest.

"Nah," he says, looking at me, holding the cup tighter. "That's alright. I prefer this one."

I exhale all the oxygen I have left in my lungs.

Fuck me.
No, really.
Please.

CHAPTER 3

Carrie glances back and forth between Dax and me, completely immersed in whatever is building between us.

"Suit yourself!" she says cheerfully before turning to me with her lips still pursed and one eyebrow turned up. "But the next one is on the house. I'm not entirely sure how drinkable that one was. My very hard-working, but under-achieving, nephew seems to be allergic to New York coffee culture."

"I'm not the least bit sorry," Dax says, keeping his eyes on me.

He takes another drag from the cup, which sends blood pumping down all four of my limbs and I have to shift on my feet to make sure they're still planted on the ground. Carrie smiles back at me, not blinking.

"Right," I announce, still reeling from the way he practically just sucked my lip mark off his cup.

Dax gives Carrie a little nod goodbye then turns toward the door, extending his hand, a signal for us to walk out together. My shoulder brushes his arm while he's holding the door open and it sends my pulse flying.

Cool it, Abs. This is just a random meeting over random coffee. You're probably about to walk in opposite directions, back to your own corners of the world.

My stomach drops at the thought, unsure of what'll happen next.

"Which way are you heading?" he asks.

I point, and Dax grabs my arm, looping it through his elbow, holding me close to him as the morning crowd rushes down the sidewalk all around us. He walks slower than all of them, forcing us to shorten our pace until it feels like we're taking a Sunday stroll through Central Park instead of being lost inside the herd of commuters pounding down the pavement.

My mind and body fiercely deliberate as we walk. Pleasure versus logic, touch versus trouble. Each part of me remembers everything that unfolded between us, and yet nothing in me seems to have learned any hard and fast lessons from the last time things ended between us.

The last time I ended things between us.

I close my eyes and relinquish control, letting him lead me for a moment so I can collect myself while feeling his body press against my side. This invisible thread between us feels more like a power line, bouncing electricity back and forth as I do my best not to react.

"What brought you to New York?" I ask.

"I was supervising a few of our newest junior partners here in a negotiation. But I just got the call that they won, so I fly back to L.A. tomorrow."

"You're *supervising* junior partners?" I manage to kick out a weak laugh at the end. It would be funny knowing Dax was here to supervise a group of *junior partners* if it wasn't for the fact that it's just plain annoying.

"You know how *junior* partners can be," he adds, sarcastically.

"Not yet. I just got promoted to senior associate, and I was pretty proud of myself for that until just this very moment, actually, so thank you very much."

I bump his hip with my elbow.

He bumps me back gently, but the placement of his elbow against my ribcage, right where my bra line hugs my skin, catches a breath in my throat.

"I told you to come work for me after we graduated. I know you were hell-bent on joining one of those big national firms here, but I would have promoted you a long time ago." His tone is light, but I know he's serious.

I scoff, thinking of how to change the subject. There's another reason I didn't follow him to L.A., and it has nothing to do with me turning down the job offer from his mother's firm.

He continues, "Then again, I'm not sure I could have managed to supervise you without making it horribly obvious to the other associates that you were" — he clears his throat — "my favorite."

I don't look over, but my body pounds in response. I focus on walking straight instead of stumbling over every crack in the sidewalk that's suddenly jumping up to greet me.

"Probably for the best that you turned me down since that sort of thing in the workplace isn't really looked upon highly these days," he adds.

Lord help me not to fall.

"Dax Harper," I say, shaking my head. "All these years later and you haven't changed at all, have you?" I stop abruptly so he'll face me. Then I can't help it. I grin at him as if not one single day has passed. His eyes meet mine, and I know he's right there with me.

"Some things never change," he says, dropping his voice, like a secret between old friends. "At least that's what I'm hoping, running into you like this."

I swallow, conjuring up every bit of my self-control as we start walking again.

"Oh, that was a long time ago," I remind him, briskly. "Before . . ."

But I don't finish.

I feel his eyes on me as we walk. *How is this happening?* Here we are, after accidentally swapping saliva on the rim of his cup two thousand miles away from the last time we rolled out of bed together.

Without any warning, Dax plants a foot squarely in front of me on the pavement, bringing us both to a halt.

I nearly run my mocha into his belt, then I look up at him, squinting into the morning sunlight streaming out from behind his head. His eyes, suddenly serious, stare down into mine.

"What are you doing later?" He knit his brows together, as if asking that question just took on some new level of concentration.

I start, "Well, I'm—"

"Nah, fuck it. Cancel whatever plans you have. Let me take you out."

"Take me out?" I blink up at him.

He nods, grinning again, like nothing about this idea is out of the blue for us. When in fact, everything about this idea is out of the blue for us.

"We don't really *go out*," I remind him, slowly. "We've never gone out for dinner. Hell, we've never even gone out for coffee. So, if you mean you'd like to see my apartment later, I can certainly—"

"Exactly," he says, stopping me again. "All the more reason why we should. Me taking you out will give us a chance to catch up. Properly. Not on a sidewalk with all eight million New Yorkers heading into work. Let's make a date out of it."

He pulls me back as a teenager on a hoverboard swerves past us, narrowly missing my toe.

I brush my hair back, flustered. "A date? *Us*?" I start my poor excuse for deflection, but the look on his face brings my lips to a close. "Okay, what?" I ask. He's barely holding in a laugh. "What's that look for?"

"Nothing." He purses his lips.

I raise a brow, waiting for him to go on.

"It's just . . ."

I raise my other brow to match the first, waiting for him to finish. "What?"

"Consider it highly overdue then. I should have taken you out properly back when we were — well, you know. Back when we were . . . whatever we were."

I drop a hand to my hip.

"You really don't have to make up for lost time," I assure him, my own lips deceiving me at the thought of Dax and I sharing a meal over the top of a bread basket. Hardly our style. My top teeth clamp down on my bottom lip to stop myself from giving a full-on-shit-eating-grin over this — very out of left field — dinner proposal from a man I've fantasized about spending just one more night with.

"It'll be fun." He tilts his head. "You do still have fun, don't you?"

"I know plenty of things that are fun," I say, lowering my voice. "None of which need to involve white tablecloths and a dinner bill."

"Ah, a white tablecloth." He snaps his fingers. "Excellent idea."

I stifle a laugh. "That wasn't a suggestion."

"I take it back. Asking was just a nicety. I'm not giving you a choice." I watch his eyes darken into that *I'm in charge now* look that he used to give me right before completely dominating every last inch of my body. He adds, "You know what?"

I grimace, almost afraid of what he's going to say next. I shouldn't be so anxious over the idea of catching up with an old friend over dinner, but this isn't just any old friend. And what sounds like a simple dinner has the potential to open up a whole can of worms that I'm not sure I woke up this morning wanting to open.

"What?' I ask, scrunching my nose.

"It's happening." He gently presses a finger into my chest, just below the line of my collarbone, then nods, topping it with that unmistakably mischievous grin — the one that makes my skin prickle, just waiting for him to make good on his silent promise of good things to come. "I didn't know if I'd run into you while I was in New York this week, but now that I have, it just seems like some sort of a sign."

"A sign?" I ask, weakly.

"It's happening."

I part my lips, waiting for the correct words to come out, the ones that let him down easy. We excel in the bedroom, but dinner outside the bedroom? We're talking uncharted territory here.

My jaw hinges open and shut as I stand frozen on the sidewalk.

It took me too long to forget Dax the last time we had a chance at making a real go of things together. I haven't gone out with anyone in months, hell, at this point it might be years! And it's suited me just fine.

I'm married to my work. I practically live at the office.

I have goals that can't be derailed by some guy — *this* guy — taking up space in my head.

I'm not even sure I have time for dinner out, or a good romp in bed if that's where this is all headed. Even if it's the kind of romp that makes me want to pull my own hair, and curls my toes, because it feels so fucking amazing to have him with me that I can't think of anything else but the way his tongue has itself wrapped around mine while he grabs my face and pulls me back and—

Nope, don't even go there, Abs.

He starts to walk backward in front of me now, grinning like a Cheshire cat, egging me on for an answer. I just shake my head, laughing at the look on his face until it hits me squarely in the gut.

This isn't just anyone asking me out.

It's Dax.

The one man I've never been fully able to forget.

He stops walking a few feet in front of me, and then . . . If lowering his voice is meant to draw me in, it works. "You really haven't changed at all, Abs." He shakes his head, running a hand through his hair, like he's still trying to take all of me in.

"I can't believe you're here," I say, quietly. "What the hell kind of luck is this?"

He moves forward, closing the gap between us.

"Then we should make the most of it." Smiling down at me, he's so close that I can feel the vibration of his chest when he speaks. Then he studies my eyes, tucking a stray hair behind my ear. It sends a delicious wave of desire though me. "What's this look for?"

I narrow my eyes, wishing he could just read my mind instead of me having to spell it out for him. "Are you really ready to open up that can of worms again?" I ask.

"It's only dinner," he says casually, but his grin says otherwise. I look at him skeptically. "Alright, gorgeous, don't tell me you're afraid of actually falling for me if we spend a little more time on opposite sides of a tablecloth tonight?" His eyes darken. "Maybe a candle or two?"

I laugh, and push him aside to start walking again, like what he's just said is utterly ridiculous when really, what I want to say is, *Yes, Dax Harper, that's exactly what I'm afraid of.*

CHAPTER 4

Dax, one week ago

Silas is standing by the wall of windows in my office. A dart is pinched between his forefinger and thumb, brows raised in disbelief like he can't believe I'd have the audacity to say no to him.

His point has already been accentuated by the last dart he let fly into the target on my wall, which narrowly missed the bullseye, landing just outside the center.

"You have to go, bro," Silas insists.

Maybe I *would* be out of my mind to blatantly refuse him.

I pour myself a splash of bourbon from the bar cart I gifted to myself the day my mother, a.k.a. my boss, moved me into this corner office of her L.A. branch. It may seem like a weird gift to oneself when given a gilded prison cell by a parent, but I knew I'd be spending a lot of time here and I wanted to make it more bearable. Particularly when Silas was in town, like he is now.

"What do you think of that stuff, by the way?" he asks, relaxing his brows just long enough to angle the tip of his dart toward the fresh glass of Kavalan in my hand.

Silas' assistant had a case of his favorite bottles sent over before his arrival from Boston last week — Michter's 20 Year, Kavalan Solist Vinho, Old Rip Van Winkle — all at least a few thousand dollars, with the exception of Old Rip. That one cost roughly the same as my first annual salary out of law school. I hadn't had the heart to try it yet. Seemed wrong to open the bottle without him.

"I prefer Maker's Mark," I say, ribbing him a bit before taking a sip.

Shit. Even I can't keep a straight face after tasting that.

"Damn." It comes out more like a sigh and I hold the glass up to my eyes, inspecting the tumbler like it contains actual gold and not just absurdly expensive alcohol. I tip it up toward Silas, showing my approval, watching the way his face morphs into a triumphant grin.

"Don't even bother trying to play me," he says, turning back to the dart board across the room. He narrows his eyes before letting the next one fly, hitting the outer ring of the center. Competitive, even when playing against only himself. "That shit is the best you've ever had and you know it."

I pour a good amount into another glass for him, knowing he won't object, and he clinks it against my own. I hope it's enough of a distraction that he stops peppering me about going to New York for him.

"Now, back to what I was saying," he says. *No luck, of course.* "What's your issue with New York?"

"I don't have a problem with New York," I tell him, tightly. "Lovely time of year to visit. The trees in Central Park are stunning in October, I hear."

"Then explain to me why you're trying to dodge a trip out with the juniors for this negotiation. *You* represent me, bro. Not them."

"The *firm* represents you, Si," I remind him, "and the junior partners are perfectly capable of handling this one without me."

"See, when I think of *the firm*, I think of you. You *are* the firm here," he says.

"My *mother* is the firm," I correct him, referring to the founder and managing partner of the entire Harper and Associates legal operation, which comprises a vast number of offices scattered across the country from here to New York.

"Ah, Mrs. H," he says, smiling, pausing ever so slightly before throwing another dart across the room. This one lands just above the last. "I remember when she dropped you off at the dorm for the first time. Even back then I was right to be terrified of her."

I take another burning sip from my glass, thinking back to the day my mother and father dropped me off at Fox Glenn boarding school.

I was thirteen.

My parents took my body-sized duffel bag into the dorm room, as I watched Grant and Silas, the occupants of the neighboring room, peek their heads around the corner, studying me in the same way you'd study a new pet or a kid that you may want to befriend, or torture, depending on the situation at hand. I stared back at them in that awkward way only young kids can get away with. Lord, I miss being able to size someone up like that. A lot of issues might be cleared up as adults if we could just size one another up outright and without pretense before getting deep in the mix of things.

At first glance, Silas and Grant reminded me of a pair of mismatched socks. The same manner of species in every sort of way, but somehow *different*. Both born and bred to be there — two thirteen-year-old boys who looked just as excited as I felt for an extended adventure away from home. Anxious for that defining moment when all the parents would swipe at their eyes and drive off, leaving us boys on our own for the first time. Away from home for weeks — no, *months* — at a time with only each other to depend on.

My mother, the honorable Mrs. H, had been right to warn me of Si before leaving, while my father merely grinned at the three of us, looking like he must have been remembering what it was like to be a young boy left on his own for the very first time.

Wide-eyed and confident beyond his years, even then, Silas had the look of a kid who charmed the mothers with all the right answers before trying to seduce them once the fathers had left the room. My mother had known with just one look what it took me a whole semester to figure out. That these kids were trouble — the best kind of trouble a boy can have, really. The classic kind of boyhood trouble that movies like *The Sandlot* or *The Goonies* were made of. The type that makes for lifelong friendships and stories retold in wedding toasts for years to come. I hadn't known it then, but those boys — along with my own roommate Ryeson, who would show up a few hours later — would define my childhood, and eventually who I was, long after those more innocent days had ended.

Like all good boarding-school boys, I only heeded my mother's warnings until she was out of the building, and waved dutifully from the window as she and my father drove slowly down the gravel drive. They were barely out of the towering, iron-clad gates of the school before I walked out of my own room, rounded the corner, and went straight into theirs.

We all had a place within that group for the next five years — Grant, Silas, Ryeson, and me. Between the four of us, I was the balancing act. The one who was level-headed *and* charming enough to keep us all enrolled. Like Grant, I was smart as a whip but had the wit to back it up. And thankfully, by that point, I was also cultured enough to know that having street cred with the right administrators was imperative in order to have the freedom to rebel outside the classroom without worrying too much about whether or not I'd be allowed to come back again the following year.

Kids like Grant could recite the handbook while kids like Silas knew it only well enough to know how to break the rules listed inside. And while Ryeson was adept at ignoring the rulebook altogether, I could decipher it. Study it just enough to find the loopholes. Note where the language was just vague enough so that when I was arguing on all of our behalf before the headmaster, I could do so like my mother might.

Like Mrs. H.

"Not enough interest in tech," I'd overheard my father saying one evening in a hushed tone when I was barely eight years old. "He's going to have to follow in your footsteps, Norah, not mine. His future's at the firm, not in my business."

And that was that. My path had been decided. Starting the next day, my mother began grooming me for a future life at her firm. Showing me how to debate each point I made at home, as if I were already stating my case in front of a judge. She taught me — not how to argue — but how to *win*.

And yet, from the age of thirteen, the only person I could *never* win against was the guy throwing darts against my office wall today.

Silas drops onto the leather couch. All this talk about New York has made my memories of Abby resurface, even after I've spent years stuffing them down where they belonged. Out of sight, and out of mind.

"What, you're suddenly afraid of flying?" he asks.

"Don't be ridiculous," I tell him, brushing off the whole line of questioning.

"Do I need to get Ryeson on the phone to give you a little pep talk now that Grant's—?" He's pulled his phone out, like he actually might call Rye. Then his face falls, staring past the phone to the floor. Out of all of us, losing Grant last month hit Silas the hardest. They were always closer than the rest of us, more like brothers than friends, and he gave everything he could trying to save him there at the end. Considering how much Si has gone off the rails recently, I can tell that Grant's death is nearly killing him, too. More than he's willing to admit. First his father — who left his entire empire to Si after his sudden passing two years ago — and then losing his best friend Grant in the last month. The strongest among us would tailspin in both those scenarios, but the pile of money Silas has at his disposal has always made his tailspins particularly epic. Plus, the media has repeatedly reported on his antics to a nauseating degree, since the headline clicks alone are likely making them millions.

I watch him blink, face still frozen, looking toward the floor. It's impossible to ignore the sudden change in his demeanor.

"Si, have you talked to Jules since the . . ." I start to ask, gently, but can't finish. Jules, Grant's fiancée, has been furious at Silas since his father died and the young business heir's shenanigans, with Grant by his side, began to fuel ever-increasing interest from the media.

His eyes ignite, but he ignores the question.

"Ryeson can explain how the company jet works, if that'll get you on it, although the last time I asked him to explain aviation, he just gave me that goofy smile of his and called it *magic*." Silas flutters his hand out like he's spreading imaginary pixie dust across my office, but there's a sharp edge to his voice that wasn't there before.

Ryeson operates the private aviation company that Silas uses to manage his fleet of airliners, all of which were inherited from his father.

"I've never been afraid of flying," I retort, annoyed that I can't seem to shake this conversation topic, though not surprised in the least, given my history of losing against this particular friend. I'm not sure why he trusts me to do his legal work, except for the fact that the book of business was basically passed down to me the day his father — my mother's client — died and Silas was forced to take over the whole Davenport Media empire.

Silas stares at me expectantly, waiting for the gig to be up. For me to tell him why I'm not too keen on the idea of heading back to New York to do his company's bidding. It's a big city, sure, but I haven't seen her in at least six years and I have this strange, gut feeling that if I went, I couldn't trust the universe not to have me bump into her. And then for me to not try to make the most of it when I did.

I run my tongue along my teeth, considering how to put this.

"You represent Davenport Media and all of our dealings," Si says. "You can't just not oversee the negotiations regarding acquisitions in New York without telling me why."

"It's not what you think," I say.

"Then what is it?" He drains his glass in one gulp before setting it down empty, rising to collect the darts from the board. I estimate that gulp cost him a few hundred dollars or so.

I clear my throat, ready to steer the conversation off in another direction, but apparently the pause and tenor of my throat clear is enough for him to see right through me.

"Oh, Jesus Christ, you can't be serious," he says, pushing his forehead into his hand. "You're still hung up on her. You don't want to go because Abby's there." His face morphs into a dark grin. "That must be it. I always knew she was more to you than just a fuck buddy situationship."

"Hey," I say sternly. "Watch your nicknames, Si. She wasn't a—"

"If not a fuck buddy, then what was she, exactly?" he interrupts, throwing another dart at the target on the wall. "In your own words."

I frown, unsure how to label what Abby and I had back in law school. "Abby was—"

"Your girlfriend?"

I scoff. "No."

"Your good-time girl?"

"God, no. What? What does that even mean?" I roll my eyes and turn back toward the cart, throwing the rest of the bourbon down my throat. It burns, but at least it's distracting me from Silas' interrogation. "Not everything needs some ridiculous label."

He narrows his eyes at me, dart paused in his grip, that familiar know-it-all expression stretched wide across his face. "That's what someone who's still hung up on a girl might say."

"Christ, Si, it's been years. Plus, she's the one who never wanted it to be more than a physical thing."

"Beside the point. Listen," he says, turning toward me. "Wouldn't the possibility of tapping that friends-with-benefits whatever" — he pauses to curl his fingers in exaggerated air quotes — "have you racing back over there at the chance? If it was me, I'd be chomping at the bit to stir things up with her again, and you know I would. Abby's hot."

"What am I supposed to do, call her up and say, 'Hey Abby, I know we haven't spoken in six years, but do you want to grab dinner Tuesday night in New York?'"

He blinks at me as if I'm a total idiot. "Yeah. You do it exactly like that. I don't see the problem."

"I don't want another meaningless hookup," I say, cringing at my words as they come streaming out of my mouth. It might be the truth, but Silas isn't going to let me declare something like that and let it slide. "Anyway, she lives on the east coast, and I'm over here. Whatever happened — if something were to happen — it wouldn't last past the night."

"And there's a problem with that?"

I shrug.

"You want a relationship?" he asks, looking more thoughtful than I would have guessed he'd look before that question came out.

"Why are we arguing about some fictitious meet-up that's never going to happen?" I ask, staring across the room. Then I grab another bottle, bracing myself for the onslaught of ribbing about to come my way. "I mean, if we're talking in general, then yeah. I'm getting tired of doing the same shit."

Si lowers the darts. "Yeah, man, I get that."

I stare at him. I would have never pegged this particular friend as a softy in the relationship department. I've watched him bounce between women for nearly two decades now, but maybe losing his father, then Grant, has softened him up just the slightest bit.

"No, seriously. Hooking up with a bunch of women is a riot, don't get me wrong, but there's something pretty empty about it at the end of the day," he admits. "If I could get exactly what I wanted in a woman . . ." — he pauses, that hundred-yard stare taking over his eyes before snapping back to the room — "I would settle down for life, I swear to God."

He doesn't have to say her name for me to know who he's talking about. We both let a moment pass before Silas throws another dart, this one with about half the gumption of the others.

He turns back to me. "Rip off the Band-Aid. Just call her before you go." There's a softer edge to his voice now. "Life is shorter than we know, bro. If you do run into her there, just take her out. See where it goes. Don't be a wuss about it."

I pour another splash of bourbon in my glass, then fix my jaw. "It's highly unlikely I'd run into her anyway," I say, glancing out the window.

"Well, figure it out. You're going next week," he says, pulling the darts off the board and morphing back into client-mode before stalking over to the spot he was throwing from before. He sends another dart flying across the room but it hits the metal rim of the target with a metallic *thud* before bouncing to the floor. "You want me to go with you?" he asks, cocking a brow. Then he shoots me that famous look that gets him plastered all over the tabloid papers as one of the hottest wealthy bachelors under thirty-five. Probably doesn't hurt that he looks more like a fitness model than your typical run-of-the-mill inheritor of a staggering fortune.

"Nope," I say, quicker than I mean to.

He laughs.

I like to think he's only teasing, but Silas is the type that would actually usher me onto his jet if he thought a bit of fun was dangling on the other side of the country. And getting the chance to rib me about Abby — or even track her down, just so he can watch the awkward reunion unfold between us — has Silas written all over it.

"No . . . but thanks," I add in a more subdued tone. The idea of him showing up at the office in New York with Abby under one arm like a little trophy, ready to hand her over to me, makes my stomach roll. "I'll go. You don't have to ask again or threaten to go yourself. Big city, right?" His face shifts wickedly, like I've just given him an idea. "Don't get any ideas, Si," I add, ruefully.

He chuckles. "Dude, you push multi-billion-dollar deals for me without losing any sleep, face down some of the most aggressive attorneys in the country, and yet, you're this concerned over the possibility of running into a fling from forever ago?"

"Six years."

He laughs. "Okay, then, six years. You've had six years to get over this chick. And the chances of running into her are slim to none, like you said. Unless . . ."

Silas pauses to rub the thick stubble across his jaw.

"Unless what?" I ask, hoping to get ahead of whatever he has rolling around that thick skull of his. "Seriously. Just forget I said anything." I hold my palms up as if surrendering. "I'll make sure the juniors get the deal done then be back by the following day. We have to get moving on the Kipsee deal next. No more wasting time on the smaller details of that one. It might be too late to—"

"Just go for it, man." He's pushed back to Abby. "Call her up. Tell her you're going to be there next week. Maybe she'd be up for, oh, I dunno, a private conversation or something. Start there. Did you ever even take her out? Like, properly?"

"What do you know about *properly* taking a woman out?" It's my turn to laugh now.

"Wouldn't you like to know?" Silas winks before holding the last dart up to his eye and taking quick aim. The dart lands squarely in the bullseye with a heavy thud. He turns to me, holding his arms out as if he's just won the lottery, and says, "Now, if that's not a sign of how things are going to go for you when you get there, then I don't know what is. You'll thank me later. Now go tell your PA to book your flight."

CHAPTER 5

Dax, New York

By some miracle, I haven't bumped into any of the fast-footed commuters rushing down the sidewalk in a jumbled heap around me, each like a wild-eyed salmon shooting down the river during spawning season. I continue walking backward with my eyes stuck to Abby's.

I should turn around to make sure I don't accidentally bump into the wrong person, maybe one who won't take it so well, but I don't want to take my eyes off her just yet.

Abby has always been predictably unpredictable. A flight risk if you push her too much, but also likely to hide behind some invisible wall if you don't. If I risk taking my eyes off her now, she might not be there when I turn back. Spooked and lost in the crowd.

"Abs, if this isn't Fate, I don't know what is. And I know you don't want to mess with Fate. She's a real angry son of a gun when you fuck with her." I'm smiling.

Her face melts into the start of a slow-moving smirk.

Time to dig my heels in.

Literally.

We come to a stop, the type of stop that would involve a screeching car sound if we were two characters in a cartoon instead of two caffeinated ex-whatever-we-are on a sidewalk at eight-thirty in the morning.

She nearly bumps into my chest. But, in true Abby form, she avoids my gaze, looking down at her feet, then at a shockingly tall woman passing by, then at a pigeon that's holding an entire quarter hamburger in its beak. She's finding every opportunity on this street to avoid my eyes right now.

What the hell happened between us that you won't even risk getting dinner with me?

I study her face while she feigns distraction. The curve of her nose, leading to a perfect point, nearly elfish in appearance with her tiny features and big, amber eyes — almost always hidden behind a pair of thick, black-rimmed glasses such as she's wearing today. The mop of dark hair pulled up out of her face, wrapped into a messy bun with a pen pulled through it on top, as if holding it up.

When I took that phone call outside the coffee shop nearly an hour ago, finally hearing from the junior team that their last round of negotiations had been successful — Silas would be happy — I'd forgotten about my order on the coffee shop counter. Halfway back to my hotel, I turned around to go back and grab it, knowing I'd be leaving on a flight instead of spending any more time here in New York. I spent the entire walk back to the shop debating whether or not I should just call her up, Silas' words pinging around in my head. See if she was free, because . . . why not?

But — when I'd walked into the coffee shop, ready to grab what was sure to be a lukewarm drink off the counter — I'd seen her.

Against all odds, there she was.

Standing at the pick-up counter. Ripping little pieces of a pastry out of a bag and popping them into her mouth as she watched an argument unfold between the guy behind the register and an angry customer a few feet away.

I barely felt the smile that stretched across my face while I watched her chatting with the woman behind the counter, debating whether or not I should walk back out the door to let our past stay in the past, or if I should cross the room to open things up between us again — like a scalpel, slicing open an old scar.

But then I saw it.

Even from across the room, clear as day. The cup sitting right beside her with my name scrawled across the side — the big, loopy D making it obvious.

But it was the berry-pink lipstick matching her lips smeared across the rim that made me start walking toward her. Made something in my gut whisper, *there it is*.

Against all odds, *the answer*.

How, in this entire micro-universe that is New York City, had my cup had the good fortune of meeting Abby's mouth this morning?

Fuck.

Sometimes Fate makes itself hard to ignore. Throwing subtle signs out, slowly pushing you in the direction you're supposed to go, taking its sweet time to guide you there.

But other times, Fate screams obscenities in your face until you can't think of doing anything else but charge down the path it wants you on, whether you really believe you should go there or not.

My feet made the decision for me when I saw the cup — before my brain could catch up. Walking forward, compelled only by the knowledge that she was there.

I'd forced myself to make the most mundane small talk with her — the woman I'd been half-hoping not to see, waiting for her to look over and notice that it was me.

So, after all that, can she really turn me down?

Of course she can.

This is Abby we're talking about. Leave it to her to take the best-laid plans — t's crossed and i's dotted by Fate herself — and hurl them all into a burning inferno.

"Abby," I say, grinning, waiting until she's ready to stop pretending that pigeon wrestling the burger in its beak is more exciting than our random shot at this.

She turns back, folding her arms across her chest. "I can see why you're as successful as you are. Relentless in negotiation, Mr. Harper."

I shake my head, looking down at the sidewalk. A far less poetic response than I'd had in mind, but we've managed to avoid the incinerator so far, so I'll take it.

"Do you realize how much had to happen to put us at the same coffee counter this morning?"

"I know," she whispers, scrunching her nose. "And that's kind of the problem."

"Live a little, Abs." I nudge her. "A girl's gotta eat, right?"

She pushes her glasses back up the bridge of her nose.

"Your logic is impeccable," she assesses, a grin spreading across her face.

"Eight o'clock?"

"Make it eight-thirty," she concedes.

Done.

She bites her lip like she can't believe she's giving in.

I reach for her chin, giving it a little squeeze before turning on my heels to walk forward so she can't see the shock simmering in my eyes.

"It's a date," I say to the next stranger to walk past us — an elderly woman with a stout bulldog on a leash.

"Whoopie!" the woman trills, pumping a fist above her perfectly white head of hair. I think she might be drunk.

"Don't make this weird," Abby says, flinging a fist out to give me the slightest gut punch without looking over. "We're just catching up."

"Over a white tablecloth," I remind her. She rolls her eyes, but it does nothing to stop the amusement taking over her face. I lean closer as we walk. "That whole fancy tablecloth thing was your idea, not mine," I add, lowering my voice.

She bumps her shoulder into me, grinning, but this time she keeps it there as we continue walking.

"You've got one hour tonight," she says, side-eyeing me.

"One hour?" I narrow my eyes back at her. "Oh, I get as long as it takes to eat a full meal. Plus, what's a full meal without an appetizer, dessert, maybe a round of cheese, a salad . . ."

"Appetizer," she negotiates. "Plus an entree."

"Make it a big one, then," I tell her. "And you'd better plan on chewing it real slow."

"Oh, I wouldn't have it any other way," she quips back, a hint of sarcasm in her voice. "Big and slow. Got it. Although, something about that description sounds oddly familiar . . ." She glances back over her shoulder with a huge grin as she hops off the sidewalk. "Don't you think?"

My heart clenches in my chest.

"Same number as before?" I call out a bit louder as the space between us grows.

"Hasn't changed!" she answers, spinning around to give me one last goofy grin before turning her back to me once more.

"Some things never do," I mutter under my breath as I watch her walk away.

CHAPTER 6

Abby

Olivia might be across an ocean, but she's not letting that stop her from judging the very not-sexy outfit I put on this morning before knowing that a date with Dax was in my future.

"Please tell me you're not wearing that tonight," my best friend says, squinting at me through the phone screen.

I have my cell propped up on my desk with FaceTime open so we can have lunch together. Well, lunch for me and breakfast for her since she's five hours behind in Hawaii.

"It's not like I knew this was going to be happening," I tell her, looking down at my navy blazer. "Would it help if I took this off?"

Without waiting for an answer, I peel the blazer off to reveal a silky, white camisole underneath.

"Yes," she confirms, leaning toward her phone to inspect the upgrade. "Shoes?"

I pull my feet out from under my desk to examine the highly sensible flats I'm wearing before shoving them right back where they came from.

"Not showing you, Liv," I say, forcing back a laugh.

"Don't tell me you're wearing those orthopedic clogs again," she says with a groan.

"Actually, my highly sensible Danskos are safe at home," I answer before my laughter grows well past the point of stifling it. "I'm in suede flats, perfectly presentable, but I could quickly run back to grab them if you think they're the right choice," I tease.

"Don't even joke about that." She looks horrified that I'd have the gall to suggest it. "Do you still have that extra set of heels in the closet there?"

I pop out of my chair to open the coat closet next to my office door. Sure enough, there's a pair of nude Louboutins on the floor, red soles and all.

I grab them, then hold one up in front of the camera lens.

"Perfect!" She cheers, clapping her hands.

I peek out from behind the shoe.

"How did you remember they were in there?" I ask.

"First of all, those are the most memorable shoes you own — they make your legs look, like, six feet tall. And second, the last time we went out before I moved, we stopped by your office at the end of the night to swap your heels out for your office clogs because your feet were killing you."

"But that was forever ago — like, before you went to Hawaii and left me here all alone with your cat." I try to think back on whether or not I've gone for a fun night out since she left.

"I figured they'd still be there," she says, grinning. "I'm glad he's taking you out. Those shoes *need* to be taken out at least once more before you pass away in that office, probably still clutching your laptop to your chest. Really, he's doing the shoes a favor — don't you dare change your mind, or I'll have to come collect them. Give our little friends a second life outside your shoe closet."

"As long as it's for the shoes," I say, sighing happily.

"And I hope you get a lot more out of tonight than a field trip for those babies," she adds, grinning.

I laugh, but I'm on the same page.

"I hope so, too. Personally, I would have skipped the dinner part and gone straight to dessert, if you know what I mean, but he was pretty adamant about *catching up* beforehand." I curl my fingers in air quotes.

"It'll be good for you to catch up . . ." She pauses, studying my eyes, suddenly looking a bit more serious. "You know, I worry about you sometimes. The last time you considered going out with a guy long-term, it was that one from undergrad . . ."

"Chad," we both say at the same time, then shudder in unison as if a chill has just taken over both our seats, an ocean away. After a three-month relationship, Chad cheated on me with one of our mutual friends when we were rooming in college, and that was the last guy I ever committed to. I know my lack of relationships goes back to a few of the skeletons I keep mummified in my closet of memories, but that's just the way I'm built now. Not much I can do about it, and so far, it's served me better to accept this about myself than to try and change it.

"You don't have to worry about me. I'm perfectly happy," I say, digging through the Styrofoam container of salad my paralegal preemptively ordered for me, knowing I'd be at my desk again for lunch.

"I know you're *happy*," Liv answers, gingerly. "I just think you could be happ*ier*."

"I wouldn't know."

"Because you won't allow yourself to fall for anyone. Like in a *real* way."

"You're not talking about Dax, are you?"

She sighs at the screen, then pops a sushi roll into her mouth.

"Do I really need to answer that?" she asks, chewing.

"Dax lives in California, so why would I let myself fall for him *now* when I wouldn't back when we were living on the same campus?"

"Because you've never been able to forget him," she points out. "And I think you did fall for him back then. Which is why you ran at the end."

I distract myself with another forkful of salad, refusing to respond.

"Just think about it," she adds, gently. "You deserve to find your person."

"You're my person." I point the prong end of my fork at the screen.

She raises her brows. "Always," she agrees. "But you know what I mean."

I shrug.

"Nothing about tonight has anything to do with me finding my person. Even if we have the most magical time catching up, we live on opposite sides of the country — and besides, I don't know if I'm ever going to have *a person*. This will just be dinner and hopefully a nice fuck, for old time's sake. I don't need to make it any more complicated than that."

"Sex is always complicated," Liv says, sweetly. "Especially when you harbor secret feelings for the person you're with. Everyone who says it isn't is just lying to themselves. But if this is strictly for the sake of those shoes getting out there, then by all means, lie away."

***

Before the menus have even been opened, Dax is making declarations about how tonight's going to go. But I'm hardly able to pay attention to the rules he's mapping out because he's apparently taken the time to change from the black shirt he wore earlier into a more casual sport coat and chinos. Both are tailored to fit him so well that I had to do a double-take when he stood up to greet me, kissing me lightly on one cheek before pulling my chair out for me to sit down.

As if that silly role play wasn't distracting enough, the change in clothing has made it hard for me to see anything other than the way his green shirt brings out the mossy undertones of his hazel eyes in the golden candlelight flickering on the table between us.

Of course, he has chosen a place with white tablecloths and candles, playfully smirking when I mention it.

"How did you get a reservation here so last minute?" I ask, interrupting him just as he's saying something about us not discussing work tonight. "Doesn't this place have a Michelin Star or something?"

"My client — more of a longtime friend than a client, really. He called in a favor earlier today when I told him our plans for tonight."

"You told your client about me?" My eyes widen. Bold move for a simple meal between two old friends.

"Did you not hear my one rule for tonight?" he asks, closing his menu.

I blink at him. "No." I was too busy staring at the candlelight flickering in your eyes. "What rule?"

"We're not talking about work. At all," he says, firmly. "We could talk about cases and clients all night, I'm quite sure."

"Right."

I inhale deeply and open my menu back up, wondering what else there is to talk about besides work. It's all I do.

I wish I'd had more time to start up some hobbies today, like fencing or jujitsu over lunch maybe, just so I'd have something interesting to offer up about myself right now.

I peek over the top of the trifold at him, hoping he'll think of something to ask me since my mind is spinning around like a silent record. I swear he somehow got more attractive since leaving the coffee shop this morning.

"Tell me something I'd never guess about you," he says, glancing through the appetizer options. "Something that has nothing to do with work."

Ugh.

I rack my brain.

He peeks over the menu to watch me think.

Something he'd never guess? My entire existence in New York is shockingly predictable.

I panic. "Uh, well, there's someone new in my life," I blurt out. It's the most mind-blowing thing about me lately, though it's still nothing to write home about.

He closes the menu and sets it down on the table, giving me his full attention.

"Now that's not something I was expecting you to say," he says, coolly.

"Liv gifted him to me before moving. His name is Toby."

An intriguing mix of confusion takes over Dax's features, making me laugh.

"*Gifted*? She *gifted* you a guy named Toby?"

"Toby's a cat." I smile, watching his shoulders uncurl from his ears. Payback for all the blushing he made me do earlier today.

"Toby stayed with me while Liv took a sabbatical in Hawaii. I don't know if you caught all that *Good Day Show* drama over her failed marriage proposal a few months back?"

He nods grimly. I'm not surprised. Dax and I were still hanging out in law school when Liv got her first job at *The Good Day* station, and I used to make him watch clips of her earliest cameos on the show. It was only a year ago that she was asked by her producer to propose to her boyfriend on-air during the show's Valentine's Day segment. No one ever imagined Rex would say no, but he did. The live footage and aftermath sent her reeling all the way to Hawaii for a few months while things calmed down at the station.

"Those memes with her reaction were brutal." He shudders. "I think most of them went viral. How's she doing now?"

"Amazing. She fell for island life, so I lost a best friend but gained a cat. Poor replacement, but fortunately, we'd kind of bonded — Toby and I — by the time she decided to stay there indefinitely. She says the bonus of me having Toby is the reassurance he provides her — that I'll go home often enough to feed the poor thing and twirl a string around for him to grab every now and then instead of dying young and alone at my desk."

I swallow, wishing all that hadn't just tumbled out of my mouth.

"Liv had to give you her cat to ensure that you'd leave your office sometimes?" Dax shakes his head. "If only our younger selves could see us now . . ."

"Pathetic, I know."

"Is it working?"

"The part about me leaving the office to go twirl a string around for him every day?"

"Yeah."

"Nope."

"How does poor Toby survive then?"

"I have a cat walker. Like a dog walker, but for cats. Carla is her name. I think they're best friends — Toby and Carla. Truthfully, I'm a bit jealous of her. Sometimes I use my cat cam from the office to peek in on them and see just the two of them chatting away. Lots of heavy petting."

He snorts. "Of course you do," he adds, sarcastically.

"And I do go home more now than I used to. Toby livens up the place, and I like having him there. Although, I get the sense that he's very unimpressed with me. I've had to convince him to like me with bits of catnip and liver treats and whatnot, but it's worked. Kind of. Now, we watch old comedy movies and eat chips together when I do make it home. He absolutely loves *Fun with Dick and Jane*."

Dax doesn't even try to hide his amusement, resting his chin on the heel of his hand while his eyes dance in the candlelight, because apparently he *had* to go and pick a restaurant with candlelight.

Unfortunately, I go on.

"For better or worse, I'm a very boring human being." I bite my lip.

"You are anything but boring," he says, hiding a smile behind his fist.

"It's this profession though, right? I'm a bona fide workaholic with nothing else but a cat who half-hates me at home to show for it."

There I go, blushing wickedly again. I subtly peek at my watch, wondering how much longer I have to wait until we get out of here and move on to the next portion of our evening.

He drops his hand away from his mouth and picks the menu back up.

"Honestly, you're like a breath of fresh air compared to the girls I usually go out with."

My heart warms from the compliment, but it quickly turns into a frown when I imagine the type of girls he *usually* goes out with.

"And even though you practically live at your office, minus the nights you're at home watching *Fun with Dick and Jane* with a cat, you've only just made senior associate?"

"I thought we weren't talking about work," I point out, trying to steer the conversation as far away from me as possible since it seems to be going so well.

"You're the one that brought it up," he reminds me.

"Right."

I pick a ragù bolognese off the menu, then place the menu down next to my water glass and look around for the waiter. I'm not used to relaxing, or doing much besides speed-eating in between meetings.

"Well, regardless, I'd love for you to meet Toby," I tell him, smiling in a way that was meant to be suggestive, but may have come up a bit short, based on how antsy I feel.

"At some point, sure," he answers lightly, taking a sip of his water.

Okay, maybe this really is just a platonic catch-up for him after all.

The waiter arrives to take our order. My bolognese, roasted salmon for Dax, and a bottle of wine for the table. Great. Then I settle back against the booth.

"You look beautiful tonight, by the way," he says.

I snort, nearly feeling the water whiz back up into my nose. I was smart enough to trade my flats out for the heels (thank you, Liv), though the whole effect hardly conjures up a compliment with as much depth as *beautiful*.

"Please," I tell him, rolling my eyes, ignoring a tiny flutter in my stomach that's suddenly grown a bit larger. "You really don't have to butter me up. I came straight from work and slept in my office last night. Do you ever sleep at your office?"

"You've never had to try hard to look beautiful," he says, bumping my knee under the table with his. He nudges me a few more times while I try to focus on taking another sip of water without dribbling out the side corners of my mouth since I can't stop smiling. He holds up two fingers and moves his leg away. "And that's strike two for bringing up work."

Shit.

"Sounds mildly threatening." I frown. "What happens after strike three?"

His eyes begin to dance with the candle. "You don't want to know."

But the look on his face has the opposite effect. It makes me want to take the bait. I take another gulp of water and swallow it all down — the water and the butterflies — wondering where the waiter is with the bottle of wine we've just ordered.

I shrug.

"Maybe I do want to know what happens on strike three," I tell him. "Might be worth it."

"Don't say I didn't warn you," he says menacingly. "But you're not going to like it."

"Doubt it," I shoot back, grinning. "I might like it a lot."

He grins wider than me, and the whole room behind him all but fades away.

I blush too easily, glancing down at the table to mask it, but look up just in time to see his gaze traveling down to where the satin fabric of my camisole dives down into a V.

I clear my throat, and his eyes snap up to meet mine.

We both begin to laugh.

The fact that Dax is here for one night before heading back to L.A. tomorrow makes everything between us feel a little less permanent. Like an innocent flirtation in a hotel lounge between two people who might only be there for one night. No matter what does — or doesn't — happen will be over by tomorrow, the moment he steps on a plane.

"So, if we're not here to talk about what-shall-not-be-named," I say, fighting the urge to say work, "and you're heading back home in the morning, then what else is on your to-do list for New York?" I hope he'll be bold enough to say, *me*.

"There's plenty I'd love to do while here," he says, sitting back, resting his napkin across his lap. "But I'm out of time, really."

"Ah, but not quite," I point out. "So, if you only have one night left in this city to do anything at all, what would it be?"

"You tell me what I should do. You've lived here long enough."

I sit back and study him while he waits.

"Well, I'd probably start right here at this fancy restaurant eating some of the best food in the world with an incredibly well-chosen dinner companion." I'm half-smiling. "Excellent plan so far."

"Good." He nods. "And then?"

"Then, since all the shows will be over by the time we get out of here, I'd probably do a late-night stroll through Times Square so you can take the requisite tourist photo with all the famous billboards lining the streets behind you."

"Nah, too crowded." He shakes his head.

I narrow my eyes at the ceiling so as not to stare at the way his lips barely part in the center as he watches me come up with something more fitting.

"Okay then, a very secluded moonlit ride up to the top of the Empire State Building," I try next, leaning in.

"Getting warmer," he says. Half his mouth twitches up into a lopsided grin. "Still a bit too touristy for me, though. I want a real, homegrown idea from a native New Yorker."

I ignore the fact that I'm not a true native New Yorker. Tiny detail in the grand scheme of things.

"Nothing too touristy. Got it." I bite my lip. Then I rake a hand through my hair, wanting to get this next idea right on the money. "Then, I'd have my wonderful dinner companion walk me down her most favorite street, popping into all the dimly-lit lounges and cute little bakeries that stay open too late serving martinis and pastries for people who wor—"

I clasp a hand over my mouth before the full word comes out.

He stifles a laugh.

"That doesn't count," I mumble, sliding my hand away.

He laughs, nudging my leg again under the table.

"Barely, by the skin of your teeth. Go on," he says, sitting back in his chair again. "I like where this one is going."

"After trying at least one bite or beverage from all the best shops on the way, I'd ask my fine dinner companion to be shown the best view in the city. One that only she knows about."

He tilts his jaw and studies me, clearly intrigued now.

"Which is?" he asks.

"Well," I start, leaning in, "I'd venture to say that—"

But the waiter arrives to lay all our food out across the table, taking his sweet time to ceremoniously uncork the wine and pour both of our glasses half-full before informing us that the entertainment will grace the restaurant shortly.

Once he has left, I settle back into my chair, the spell of that moment nearly broken.

"You were saying?" Dax asks.

"I guess you're just going to have to wait to find out about that view," I tell him, grinning.

"Maybe not," he says. Then he takes his wine glass and holds it up, waiting for me to take mine in my hand like him. His eyes shine with mischief.

"To the best view in the city," he says, clinking our glasses together. He winks. "And to not having to wait around to find out what it is, since I've already got it right here."

CHAPTER 7

Abby

I push myself out from the table, making more room for the next course. Dax might be the only person in the world to order a post-dinner appetizer. And now, he's ordered two, even though we hardly touched the first, before settling on the chocolate soufflé for dessert. I'm not even sure what makes a soufflé any different than the chocolate cake on the line right below it, but I have a strong feeling that he chose it simply because the menu states it'll take an extra thirty minutes to bake before it arrives at our table.

"You two okay with waiting around that long?" the waiter asks, eyeballing us both with a stack of plates balanced down his arms that he's just cleared from the table next to us. We've already seen three other couples come and go from that table since we arrived, and there's a fourth couple being seated there right now.

"I can't turn down a freshly-baked chocolate soufflé. Can you?" Dax asks, eyes gleaming like a kid who's just discovered a secret stash of cookies his mom and dad hid in the closet.

I roll my eyes in a full circle before landing them back on his. And yet, I'm secretly not mad about it. Sure, I would have loved to be finishing my third orgasm with him by now, but I'm having a surprisingly fun time catching up with him. So much that I've hardly noticed time passing. He's kept me laughing all evening with stories about his life back in L.A., which sounds far more endearing than mine.

"Why do I get the feeling you're just trying to buy more time?" I narrow my eyes across the candles which have shrunk to mere nubs by now.

The waiter looks pointedly between us.

"That's not a no." Dax smiles triumphantly, then turns to the waiter. "Which means it's a yes. We'll go for it. Thanks."

The waiter sighs — like, legitimately *sighs* — before nodding once and heading back to the kitchen with his stack of plates.

"Why do I get the sense that we've overstayed our welcome?" I whisper, grinning.

Since Olivia moved to what feels like another world, I suppose I've been more starved of face-to-face friendship than I realized. Tonight has felt fun compared to the rigid, downtrodden colleagues I usually share a quick lunch or happy hour with. We usually end up with the whole table complaining endlessly about nonexistent work–life balances and then storm back into the office together, parting ways at the water cooler.

"I'll leave him a tip that makes it worth it," Dax says. "Promise. Everything about tonight has already been worth it."

I like the grin that stretches across his face, but it's the look in his eyes that makes my eyes flutter down toward the table. My stomach twists in a knot. I wasn't expecting to have this much fun.

"Are you ordering soufflés and appetizers so you're too stuffed to bother with that walk I suggested earlier?" I ask.

Dax erupts into laughter and smacks his fingers against the edge of the table.

"Christ, I forgot how attractive your dimples are," he tells me, completely avoiding my question. "How could I have forgotten about those?"

I purposefully wipe any dimples from my expression, though they might be permanently etched on my cheeks now, based on how much smiling I've done over the last three hours.

"I have to ask, did you really just want to come here to catch up with me?" I watch his face as I ask. "Then back home to L.A. tomorrow?"

"Isn't that why you agreed?" he asks, the look in his eye vaguely challenging me to admit more.

"You drove a hard bargain," I remind him.

"Truthfully, I almost didn't even say hi when I saw you this morning." He takes his napkin from his lap and tosses it on the table. Then he tosses the rest of what's left in his wine glass down his throat.

What?

My heart kicks up a notch. "Why?"

Why wouldn't he have talked to me?

"I didn't know if you'd want me to. Or, frankly, if I wanted me to."

My mouth goes dry.

"Well, I'm glad you did," I tell him, glancing at the empty bottle, wishing there was another splash to pour in my glass, but the wine's gone now, too. "Tonight was more fun than I expected, honestly. Why didn't you ever ask me out properly back in law school?"

He starts to say something but pauses to study the look in my eyes. The air practically thickens between us. I shouldn't have said that.

He breaks into a laugh, more strained than it was a minute ago . . . if only just.

"You're unbelievable," he says, tipping his chair back.

"Forget I said that last part," I say. "We're here now, so . . ."

"Are we really not going to address the fact that we slept together for a whole two years, and then you ghosted me one day, and I never heard from you again?" he asks.

The woman at the table beside us audibly gasps. I glare over at her, then back at Dax.

I lower my voice. "We were practically kids then." It's a lame excuse, and I know it. We weren't kids at all.

"If I remember correctly, we were pretty damn good at what we were doing back then," he says. "Nothing childish about it."

The woman coughs loudly, like she's gotten a piece of lettuce lodged there. Her date subtly nods his head toward us.

I swallow, wanting to clear this up quickly. "That's fair. But you did come talk to me at Carrie's this morning, and I'm really glad you did." I smile brightly. The couple at the table has gone silent, and I suddenly feel self-conscious. "Any interest in skipping the soufflé and getting out of here? Maybe go for that walk now?"

I exhale slowly, hoping he'll bite, then steal a glance at the woman next to us who isn't even pretending to eat her salad anymore. She and her date are both unapologetically leaning over to their left side, waiting to hear what comes out next.

Dax doesn't even notice.

"If I don't ask you this now, I might not ever ask—" he starts.

But I don't let him finish.

"Then don't," I quickly interrupt. "I don't know if I have a good answer to what I think you might want to know. But it was a long time ago. Besides, you're the one that said Fate put us both in Carrie's shop today. Focus on that. Focus on what's happening right now instead of—"

"Why did you cut things off between us . . . that last morning?" he asks.

I close my eyes, wishing he hadn't asked. My mind flashes back to the one time I allowed myself to spend the entire night at his place. Before that, I'd always forced myself to leave before accidentally falling asleep in his bed. But, I'd woken up that last morning to see his window blinds casting a shadow over the bed, each slat a black bar, the sun rising behind them. I'd stayed without meaning to, but also without actively forcing myself to go. Everything had seemed possible the night before, but the next morning I panicked and left, wanting to keep the perfect memory of him alive before it all came crashing down.

"We were graduating," I answer, briskly. "You were going to L.A. and I was coming here. There was no point in dragging it out any longer."

"Dragging what out longer?"

"I'm happy to remind you . . ." I say, letting my voice trail off.

A blanket of silence fills the table and I let it, since nothing coming out of my mouth is doing a stellar job of defusing this. But I get the sense that Dax is well-versed in the same stone-cold silence method, because he just leans into the space between us, waiting for me to go on.

The wine I've consumed tonight must be doing its job to make me feel more brazen, I suppose, because the next sentence out of my mouth doesn't leave any room for error or misunderstanding.

"So, is all this because you're just not interested in having sex with me anymore?"

I don't care that the couple next to us freeze, then stare over at our table. They've hit the jackpot of voyeuristic conversation topics a mere foot away.

Dax, however, is unperturbed.

"Who said that I'm not interested in having sex with you anymore?" he asks, lowering his voice.

"You, evidently." I cross my arms.

"When?"

"You didn't have to. You've ordered almost everything on the menu, including a fucking thirty-minute soufflé."

"Oh, that. No, I'm just not interested in meaningless *anything* anymore."

"Who said it has to be meaningless?" I shoot back before I can stop myself.

Shit.

The words hang in the air between us and I watch as Dax inhales them, a smile forming on his lips. I wish I could grab each word and stuff every last one back into my mouth.

"Ah," he says, leaning back in his chair, grinning.

"No, no, don't *ah* me right now," I say, annoyed.

"So, this isn't meaningless." He waves his hand around the table. "Was it the white tablecloth that did it for you? Or was it the candlelight between us?"

His eyes dance across the table at me when I finally look up.

"Stop being weird," I tell him. "You're making this more complicated than it needs to be."

"Sex is never not complicated," he says. "What we had was never not complicated."

"So I hear," I grumble, recalling Olivia's words from our earlier conversation.

I glare over at the woman at the table next to us. She snaps her eyes back to her salad and starts rooting her fork around in the lettuce, frowning.

I shift in my seat.

"Are you ready to go?" I ask, annoyed that we still have an audience.

"But the soufflé still has—"

"Fuck the soufflé," I interrupt and stand up.

The woman scoffs, looking nearly faint.

"*Fuck the soufflé?*" he asks.

I turn to the table next to us.

"You heard me," I announce to them.

Their eyes grow wide, not even hiding their shock at how the conversation they've been so evidently eavesdropping on just took a left turn.

"Now, stand up," I say, motioning to Dax.

"I still have to pay." He's not even looking around for the waiter.

"Fucking hell," I groan, pulling my wallet out of my purse. I only have two twenties, which is not remotely enough to cover the bill, and paying with a card will take too long.

Dax tosses one, two, three — okay, five one-hundred-dollar bills down on the table between us.

I stare back at him.

"Told you I'd make it worth his time," he says.

"Show-off," I mumble.

But, he finally stands up, causing a nerve in my stomach to snap. I turn back to the couple who now shamelessly watch us.

"Please tell the waiter that our soufflé was actually ordered for the two of you — and this should cover the bill."

"Uh, thanks," the man says, weakly. "And good luck. Tonight. With your—"

"Oh, shut up," I tell him.

Then I grab Dax's elbow and lead him out of the restaurant and out onto the street that'll take us back to my place.

CHAPTER 8

Dax

The moment Abby opens the door to her apartment, an enormous black-and-white tuxedo cat starts weaving himself around my ankles.

This vibrating ball of fur must be Toby.

She pauses behind me with her brows cinched tightly as I bend down to scratch under Toby's chin. He starts to purr audibly, sounding like a bowling ball traveling down a ribbed alley, gearing up for a strike.

"Well, isn't that something?" She sounds confused while watching him melt into me.

Toby's tail wraps around my ankles before he swoops back under my hand, purring even louder. I tell her, "All cats love to be scratched under the chin."

"No, of course he does. It's just that he never greets me like that. Usually when I walk in, it's like a bomb has gone off. He bolts behind the couch and waits there until I bring out a can of something for him to eat. I always thought it was just because he missed Olivia and was disappointed that it was me coming home instead of her, but clearly it's because he's not a fan."

"Ah, no, it must be that catnip I rubbed into my ankles this afternoon." I wink up at her.

She studies me, then smiles and brushes by. "I might need to try that."

I stand up and look around, instantly taken aback when I see where she lives.

The sprawling, top-floor apartment is eclectic and vibrant. Original artwork with distorted faces and what look to be intertwined, abstract bodies line one wall. In front of it is an emerald-green chaise piled high with an ungodly number of cushions, each a varying shade of lemon. A wiry chandelier hangs over a thick, wood-plank table. In the middle of the table, elegant brass candleholders shaped like cranes stretch up toward the light.

But it's the plants that catch me by surprise. She has plants potted *everywhere*. Huge, banana-leaf ferns and parlor palms sprout up from earthy, terracotta vessels sitting beneath a long, industrial skylight that stretches from one corner of her apartment to the other. The way she described her soulless imprisonment at the office, I had no idea that her apartment would be brimming with so much, well, *life*.

I reach out to touch the soft edge of a palm that's as tall as me.

"This is it," she says, throwing out a hand. "The place I love the most. Here in New York, anyway."

"How do you keep all this alive if you're never here?" I ask.

"I don't," she answers.

"You must have quite the green thumb to handle this in your complete lack of spare time."

"I already told you about Carla, Toby's bestie, but I also have an urban gardener that handles all this." She waves her arms around the room. "It costs me an arm and a leg every month, but it feels worth it to me. When I do make it back home, I want it to feel as different from the office as humanly possible. And with this, I'm always happy to be here. Always surrounded by living things. No matter what."

"I can see why," I tell her, admiring a little garden of succulents and herbs lined up in the window sill that perfectly frames the view of the city lights outside, catching a whiff of basil at first, then fresh mint. "It's amazing."

"It is," she agrees, wistfully. "He does a great job."

She makes her way across the kitchen to grab two turquoise glasses from the open shelving behind the sink.

"What can I get you? Water? Wine? I'm afraid I have zero food. Never here long enough to make a grocery trip worth it, but I'm pretty sure I won't be hungry until next Tuesday, based on all the stuff you just ordered. I hope those eavesdroppers enjoyed that soufflé, by the way."

I smile, but deep down I get a tinge of sadness tugging at my gut.

There's this whole vibrant, living person inside of her. One who loves being surrounded by trees and shrubbery inside her very own concrete jungle of New York. But on the outside of all this, she's built herself a bleak cage. Stuck in an office most of the last six years, not even bothering to date or form any real relationships. She seemed enamored with my lifestyle at dinner. Making comments that gave me more insight into her life here than anything else she's disclosed so far.

"Abby, why don't you work for someone that'll allow you to be *this* version of yourself?" I ask.

"What do you mean by *this version*?" she says, spinning around.

I put a hand against the wall to study an oversized, abstract painting of what looks like a woman with jet black hair and a row of thick bangs covering her eyes. Wearing a cold coat of silvery armor, she floats on her back in a mossy sea of green.

"Did you paint this?" I ask, unable to pull my eyes away from the small signature scribbled in the corner that looks a lot like Abby's name.

"Oh, that was a lifetime ago," she says, looking embarrassed. Then she turns to grab a pitcher of filtered water out of the fridge and I can't help but notice that, besides the water pitcher, the rest of the fridge is completely empty.

She wasn't kidding about the no food thing.

Then she kicks off her heels and puts a hand on her hip, chugging the glass of cold water she's just filled for herself. She walks a second glass over to me, stopping so close that our chests are practically touching when she pushes it into my hand.

"Drink this," she says. "You had a lot of wine. And I'm going to need you in tip-top form."

"I had no idea you were such a closet artist." I study her eyes and ignore what she's just hinted at, though my body instantly responds to her words.

How does this hardened woman I've spent the last six years of my life thinking about have all of *this* existing inside of her? And how come I simply never knew?

"There's a lot about me you don't know," she says, lightly. Her lip twitches gently as if she's well aware there are a whole world of secrets that she keeps to herself.

"We only went to my place in law school, didn't we?" I ask, thinking back to whether or not I was ever invited over to her place. Come to think of it, I don't think I was. Not a single time.

"Drink up, Dax," she says, nudging the glass up to my lips.

I do as she says and chug half the glass. She carefully takes it back from my hand.

"I never had you over to my place back then, you're right. But we're here, now." She slowly sets our glasses on the table behind me, making sure she brushes her chest up against me again as she does. "And you've successfully met Toby now, so . . ."

She looks up at me from beneath her lashes and I'm transported back to another place and time, when all I had to do was send her a text in order to end my night by looking into those deep amber eyes. To look into her face with that exact expression she's giving me right now. The one that always ended with both of us breathless and moaning before she returned home at the end of our night.

She grabs a hold of my belt and drags me into her until our hips are flush against each other and there's no more hiding what I want to do with her.

A longing smile fills her face, quietly triumphant, borderline smug. "So, you *do* still want me," she says.

She moves one hand down from my belt to palm the growing bulge between us, nodding approvingly.

"I've never not wanted you," I growl into her ear, feeling the heat of her breath hit the sensitive skin below my ear.

She tilts her chin up so her eyes meet mine as she moves her hand up and down against me. Her eyes catch the light of the moon pouring through her window, making the amber flecks move inside them like liquid pools of gold, challenging me.

"If that's true," she whispers into my ear, "show me."

A wave of anticipation and knowing washes through me. The same I felt just before crossing the shop to talk to her this morning, mixed with an even stronger, more familiar longing that's never gone away when it comes to her.

Abby's eyes fill mine, searching for the answer.

I might have tried fooling myself into thinking I could keep things under control tonight, that we'd be better off leaving most things between us in the past. But we both knew where this was heading. I knew the second she smiled up at me this morning.

Fuck it.

I might want more than is possible when it comes to Abby. But I'll take whatever I can get when I'm with her. And for tonight, that'll have to be enough.

CHAPTER 9

Abby

I take Dax's hand and lead him to the emerald chaise lounge, then push him back so he lands on the springy green velvet behind him.

"Sit," I say.

He bounces up off the lounge to stand in front of me again.

"I prefer to stand," he says, darkly.

"Suit yourself," I say, not exactly upset that he's already taking control.

Dax wraps one hand around the back of my neck, encircling my waist with his other, then pulls me into him until I'm sure our lips are about to touch.

I close my eyes and wait for him to meet me the rest of the way, not quite believing that I had the incredible luck to run into him again this morning. I'm rarely lucky in life, but today proves otherwise.

I melt a little in his arms, waiting for his kiss. Anxious for his hot breath to hit my lips.

We're really about to do this.

Come what may.

Any minute now.

We are about to . . . kiss, aren't we?

Aren't we?

I don't feel his lips, though. In fact, I don't feel his breath getting any closer to mine than it was a fraction of a second ago, even though it's been long enough that he should have made it there by now.

I squint my eyes and tilt my head to the side, primed and ready for some serious action, but just a few inches away from mine, his hazel eyes are open.

Wide open.

And they're dancing, like an electric samba has taken off and I'm the last in the room to know.

The hazel-green of his irises catch the city lights streaming through the window, and I'm transported back to a thousand memories of them glowing in the light of the stars between the slats of his cheap university window blinds, as he hovered above me. Except in every one of those memories, he's actually kissing me by now.

"What are you doing?" I whisper.

"I know we haven't seen each other in forever, and I know we live on opposite sides of the country, but I want this — whatever's about to happen — to mean something to you. At least for tonight."

A familiar lump lodges itself in my throat.

First, the hug in the coffee shop, and now this, catapulting raw emotions back into my life. Emotions I'd otherwise never let myself get caught up in. Emotions that should stay locked away and buried where liking someone can't turn into something that feels more like hate.

He pushes my hair back, studying my eyes while I grapple with what he's saying. That this is more than just a trip down memory lane for him. It feels like closing the loop on years of memories — and feelings — we've both had, but only one of us will admit to. It feels like a movie scene, something I've watched two actors do on screen thousands of times, but it is happening to me right now, makes my insides twist. Hard.

His words hang between us. A dare for me to tell him he's wrong, or that nothing in me feels anything for him. Now, or ever.

"That's a big want," I whisper, leaning closer to his lips, hoping he'll let me stop all the thoughts from coming out of his mouth with a kiss.

I let him take my chin and bring my face back up into his until . . .

Fuck.

There it is. He sees right through me when he looks at me like that. Always.

All those ugly parts I tried hiding from him in some dark corner of myself now stand in front of him, arms wide out, head thrown back beneath a spotlight.

He wraps his hand through my hair, pulling me in. A silent agreement on where this is going. I dissolve into his arms when his lips finally find mine. Turning me into a puddle of liquid while every concern I have left drowns beneath his kiss. I open my lips to him more as he wraps his palms behind the curve of my neck, heating my skin, pulling me deeper into his kiss, holding me so tenderly that my breath catches in my throat before I allow myself to inhale him. Again. Remembering the rhythm of his tongue, the taste of his mouth as it opens to explore mine. Gently, *so fucking gently*, as if he's afraid I might not be willing to go where he wants to take me.

But I am.

I let myself get lost in his kiss until I forget where I'm standing, consumed by the tidal wave of old memories crashing through me. As if the dam I built around his memory is bursting, devouring me, water filling every crevice like a maze until there's nothing left to hold onto. A montage of moments strung up between us, like flashes behind my eyes of nights buried under his sheets, all sweat and throbbing hearts, damp skin and decisions I never want to forget.

His movements grow more urgent until he stops kissing me, then presses his forehead into mine, our breaths matching pace as neither of us makes a move to leave this exact spot in the room.

"Okay," he says, breathing heavily into the air between us.

He kisses me again; except this time it feels more like a soft landing than a launch.

"Okay?" I repeat, unsure if that kiss just undid everything in him, like it did me.

"Okay," he says, relief filling his voice.

I sigh and drop my head back, then lean in for another kiss. I'm hardly sure that one night back in Dax's arms is something I can handle. Especially since there's only one way that opening myself up to someone like him can end.

"Are we sure this is a good idea?" I ask, closing my eyes, allowing his kiss to find me again. Wondering if Dax had been right all along, if he really should have just noticed me standing at the coffee shop and walked back out again, not even attempting to open back up this thing between us. Like a moth drawn to the flame.

"No," he whispers. I can feel him smiling against me. "But we can clean this mess up tomorrow."

I nod in agreement. Knowing tonight we have to let it be made.

CHAPTER 10

Dax kisses me again and begins working his hands up and down my spine — massaging my sore, chair-shaped muscles, like a spa and make-out session rolled into one.

My eyes ease into the back of my head and I lift my chin to give him access to my neck before I start praying to every god I'm aware of to not let him speak again, or look at me like he sees inside me, until we're finished. And by the time he starts dragging his tongue down to the tiny, sensitive spot where my pulse is hammering away beneath my jawline, I know that I'm not going to last very long with him.

I never have, but especially not tonight. He pushes both hands into my waist, massaging that next. Kneading and working the tightness of my joints, my tendons, my muscles that sit to attention in a chair, all day, every day.

His mouth returns to my lips, but his hands travel further south, massaging the generous curve of my hips that lead into two handfuls of flesh. I groan into his ear while my head falls back, relishing in the feel and strength of his hands working the tension out of my muscles and body like no masseuse ever has. It's making my knees go weak.

"The bed," I murmur into his ear.

He silently turns me around and plants both hands on my shoulders, firmly leading me forward while kneading those next. I walk slowly toward my bedroom, just to make it last longer as he circles knots and pressure points, most of which I knew were there and always told myself I'd get around to working out one day but never have.

When we get to my room, I toss every throw pillow off my bed while he kisses my neck, holding onto me from behind, and when each and every last pillow is somehow thrown onto the floor, he spins me around to face him.

I peel my top off, then my skirt, tossing them both into a heap by a nearby chair, then watch the way his eyes graze the sky-blue bra and panty set I'm wearing underneath, loving how I feel beneath his gaze.

Sexy.

Wanted.

He takes a step closer, dragging his hands down my bare skin, then spins me around, rolling his hands along my sides from behind.

"Lie on the bed," he whispers into my ear, sending a tingling shiver straight through my spine.

I look over my shoulder as I climb onto the bed. He's removing his belt, dragging his shirt up over his head.

The years have done nothing but good things to you, I want to say. But I don't. I take all of him in, instead. His skin is tan and taut all over, the shadows deep in the grooves of his abs and arms. He has more chest hair than I remember, but that little rut of darkness leading down through the waistband of his jeans is still there. And I know exactly where, and what, it leads to.

"Lie down," he says. "On your stomach."

"Oh," I say, a bit surprised. "We aren't going to . . ."

His eyes darken and he spins his forefinger around, then points down to the mattress.

I do what he says, the trust resurfacing between us making me feel at ease, as he climbs onto the bed on top of me, then presses the length of his bare chest down onto my back, the heat and pressure of him warming me from within. He drags my hair across my shoulders and down to one side of the bed before hovering his lips just over my earlobe.

He takes it in his teeth, biting gently, sucking on it before whispering, "I'm going to give you a massage first." He kisses my shoulder. "What did you think I was going to do?"

I close my eyes, and breathe out a laugh, but don't say a word. He's never given me a massage before. In fact, no man ever has.

"Where's your massage oil?" he asks.

"Where's my massage oil?" I repeat, feeling hot under my skin.

"Nightstand?" he asks, reaching toward the tiny table.

"I don't have massage oil," I say, feeling flustered. "Do people just keep massage oil on hand where you're from?" I look over my shoulder. "No wonder you think it's the *best* coast."

"Then where's your coconut oil?"

"Now *that's* in the nightstand," I say, smirking.

He kisses my cheek but gives me an amused look before pulling open the drawer.

"Oh my God, I'm kidding!" I call out, wondering what type of women he dates back in California that keep both massage oil and coconut oil in their nightstands. "Hang on, I'll grab it."

I roll to my stomach.

"You don't have any food in your fridge, but you keep coconut oil on hand?" he asks, laughing.

"As a moisturizer," I tell him, flushing again.

"Just tell me where it is," he says.

"I'll grab it," I say, dragging myself up off the bed.

"No, stay," he commands, and I lie back down on my stomach. "I'll find it."

"It's in the bathroom. Second drawer from the left," I call out when he disappears behind the door.

I take the opportunity to unhook my bra, tossing it into the corner so that when he returns, there's only a thin pair of panties between him and the rest of me.

A moment later, Dax is back on the bed, kneeling over my lower back. His knees are lodged on either side of my hips, with both his hands digging into my container of organic coconut oil. He rubs his hands together to warm them, releasing the sweet, faintly tropical scent before pushing both hands onto my shoulder blades, rolling deeply across my skin, sliding down — all the way down — to where I imagine his second favorite pair of dimples is making an appearance just above my panty line and right above my ass.

I close my eyes and groan into the mattress, feeling the weight of his body pressing down on mine, pushing through muscle knots and tension, working out any last reserves I had left in me.

His hands slide up again with firm, mounting pressure, then wrap around my shoulders and travel down each of my arms, pushing his slick palms into mine when he gets to them. It feels intimate — him holding my hands down onto the bed like this — somehow more intimate than sex.

He pauses there, keeping my hands pressed into the mattress, my eyes closed, and I'm glad he can't hear what I'm thinking right now.

No one has held these hands in years, Dax. Not even you.
And the feeling is practically shredding me.

But just as I'm about to pull mine away, cursing my fight or flight response to this shock of *feeling*, he releases me again, sliding his fingers back up my arms, swooping quickly around my shoulders, and firmly massaging all the way down my back. This time he kneads my skin even lower until he's dipping just under the waistline of my panties from behind, finding a new patch of skin to absorb the sweet, scented oil.

I groan into the bed, unable to hold it in.

"Where have you been hiding these massage skills?" I moan, my eyes still closed.

He bends in half, leaning over so his lips brush against my ear when he answers.

"On the west coast," he whispers through what I can tell is a smile.

My laugh lasts only a moment before it gets caught in my throat when he slips both hands around my sides and hooks his fingers into the elastic waistband, sliding my panties all the way off.

I'm completely naked beneath him, not even sure if I care that he's technically still clothed in a pair of plaid boxers and sitting on top of me.

He flips himself around to kneel over me, but this time he's facing the opposite way toward my feet. He starts sliding his hands back down my lower back, all the way over my ass, digging the slippery heels of his palms into the backs of my thighs, then calves, and eventually my feet, all the way to the tips of my toes, where he squeezes each one before starting the ascent up my legs, and over bare cheeks.

My entire body is coated in slick oil, heated by his hands, kneading each tender, forgotten muscle until a collection of stars begins gathering behind my eyelids, shooting blindly into the dark.

I don't know if I've ever been so relaxed, or so at ease before while lying beneath a man. Nothing about his movements feel rushed, or like there's a clear end goal in sight. It's just Dax doing something that he knows will make me feel good. Sure, he's clearly enjoying the view up there, my naked body oiled up beneath his, but everything about this feels sensual instead of sexual.

He continues massaging my legs and feet for a few more minutes before his hands start working my cheeks between his palms. Kneading and squeezing and molding my flesh as the oil drips heated drops down my sides to the blanket beneath us. When I can't stand it another second, I make my needs known.

"You know what else they say about coconut oil?" I ask, not bothering to open my eyes.

"That it's a natural lube?" he answers lightly, taking the words right out of my mouth. I roll my face over and chuckle into the mattress. "Why else do you think it was my second request after the massage oil?"

"Good," I say, though it comes out as more of a drawn-out moan while his hands roll down my skin. "Glad we're on the same page."

I let him massage my cheeks for another moment before arching my lower back and nudging one leg over to the side a few inches, hinting at what I want from him next.

A low groan escapes him, and even from here, I can feel him growing — harder, longer, thicker — right above my lower back.

"What the hell are you doing to me, Abs?" he mutters, more to himself than to me, and I nudge my leg over another inch and wait.

He obeys my silent request, tracing one hand down through the edges of my cheeks until he cups me from behind, rubbing the slick oil all the way over my ass and along each of my folds, coating me with wet heat before finding my most sensitive spot with one deliciously oily finger.

He slides in effortlessly, filling me immediately. I know I must feel tight, my walls clenching in around his one finger, and I wonder if he can tell how long it's been since I had any part of a man inside of me.

He groans again, pushing his finger deeper inside, before pulling it out, then two in the next time, groaning again as he does.

"You feel unbelievably tight," he tells me, pushing his fingers in while barely circling beneath me with a third.

I spread my legs wider, arching my back and pressing my hips into the mattress while biting the side of my fist to distract myself from the burning pleasure as it begins to rip through me in mounting waves. He drags his hands back down my thighs, then up again to find that spot between my legs, slipping more fingers inside me as I begin to moan. Then he leans his torso against my back, and I open one eye to peek down the bed, watching my toes curl while he studies his hands — sliding in and out of my body, circling and edging the mountains and valleys of my most intimate parts, remembering — to the point — exactly how I want to be touched.

The pressure.

The rhythm.

The feel of him inside.

The familiarity of it all takes me back.

I roll over, suddenly desperate to have him in me. I want him looking into my eyes when he fills me, and I want to know the exact moment we both go over the edge. To see evidence of it in the way his pupils grow larger, then shrink in on themselves, dilating deeper when his final release is through.

"Condom?" I ask through shuddering breaths. "Nightstand."

He reaches into the drawer and pulls one out. Once it's on, I drag him up by a shoulder and he flips around, wrapping his arms all the way across me, cradling my head beneath his elbow, fire filling his eyes. I pull his lips to mine, kissing him deeply, growing more urgent as his hands find and fill me again.

I moan his name into his lips.

"I want you," I whisper. His dark fans of lashes open when I repeat his name, then his eyes begin to burn, growing in intensity when he finally allows himself to push inside, filling me like hot water, expanding within my walls.

And then . . . and then . . . and then . . . we begin to move.

Absorbing each other, rolling our hips to the same song, like a slow dance neither one of us ever forgot the steps to.

Knowing that this is the way I want him to rock me, back and forth.

Knowing this is the way he likes me to raise my chest to meet his.

We give and we take slowly, so fucking slowly, that my breath hitches each time I think he's going to pull all the way out, just to push himself deeper inside me again.

"Not yet," he says more urgently, his ragged breath filling my inhale.

I clench myself around him.

"I can't wait," I moan between kisses. "I've missed . . ." *You. This. Us.* But I don't say any of it, only adding, "*everything*" as a single exhale.

He buries his face between my neck and shoulder, biting gently into the hollow just above my collarbone, sending waves of pleasure — like glowing orbs exploding throughout my veins.

Not yet, my body screams.

I want to be right here where nothing else matters.

Not yet ready for the catapult over the edge.

Keep it only physical, my insides scream.

But it's nearly impossible to send it all away.

Not when it's Dax.

And it's me.

Here, in my very own bed, of all places.

Doing exactly what we've always done . . . except this time, so different.

He's different.

He's making good on that promise. This isn't just sex.

Emotion bubbles up between us in every push and pull and kiss and moan, so familiar that it hurts.

I kiss him harder, burying my thoughts away while tugging and twisting his lips in mine, not knowing how we got here together, but knowing we're getting closer to summiting the mountain, still.

Then, just like that, it happens. As quickly as everything in me starts to clench and build into one final climax, everything else bursts open, the release harder and faster than a gunshot, exploding from the deepest part of me, sending fireworks and stars and fiery raindrops bursting out in every direction from behind my eyelids.

When I force myself back to his eyes, I watch them explode in a flash of green and gold above mine before they squeeze shut again. Wrapping himself around me tighter, harder, shuddering into me. Leaving me breathless and sweating, but held so close beneath him that I can still feel his heart, his body pulsing. Hard and fast, just like mine.

And then . . . and then . . . . and then . . . we begin the slow descent back into New York, all heat and liquid metal, like a plane landing after it's flown too close to the sun.

Again, I can feel the bed beneath me.

My bed.

His grip loosens and I lean harder into him. Too quickly, it's over.

Just like everything that happened between us before.

CHAPTER 11

Abby, the next day

I don't know what's wrong with me, but I know it's the same thing that's always been wrong with me. I can't bring myself to read the note he left sitting on my nightstand beside a somehow still-warm cup of coffee. Instead, I tuck it into my purse, only pulling it out to read when I'm almost halfway through with my workday.

And by the time I settle into my office futon for a long read, pressing the single crease to flatten the page, I've already reached the end.

The ball's in your court, babe.
Dax

CHAPTER 12

Dax, six months later

The truth of my time with Abby — however unfortunate the truth may be — is that some things never change.

CHAPTER 13

Abby

I scan my closet. Apparently, all I've purchased as an adult to fill my very hard-to-find walk-in closet here in New York is neutral-colored pencil skirts, polyester blouses, and stiff blazers.

"It's like I've spent my whole life attending my own funeral with this wardrobe," I say to Olivia, bracing myself against the door.

She snorts into the phone screen.

"What do you think I've been telling you all these years?" she asks.

"This is getting serious," I moan. "What's wrong with me? Am I thirty or ninety-two?"

I only have an hour to pack for this extended work trip to California where I'm imagining balmy weather and palm trees swaying over enticing blue pools, but apparently I don't even own a swimsuit from the last five years. My closet is a sea of charcoal and beige.

Beige, for God's sake.

"Why didn't you tell me I dress like I'm having a love affair with neutral polyblends?" I ask.

"I have," she teases. "Although I think the term fashion people like to use nowadays is *old money wardrobe*. Which works for New York."

Her tan, freckled face fills my phone screen, propped up against the wall behind my dresser, next to what is apparently my highly depressing funeral-director closet. Her cobalt eyes shine, somehow lighter in the sunlight there.

"You're going to need to get a few tank tops and shorts. L.A. is hot this time of year compared to New York, Abs. At the very least, go hit up that store near your apartment so you can throw some basic sundresses into your bag. Otherwise you're going to have the same situation I had when I got to Hawaii. I was sweating my face off, about to pass out from the heat, standing outside in a sweater, of all things. Except you might not be lucky enough to be rescued by a young Jason Momoa look-alike who just so happened to be passing by, like I was."

"In my case, I'll probably pass out on Brett's shoulder, which is more like nightmare material, but I don't have time to shop." I check the clock next to my bed. "I only have an hour to pack. Brett booked our flights for eight o'clock tonight."

"A night flight? With your boss? *Ew.* Do you think he likes to fly in his pajamas?"

I try not to picture my asshole boss cozied up beside me in some paper-thin pajama pants that don't hide anything. This trip is going to be hard enough on my nerves without adding Brett flying in his pajamas to the mix.

"Not the mental picture I want to hone in on right now," I say, chuckling. "Besides, in his words, why would we fly during the day when those are butt-in-the-chair, billable hours?"

I hold the phone camera up to my closet so she can assess the situation.

"Don't you own a pair of yoga pants?"

I crack open a dresser drawer, the contents of which have not seen light in months, pull out a pair of red Lululemons, tag still attached, and hold them up to the screen.

"There you go," she says, brightening. "Buy an *I heart NY* T-shirt or something at the airport to get you through the flight. And after that, go shopping, like, ASAP."

"I'll just order a few new things to arrive this week since I won't have time to shop once I land. I can't believe how long I'm going to be in L.A. for this merger," I tell her, shaking my head. "Of all the places. I haven't been back there in, well, forever. It's supposed to take weeks to get the deal done. Possibly longer since the opposing counsel team just got word that a new buyer is potentially coming in hot. Whatever new team is supposedly jumping in at this point is going to have to hit the ground running, but it'll still put us a bit behind according to our client's timeline."

"The life of a fancy attorney," she says. "Will they fly you back and forth every weekend? Or do you plan to just stay there that whole time?"

"They offered to fly me back and forth, but honestly, what's the point? I figure I may as well just stay there instead of spending every Friday night and Sunday morning on a plane flying across the country."

"Thank goodness for Carla," she says, sadly. "Poor Toby will really miss you."

I snort and shoot her a look.

"Thank you for lying like that, but he prefers her to me. I swear he understood what I was saying when I explained to him that he'd be staying at Carla's house while I'm gone. The joy in his whiskers was legit, Liv. You should have seen it."

She laughs and rolls her eyes.

"I would feel worse for him," Liv says, "but I do know he loves her—" She stops short and clasps one hand over her mouth.

I laugh and shake my head then wave her on to continue.

"Go ahead. You can say it. He loves her more than me."

"No, I wasn't going to say that," she argues, pulling her hand away.

I squint at the screen in time to see Liv rub her nose and look off to the side.

Liar.

"Okay," I say, relenting. She and I both know Toby is in excellent hands with Carla while I'm gone. Not only does he absolutely adore her, but she's obsessed with him, too.

"He's adaptable. And resilient. And wary of weirdos, apparently. You must have done a good job raising him, mama," I tell her.

She grins.

"Speaking of being a weirdo, have you thought anymore about calling Dax before you get on that plane?"

"Should I take the matching sports bra?" I ask, holding up a matching chili-pepper red bra with the tag hanging off the side, and ignoring her question.

She widens her eyes at the screen.

"You're not going to call him before you go?"

I stare back at her.

"Why bother with all that again? We've been down this road before. He lives over there, and I live over here. And there's nothing in me that wants to open that situationship up again." She continues staring at me like there's egg thrown across my face. "What am I supposed to do? Call him up like, *Hey! Remember when I ghosted you for a second time a whopping six years after the first time? I hear that the third time's the charm, so let's have one more go at it!*"

Liv frowns. "You'd better call him," she says, stiffening her upper lip. "The way you two keep popping up in each other's lives . . ." She whistles. "It's like the universe wants you to get something figured out."

Staring into my stupid closet, I fix my jaw and shake my head, like it'll shake the memory of Dax saying something very similar back into the past.

"Trust me, I did us both a favor by closing the door on a second chance," I say, firmly. "We're both wrapped up in our careers and live way too far away to attempt anything more than the very good time we had that night. Plus, I'm really not capable of relationships," I insist. "You know that."

"That's just what you like to tell yourself. I think it's worth a shot." She sighs. "Besides, you're going to need some serious stress relief with this deal you're working on."

"Ah, yes, The Nile Group deal." Brett and I, along with a team of associates who are all staying in New York as support, have been working on a deal to purchase The Nile Group for months. I already know this will likely be the biggest deal of my career, and Brett is co-counseling it with me, finally giving me a chance at becoming a fully-fledged partner. "See, the thing is, after you've ghosted someone twice . . . I'm not sure the term *stress relief* is the exact phrase that comes to mind when I think of Dax."

"I don't know anyone else who's held onto the idea of someone as long as the two of you have. And, besides, maybe it won't matter that it's been a few months. You guys slid right back into your old roles the second you saw each other last time, right?"

"He could have a girlfriend this very second," I remind her, shrugging. "I wouldn't know."

"He doesn't," she says.

"How would you know that?"

"Because I just checked online. He's single. Single as a fucking pringle."

I laugh, recalling the moment she said those exact words on *The Good Day Show*, causing the meme of her face to go viral.

"I need to focus on the merger while I'm there. Nothing else. This is my shot at a partnership offer."

"Ah, right, instant partnership with Brett and the rest of those yahoos at the top of the food chain there?" The only person who hates Brett more than me is Olivia.

I sigh.

As if there's been anything *instant* about becoming a partner. This promotion would mean I'd finally achieved the goal I've been chasing nearly twenty-four seven since the day I graduated from law school and took this position working under Brett.

After eight months of around-the-clock work on this deal, recently, a few backdoor rumors began swirling that another company suddenly has its eye on The Nile Group, too. That's the real reason I'm jetting off to L.A. tonight. Our client doesn't want to see The Nile Group get taken out from under us in the final moment. They want the deal done *now* without any other enticing offers coming in before we can get it done.

It's a long shot, if you ask me. Especially since I'd guess that The Nile Group is well aware that another stealth company has its eye on them, and will likely stall in order to receive their offer.

"This is the one," Brett said earlier today while going on and on about dropping everything in my life to head over to L.A. with him for the next few weeks. "Get this deal done before whatever assholes are trying to steal it out from us and you're in, Torres. You'll be one of us."

You're in — meaning I'd get a seat at the partner table. Something I've saved up and planned for since the moment I was hired.

I peel off the gray pencil skirt I wore to the office and start pulling the red yoga pants on.

"Holy shit," I say, gasping between pulls. "Either I've grown since I bought these, or I forgot how controlling the control top can be."

Liv looks amused while she watches me nearly fall into my dresser, hopping on one foot while trying to get my ankle through a tiny pant leg.

"Sit down to do that before you end up in the ER," she calls out over my grunts.

I manage to balance myself against the edge of the bed, panting a little harder as I push my toes through the second tiny leg hole.

She begins laughing all over again.

"Why would people wear these things?" I ask.

"To do yoga. You know, exercise. Relax. Something you used to have time for. Selma has a whole yoga room looking out over the valley, which you're going to need to take advantage of, if you're not going to be taking advantage of Dax's massages while there."

"Are you sure your in-laws aren't weirded out that I'll be crashing at their place while I'm there?"

"Are you kidding? When I told Dom you had to stay in L.A. for the next few weeks, he practically jumped over the top of me to call Quinton. Both Quinton and Selma offered their house up for you to use before Dom could get the full story out. They'll be in France over the next few months filming, so the timing is perfect."

"I still can't believe Dom's brother is a mega-famous film director."

"You should see their house. It's nearly as beautiful as Selma herself, and considering she's the most sought-after supermodel of all time, that should give you an idea of what to expect," she says, still sounding a bit dreamy herself. "Remember the first time I ever met them?"

I laugh, picturing sweet, ambitious Liv trying to sell her first film script idea to Quinton at Dom's urging.

"My brother- and sister-in-law are a bit . . ." She trails off, trying to find the right words to describe them.

"Wonderfully unique?" I ask, smiling.

"Wonderful. And unique," she agrees, laughing. "But yes, they're also wildly generous and are stoked to have you there. They briefed Starry about your food allergies too, so expect a thoroughly stocked, peanut-free kitchen when you arrive."

"Who's Starry again?"

"The house manager."

"Well, that was fast. It's only been, what, three hours since we made this arrangement?" I say, glancing at the clock on my nightstand, half-hidden beneath the branch of a fiddle-leaf fig tree.

I only have another forty-five minutes until I need to get an Uber to the airport.

"These people are next-level organized, Abs. They have to be. They run a Hollywood empire and spend their lives in houses all over the globe. I wouldn't be surprised if Quinton secretly employed an assistant whose only job was to eavesdrop on all his phone calls, just so they can anticipate whatever he'll need next."

I take a steady inhale, wondering if it's the intensity of these control-top Lululemons or the dizzying thought of spending the next few weeks living under Quinton and Selma's roof while attempting to pull off a deal that could change my life — in the city that has very much changed my life once already — that's making me feel a bit lightheaded. Maybe it's all of the above.

"This whole arrangement sure as hell beats you staying in long-term corporate housing next to Brett, though. We couldn't have you doing that. The gardener will also be there, by the way. Maybe a pool guy, too."

House manager. Gardener. Pool guy?

Good grief.

The only pictures of their sprawling estate I've seen are the few Liv sent earlier while trying to get me excited for at least one part of this trip — and it worked. Their place looks like paradise on earth — a collection of buildings nestled in the Hollywood Hills, perched on top of a mountain overlooking the entire valley, with a deck and a huge infinity pool that looks like it could be as long as one of our city blocks here. I still can't believe that's going to be my home away from home while we get this deal done. It's a far cry from my living arrangements the last time I was in that city.

The whole idea makes my stomach swirl like a whirlpool.

"Didn't they scare the shit out of you the first time you met them?" I ask, wondering what type of reception I might get if they happen to pop in.

"Absolutely. Yes."

I laugh at the way her head starts bobbing dramatically, as if she's remembering the exact moment they met.

"Which is why reconnecting with Dax might prove to be a nice little form of stress relief while there. Take the edge off. Stay sharp. Ain't nothing wrong with that," she tells me.

"You should have seen the way he looked at me that night." I squeeze the words out as if it pains me to remember, but inside, something inside me pulls apart, just conjuring up the way he held me, touched me in ways that couldn't be possible if we'd agreed to make everything meaningless.

"You know," she starts, "if sleeping with Dax is out of the question because he's only into emotional connections now, and you still believe that's something you aren't capable of — which is incorrect — then you're going to have to get on board with yoga. L.A. is the yoga capital of the world."

"I thought that was India?"

"If you think it's India, then you've never been to L.A.," she says, widening her eyes with a laugh. "Get ready to get your socks knocked off. Literally. The whole city likes to talk about yoga while sucking green juice through paper straws. Considering the way you hate that kind of thing, I'm legit concerned for you."

I laugh. Olivia has spent a lot of time in L.A., since that's where Dom is originally from, even though they've made their permanent home at his estate on the North Shore of Oahu.

"L.A. sounds like another planet compared to New York," I tell her.

"Just start with yoga, and if that doesn't work — which it won't, because I know you — then go for stress relief *à la* Dax Harper," she tells me, smiling wickedly. "I always liked him, Abs. A lot. I really, *really* liked him for you."

I shake my head. "We're not even going there."

"Fine. Text me once you land, and again when you decide to call him. We get to be a whole three hours closer in time difference while you're there."

"Promise," I tell her.

"And Abs . . . she says, pausing. "Permission to say something you might not like?"

"Lay it on me." I know from the way she's looking at me that she's about to impart some best-friend wisdom that, in my world, only Olivia can get away with dishing out.

"Quit being such a killjoy to your own happiness."

I wince, nodding at my own expense, but only because it's so true. "I wish I knew how." I laugh, shrugging. "I'm the worst, apparently."

"Give him a chance. Tell him you're coming to town. Let it play out while you're in the same city again. I don't have any intention of being a lonely old lady with you later in life. You're welcome to third wheel it with Dom and I someday, but I can't have you growing old alone in an office while we're over here surrounded by babies and grandkids."

A sharp pain of jealousy hits the middle of my chest. I shove it away, then force out a smile, matching Olivia's on the screen. I wish I was capable of the type of love she and Dom have for each other, but I'm not. It's just not in my DNA. If history has repeatedly shown me anything about myself, it's that. Self-sabotage may as well be my middle name at this point.

"I need to get a day or two of negotiations under my belt before I even consider adding more complications to my time in L.A. I'm feeling too jittery as it is."

"Fine. But at least get yourself a few more pairs of those yoga pants right after you land, then. If sex is off the table, you're gonna need 'em."

I laugh, and she joins in.

"Thanks for your honesty," I tell her.

"You always do the same for me. Now, go finish packing that beigey wardrobe of yours, Abs — you have a plane to catch."

CHAPTER 14

Dax

My phone dings through the car speakers just as I'm about to make the last left turn into the parking lot. That accident back on the 101 killed my commute. I sat at a standstill on the highway for so long, wedged into so much traffic that I couldn't see what was happening ahead until I passed what looked like a head-on collision. It kept everyone moving at a snail's pace. My plan to show up an hour early this morning swiftly turned into barely getting to the right building on time.

"Text from Lila Lancaster," my car's text-reading feature announces.

I grip the steering wheel. She's already texted me four times.

"Would you like me to read it?" the voice asks.

"Yes," I answer.

A robotic woman's voice begins reading Lila's text through the speakers so loudly that it hurts my ears, much like Lila might in real life, and I press the speaker button down on the wheel to save my hearing for our meeting and the scolding she'll likely have ready.

"Dax! Where are you? We're starting in three minutes. I'll hold down the fort until you get here, but you better hustle!"

I'm already mumbling, "Yeah, no shit, Lila," when the car's robotic voice interrupts with, "Would you like me to reply?"

The car automatically reads back what it just heard me muttering, as if it were meant to be sent as a reply text to Lila.

"No shit, Lila," the car repeats.

My eyes widen as the voice asks if I'd like to send that reply.

"No!" I yell, hitting a button on the wheel.

"Okay, I'll send it," the car responds.

"Cancel!" I grumble, hitting another wrong button on my steering wheel as I maneuver around a family of ducks that's taking its sweet, sweet time to cross the road right in front of the parking lot entrance I'm trying to turn into.

"Sent!" the voice responds cheerfully and I swear there's a hint of smugness in the typically monotone voice.

My jaw drops, but I can't help but laugh.

"Fuck," I say under my breath, choking back another chuckle.

I need to update my phone. It's been acting out all week.

"Text Lila," I say, after pressing the correct command button on my steering wheel.

"What would you like to say to Lila?" the car speaker asks.

"Sorry, stupid phone malfunction. Be there in two."

"Sorry, stupid. Be there in two," the car repeats back. "Shall I send it?"

"No!" I yell, hitting the steering wheel's button in another slight panic to stop the text from sending.

"Sent!" the voice chirps again.

"Ugh," I groan, pushing back into the headrest, still waiting for the last duck to cross. But when I imagine Lila's face as she opens up those last two texts, I crack into a smile.

Yeah, she's not going to buy that it was just a phone malfunction, but it's at least a *tiny* bit funny. I start laughing a little too hard, all by myself in my car. The steel in Lila's eyes when I finally get in there for this meeting is going to be epic. As it should be, considering the magnitude of what's at stake today, but for some reason, this only makes me laugh harder.

I'm not worried about our deal. Silas has enough capital to buy anything he wants, and if The Nile Group is suddenly on his must-have list, then that's what Lila and I are going to get for him.

After sliding into a parking spot, I manually shoot Lila a quick apology text, blaming it on my phone needing an update, then I jump out of my car, briefcase in hand.

Of all the days to be late. I've worked my ass off on plenty of high-stake negotiations, but this one is shaping up to be a hostile takeover, considering The Nile Group has been courted by another company for nearly a year at this point.

My firm's PR team has been working endlessly to put Davenport Media in the best public spotlight in the lead up to this moment. Today we will surprise everyone by putting our offer on the table. I have a feeling we're going to need every last bit of corporate power we can possibly exert once Silas' intentions are known. There are already two other offers on the table, both from stealth companies that have been trying to keep their offers under wraps. That is, until Silas' head of development got a whiff of their long-standing attempts.

And now, here we are.

After jogging across the parking lot, I pull open the front door of the mega office building full of rented-out conference rooms — *neutral territory*, I remember Lila saying once she'd been able to collaborate with the other potential buyers and get everyone meeting here today.

The door lifts off my fingertips as someone walks in behind me.

"Thanks," I say, without turning around.

Then I head straight to the metal detector line, already unbuckling my belt while sliding my shoes off using only my toes. I toss everything onto the conveyor belt, including my briefcase and phone, before walking through the detector with my hands held up over my head like I'm the main attraction on a shooting range.

"In a hurry today, bro?" Randy asks on the other side before waving his handheld detector over my outstretched arms and down each one of my legs.

"Lila is probably catching fire at this very moment out of sheer rage," I tell the security guard, whom I've gotten to know over the last couple years of having acquisition meetings for various companies at this conference building. "Accident on the 101. Stopped for well over an hour. Should probably have called the company chopper in to get me outta there."

Randy chuckles, knowing I'm only half kidding.

"You know the machine is running slower than usual today, too," he tells me, eyeing the tattered belt that's slowly passing through the ancient tunnel at a snail's pace. "The world's conspiring against you today, man."

"Trust me, nothing is going to stand in the way of this deal going through," I mutter. "Not even the world conspiring against me."

However, as I stand near the conveyor belt on the other side of Randy's manual check, waiting for my belongings to make it through, I realize that I may have underestimated the universe.

I'm tapping my foot when a spicy waft of vanilla perfume hits me. It smells just like the tiny amber bottle of pure vanilla extract my grandmother used to hold under my nose for a sniff before we added it to her biggest ceramic bowl — the one with the halo of chickens around it — as we made her famous sugar cookie recipe. Something about the sweet scent transports me back to her kitchen, always so calming and warm.

Someone else is waiting for their belongings to make it out of the ancient machine, and they move in a little too close to my side. I step about six inches away and clear my throat.

"You look exhausted," the waiting woman says, leaning over.

I must be hearing things because the voice sounds a lot like Abby's, but why would Abby be here?

I blink a few times, trying to clear my mind of her memory. It's been months since we saw each other, but it's like she lives just below the surface of my mind. And now I'm hearing her voice in L.A., of all places.

The security operator pauses the conveyor belt to stare at me, then shifts his eyes to the person standing too close to my side. I widen my eyes at him then swivel my head, following his eyes right to—

No.

It's Abby. Abby is standing right beside me.

What the fuck is she doing here?

She grins nervously.

"Maybe a little matcha would help you wake up?" she asks, scrunching her nose.

My breath quickens when she speaks.

I look around, first not believing my ears, and now, my eyes.

Her dimples, my weakest spot on the planet, deepen. Her thick, black hair is piled high on her head in a perfect little bun with tortoiseshell glasses framing her sharp, amber eyes. She's wearing a navy business suit, and the same nude heels she wore on our last night together.

A sudden memory of those shoes heaped in a corner of her bedroom hits me right below the belt.

"Abby?"

Before the mirage can disappear, and before I can think twice about what I'm doing, I step toward her, wrapping her into an unexpected hug.

"Dax," she sighs my name like she's embarrassed to see me, but her breath tickles my ear, just like it did the last time we . . . When I . . .

Fuck.

I loosen my grip, remembering the unanswered note I left on her nightstand.

I pull her arms down from where she's looped them around my neck and take a step back.

She looks down at the space I've just put between us, and swallows.

"What are you doing here?" she stammers, looking around.

"Me?" I say, forcing a more professional tone into my voice. "Working. You?" While I'd love to believe she tracked me down to make amends, she looks ready for a meeting, coffee cup in hand. The same berry-pink lipstick stain across the rim.

Fucking hell.

"Me too," she says, before tearing her eyes away to look down the length of the conveyor belt for her own bag. My briefcase is nearly out of the black tunnel. I pull it the rest of the way out and see her briefcase coming through next. I should run to my meeting, really I should run out of this entire building since there's a good chance I already know how this might play out. But I decide to wait another thirty seconds for hers, too.

"Unless, of course, it turns out that I'm stalking you. What a turn of events that would be, eh?" she says, adding a nervous laugh at the end.

I can't bring myself to join in. This building is full of conference rooms that can be rented out to serve as neutral ground for contentious negotiations, but considering that we're both in mergers and acquisitions, the odds of us walking toward the same conference room right now is still too high for comfort. And I don't think she realizes yet what might be happening.

I catch the moment her eyes dart down to my ring finger — so quickly, I nearly miss it.

I hold my empty hand up, just to make her squirm.

"Eloped last month," I tell her, frowning.

Her eyes flash to mine, lips parted like she's about to protest, then thinks better of it.

"Ring hasn't come in yet but it's beautiful. Princess cut. Two carats. You should see the way it sparkles in the light," I add.

She purses her lips and rolls her eyes, trying to hold back a smile while not bothering to lift her own empty hand.

Just as I'm about to tell her I'm kidding, my phone rings.

It's Lila. I shift my briefcase to my other arm and hit the red button to reject her call, then add, "Joking. It's an emerald cut. Princess is so last year."

Abby narrows her eyes at me while I shove my phone back into my pocket, knowing another call from Lila is bound to start at any moment.

"I need to get going," I tell her, backing away from the security station toward the main screen with all the room schedules and names to check where I'm headed.

"Wait," Abby says, grabbing my elbow, latching on, like not a day or six months has passed since the last time we stared into each other's eyes as the world around us disappeared. I stiffen my spine, but don't turn her away. "I'm running insanely late, but I'll walk with you, at least to the board with all the room numbers. Which direction are you headed?" She quickly looks around the foyer of the enormous building for a sign.

"There's a screen with room names and schedules down here," I say, eyeing her, while picking up the pace. I force myself to walk beside her, praying this is just a heart-stopping coincidence and we're not on our way to the same bloody conference room.

Am I a little peeved about how things ended between us a few months ago?

Yes.

But am I also a man who finds the woman practically jogging beside me completely irresistible?

Also, yes.

My pulse picks up speed as we approach the display board, praying our eyes don't land on the same room number.

"So, what have you been up to?" she asks, just as casually as one might ask about the weather.

I turn toward her, frowning.

"Seriously?" I ask, visually scrolling down the list of room numbers.

"Seriously, what?" She runs her finger down the list. I watch where it lands.

Are you fucking kidding me?

Adrenaline starts coursing through me, but I don't mention it to her yet. We have a few things to work out before I blow her whole day up with the next set of news.

"You never called me after New York," I say, walking toward a collection of arrows and room numbers mounted on the wall. Sure enough, Abby sets off right beside me. We both turn down a long hall to our right and she loops her elbow tightly through mine.

"I know," she says, keeping her voice low so no one passing by us might hear. "I hope you're not upset about that. But I really think I did us both a favor."

I laugh. *Christ.* Then, I drop her elbow from mine and shoot her a look that says, are you delusional?

"What?" she asks, looking surprised.

"What makes you think you did us both a favor?" I ask sarcastically, increasing my pace. "Enlighten me."

"Well, it was still a really great night," she points out, skipping to keep up.

"You sound like you're dictating a thank you card to your grandma," I interrupt as we turn a corner down another long hall.

She scoffs.

"Dax, you live way over here. I live over there. I thought about calling, I really did, but," she admits, shaking her head, "I just thought it might be best to let us do what we do best."

"Sleep together and then act like it never happened?" I ask.

"While keeping it no strings attached," she adds, looking pleased, as if I finally get it.

Is she serious right now?

"You didn't think you should have at least called before you flew across the entire country here to L.A., because we're both M & A attorneys and it might be really awkward if we ran into each other like this?"

"Just like you called before you flew across the entire country to my city for work?" she shoots back.

I frown. *Fair.* "That's beside the point."

I left the ball in her court, and that's where it's stayed ever since. Grown moss all around it, even.

She looks in my direction, assessing the slight dodge from her not-so-subtle play, but my phone pings again, pulling my attention away.

I curse under my breath.

Three more missed texts from Lila and I'm now officially running nine minutes late.

"Okay, I get it. I do," she says, still keeping up beside me as we both turn down another hall, following a sign with more room numbers and arrows plastered across it. Her voice softens. "Brett booked this work trip only yesterday. I'm going to be in L.A. for the next couple of weeks working on this deal. It's huge. Like, career-making level of huge. I didn't plan on running into you like this on my very first morning here. But, now that it's happened, we should find time to catch up!"

I come to a halt.

She skids to a stop beside me, wilting as she realizes the phrase she's just used.

"Sorry, bad choice of words." She grimaces. "I'd love to talk, but not like this. We're both running late for our meetings so maybe I can call you later?"

Fucking hell, Abs. You're giving me whiplash.

I fight the urge to correct the plural use of the word *meetings* to just one, singular, potentially explosive *meeting*. Then trudge on, doing my best to ignore the confusion bouncing through my mind — a mixture of sweaty, sheet-clutching anticipation and doubt — while painfully aware of what we're about to walk into in, oh, thirty seconds or so. Give or take. I glance at Abby, who's still blissfully unaware.

She's still practically jogging beside me to keep up.

"No hard feelings," I say. "We don't need to catch up. I'm good. It's fine. You're right, you did us both a favor."

We pause on the corner while Abby checks another sign with room numbers and arrows, pointing us to the right.

"One fifty-six," she repeats the room number to herself before setting off to the right, the last hall with only a few doors along the way.

Jesus Christ.

I walk faster ahead but she manages to keep up.

"We must be in the same hall," she murmurs under her breath. "And not to beat a dead horse, but if it makes you feel better, maybe you changed my mind about a few things that night."

I scoff.

"Your silence afterward could've fooled me," I deadpan. "But I get it. You're not really one for meaningful connections, so . . . mission accomplished."

She shakes her head grimly, facing her eyes forward.

"I swear I was just trying to save us from trying something that was doomed to fail in the end," she says, pushing forward. "I've never pretended to be good at this kind of thing."

"What kind of thing?" I ask, challenging her to spell it out for me as the numbers over each doorway quickly lead up to one fifty-six. "Put a name on it so there's no more confusion here."

She silently glances over at me. We're running out of doors, which means we're also running out of time. And I still haven't broken the news to her that we're about to spend a lot more time together over the next few weeks, whether she wants to or not.

"We're short on time and I don't want to get into all that if we don't have time," she says. "I'm almost to my room. Where's yours?"

"Uh, it's coming up," I say.

As annoyed as I am, I also don't want to end this on a sour note before we go into this meeting.

"Would you be up for a late dinner?" she asks. "If not tonight, then maybe tomorrow? A guy's gotta eat, right?" She smiles faintly.

97

I face forward again, sneaking glances her way as we both slow our pace.

There's only one door left.

We both come to a stop right in front of it.

She turns to face me.

"Well, this is me," she says, sighing.

The sign above it reads *one fifty-six*.

My heart thumps up to my ears, knowing what's waiting on the other side of that wall.

She grasps the handle without pushing it open, claiming it as her own.

I grab the handle over her hand and pull it back to keep the door shut. She slides her free hand onto my chest as I do, concern filling her eyes. She must think I'm trying to buy more time with her before our conversation ends, which I am, but not for the reason she's probably thinking.

"Dax, I've got to go in now," she says, sidestepping in front of me. "I'll call you to finish this conversation."

I need at least fifteen seconds to warn her before we walk into that room together.

"I need to tell you something," I finally say, pushing her hand off my chest in case someone walks out. She takes it as a sign that I want to hold her hand and keeps her fingers laced in mine.

"I've got it, Dax," she says, squeezing my hand, thinking I'm just trying to open the door for her.

She yanks on the door handle again, but I keep it firmly shut with my hand over hers.

"That's not why I followed you to this room," I start. Any second now it's going to register. "We're going into the—"

"Dax, seriously—" she interrupts.

She's about to yank on the handle again, but her face erupts as it sinks in. She studies my face, jaw drops, and takes a step back, letting her hand slide off the door.

I nod. "Yep. This is my room too," I tell her.

Her eyes widen.

She blinks.

Twice.

Three times.

There it is. A full-on shit sandwich combo with chips smacking her right between the eyes.

She takes a bigger step back.

"Oh my God, Dax, don't tell me—"

I shake my head, as if I'm the one to have something to apologize for even though I'm just as blindsided by the situation as she is.

Just then, the door jerks open from the inside, leaving my hand frozen in the air where I'd just been holding the bloody thing shut.

Abby and I quickly jerk any touching body parts back to our own respective sides.

Lila is standing on the other side, shifting her eyes between us, painting us red with her stare like we're standing at the epicenter of some great conspiracy theory. One millisecond later, a sour-looking man I've never seen before steps into the frame.

Abby turns toward them, her mouth slightly ajar.

"There you are, Dax," Lila says coolly, crossing her arms. Her eyes dart quickly between Abby and me. "I was about to tell them to send out a search party for you. You're never late. And those texts you sent back were . . . not very descriptive on when you'd be showing up." She narrows her eyes at me, tightening her lips.

I force a smile, remembering the texts. She has every right to be annoyed.

"There's a reason for that," I start to say, but Abby spins back to me, her jaw opening and shutting like a fish out of water.

The ferocious bulldog-looking bald guy next to Lila pipes up next. "Where have you been?" he barks under his breath, glaring at Abby.

And, this must be . . .

"Brett, hi, I'm here now," Abby says, breathlessly.

Somehow, she instantly manages to collect herself, morphing into the very picture of professionalism.

"Accident on the highway. Total lack of subways here," she adds, stiffly. Then she turns to me, all manner of apology suddenly gone from her eyes before adding, "If we're all here, let's get started then, shall we?"

CHAPTER 15

Abby

I close my eyes and exhale a steady stream of hot air before turning all the way around in the driver's seat, looking for any sign that says I'm still going in the right direction.

"He *what?*" Olivia yelps into the phone, sounding just as shocked as I was this morning when Dax failed to explain that he and Lila were there for The Nile Group, too.

"He and Lila are trying to steal The Nile for their client," I tell her. "I had no idea there was a potential hostile takeover in the works, but I should have known it could be a possibility once I heard Davenport Media was showing interest. Somewhere in my brain, I should have recognized that Dax and Silas Davenport might be connected legally. They are buddies from their boarding school days, but I had no idea that he was solely representing The Davenport Media Group now. There were rumors of another party wanting to enter the negotiations — which Brett knew more about than me, going into this morning — but I never saw this particular left turn coming."

"Wait, Dax went to boarding school with Silas Davenport?" Liv asks, sounding impressed.

I sigh, feeling lost — and certainly in more ways than one — but hoping the gate I've been trying to find for the last forty-five minutes is the one I've just pulled up to. I've already tried two other gates on my way here since none of the directions to Quinton and Selma's estate are based on actual street names after a certain point and only mention random landmarks. Apparently it's one of the ways they try to maintain a private residence here in L.A. with all the paparazzi roaming around.

"I think I mentioned that to you at some point?" I say, feeling distracted, looking around for any sign that this gate belongs to a famous movie director. But all I see is a fake boulder in front of a very nondescript metal gate.

"Have you kept up with Silas in the media?" Liv asks. "The guy's apparently a bit of a loose cannon, although, from the look of most media coverage he's definitely figured out how to have a good time with that pile of money he inherited a few years ago."

"Wonderful," I mutter, studying the dark gate in front of my headlights, praying that this is the right one.

After a full day of fending off Brett, who's somehow managed to act more stressed than usual, along with a pack of overzealous hyenas coming in hot from Dax's firm — and who had the audacity to threaten a hostile takeover of The Nile Group if we don't all agree to capitulate — I'm really too overwhelmed to zero in on our opponent's rich-boy party habits right now.

I push the brake pedal to the floor and resist the urge to press my forehead against the steering wheel for a nap. Instead, I let out a heavy, soul-cleansing sigh — praying with my last ounce of strength that these gates truly belong to Selma and Quinton and I won't be forced to drive back to that awful hotel from last night.

Brett and I stayed in separate hotel rooms near the airport last night after getting in late from New York, since I didn't think I'd have the energy to find my way over to this house following a cross-country flight and a full day of work. But now, I'm wondering how I had the energy to navigate through L.A. traffic after our meetings today (without any accidents, thank you, although there were a few near misses) to find this place. A place that's so deeply shrouded in secrecy that a clearly marked street sign is apparently too much to ask for.

This would all be quite thrilling if I wasn't so freakishly exhausted.

"Hang on, Liv, I'm pressing the rock's speaker button thingy now," I tell her, wearily.

"Oh, you made it!" she squeals.

I wish I had her energy right now.

"God willing," I mutter back, feeling a slight wisp of excitement twist through me at how excited she sounds.

I would hold up the FaceTime screen for her to tell me whether I'm at the right entrance or not, but all these gates and rocks look the same to me.

I lower my window, then press the tiny red button set into that enormous faux boulder. There's a bunch of holes all over one side, which must be a speaker. I notice a tiny little camera lens off in the top right corner and force out a smile, trying my best to look bright-eyed rather than haggard to whoever might be watching on the other side.

As soon as I hit the red button near the speaker, a bright, white spotlight shoots out of the trees behind the fake rock, blinding me.

I shade my eyes with one hand and stare into the camera, hoping to be let in, or for something to be said other than *leave the premises* — as happened at the last two places.

"Uh, hello?" I prompt, after a moment of silence, then press the red button for a second time.

The speaker gargles to life, and a woman with a voice like butter answers.

"Good evening."

"Good evening," I echo, probably louder than I need to. "Uh, I'm Abby Torres. Sent by Olivia."

Silence.

"Olivia and Dom — erm, Dominick Bryant? Quinton's brother? I think you're expecting me? Is this Quinton and Selma's home?"

"Oh, of course, hon."

Hun?

"Thank God," I mumble to Olivia.

"One moment, please. Just double-checking that you're who we're expecting. If you'd just smile real big up at that camera lens, please, dear."

I squint my eyes up toward the camera lens, but the happiness on my face is real.

I finally made it.

"Perfect. Oh my stars, you are just beautiful! Okay, head on in, honey."

The gate in front of my car suddenly unlatches itself and then swings open on a silent hinge.

"This could be the start of a really bad movie," I whisper to Liv, hopefully quiet enough that the woman talking through the rock can't hear me. "You're sure I'm in the right place?"

"Go ahead and follow the driveway down and to the right," the woman says through the hidden speaker. "You can park in the circle drive in front of the doors when you arrive at the main house."

"You're all good," Olivia chimes in. "You should see it during the day. Probably a bit dark there right now, but you're fine. Seriously, just wait until you see the place. And Starry is just the best."

The speaker clicks off.

"Uh, thank you!" I call out, a moment too late.

"In fact, I think that was Starry who answered," Olivia adds. "House manager, though she's more like everyone's favorite grandma."

"Everyone's favorite grandma?" I ask, feeling that old familiar pang — like a thick root lodged in my throat. A root because it's been there as long as I can remember. Longer than most things I can recall, like it was there first and I simply grew to exist around it, growing thicker at any mention of family.

"You're going to love her," Liv says.

"I'm sure I will," I say, picturing the type of grandma I've only ever seen depicted in sitcoms or movies full of smiling, happy families. The only grandmother I ever knew was Grandma Tally, and she died just before I turned eleven. She lived alone in Kansas, so I only met her twice when my aunt and uncle took me down to visit, but when I did, she served me grapefruit pie and yelled at me when I accidentally used her dog's toothpaste instead of my own since it was sitting in the bathroom drawer. I'd fallen asleep with a gritty, meat-flavored film crunching between my teeth each time I accidentally let my top jaw touch my lower one — and wondering why I didn't get the type of grandmother that baked cookies and gave cuddles instead of what I experienced on that awful trip.

The gate swings open slowly in front of the headlights. I refocus and ease my foot off the brake, slowly inching the car forward. I tell myself that what I'm doing is totally normal — driving up to a dark house alone at night, in the middle of a deserted mountain road above an intimidating major city, and being trapped behind electronic gates that someone I've never met before has control over.

Totally, totally normal.

I wish I had Dax in the passenger seat for all this.

"You sure I'm in the right place?" I ask Olivia, creeping forward. "What if some nice-sounding sicko just let me into their gate? Someone that doesn't care who I am as long as I'm a piece of fresh meat for the taking? I might not look super cute right now, but definitely cute enough to kidnap."

She laughs, and I bite my lip down hard as I make my way down the long driveway. Olivia continues cracking jokes about getting tortured by Selma's professional house staff, while wondering aloud whether or not that would be the worst way to go.

"You might feel like you've died, but gone straight to heaven when you get there," she assures me. "Trust me."

As I continue on toward the house, I imagine Dax holding my hand to steady me as we make our way silently through the dark, reassuring me that everything is going to be fine. But, let's be honest, he'd have to forgive me for what I pulled on him after our rendezvous back in New York.

I force the thought out of my mind. We just need to finish the conversation we started earlier, before Lila and Brett flung that door open on us. I'm certain they didn't notice Dax and I pulling apart. Besides, I'm sure Brett would have mentioned it to me by now if he had noticed anything funny going on between us.

I stare up at the tunnel of trees I'm driving through, starting to feel a little bit like Belle from *Beauty and the Beast*, making my way through the great and forested unknown.

"Tell me when you can see the place," Liv says.

The route becomes more peaceful as I meander through an apparently unending line of willowy aspen trees lining the subtly lit driveway. My headlights reflect off their smooth, dove-white bark beneath a thick canopy of fluttering leaves.

"This place is pretty unreal," I tell her. "How long is this driveway?"

"You're not in Kansas anymore, Dorothy," she says, dreamily. "Open your window and smell that fresh air. They built the place way above the smog there. High enough to get that famous sun and ocean breeze that first brought people flocking to L.A."

I lower my window again, dropping one hand outside to feel the cool night air trickle by, like water slipping across my skin. It smells faintly of the saltwater mixed with dampened earth from the light sprinkle of rain we got earlier tonight, and I take a deep inhale, filling my lungs, allowing myself to feel the first real nudge of excitement since I landed on another planet last night. I already love how green and natural it is up here — a far cry from the concrete jungle back home, with the exception of my apartment overflowing with plants.

Around the last bend in the driveway, a beautiful French-chateauesque house — no, a legitimate chateauesque *mansion* — comes into view, surrounded by a line of antique street lamps. They're lined up in the style I remember seeing along the Pont Alexandre III in Paris, except that instead of reflecting into the Seine River, these lamps are reflecting into a shallow creek, which winds along the front of the home and driveway, nestled beside what looks like a gravel walking path.

The whole view reminds me of Paris, a mini City of Lights.

"Whoa," I say quietly, keeping my eyes fixed on the three-story main building that's surrounded by a sea of sandstone and cut grass, carefully crafted to create a green and tan checkerboard effect upon the ground.

I glide the car up to the apex of the circle drive, coming to a stop just a few yards down from a pair of enormous arched doors made of twisted iron and deeply tinted, warbled glass.

I'm half-expecting the cast of *Downton Abbey* to parade out those enormous double doors to greet me.

"This place," I sigh into the phone. "I'm not sure that I deserve to stay here."

"I know, right? I'm not sure *any* of us do. Not even Quinton and Selma."

"Wish you were here," I tell her, feeling a pang of loneliness. The same one that crops up every time I experience a moment that makes me wish I was sharing it right beside someone else.

"I do, too," she says. "But you're going to feel at home the second you meet the staff. Everyone there is beyond nice."

"Thanks for setting this up." I don't bother to remind her that I've never, not once, felt *at home*. "Beats the hell out of staying next door to Brett at that hotel."

She chuckles.

"I can't believe they actually tried to stick you in a hotel next door to Brett for multiple weeks. Haven't they at least heard of Airbnb?"

A light flicks on from the inside, casting a blanket of light across the flat hood of my rental car.

"Someone just turned on a light," I whisper. "I think that's my cue to get out of the car."

"Good luck!" she calls. "Let me know how tomorrow goes."

"Lord, help me," I groan. "Love you."

"You too! Tell them I say hi," she says. "I guarantee you've never experienced anyone like Starry before."

"I have a feeling I'm about to experience a lot of things I've never experienced before," I say.

"I know," she says, not forcing me to go through the long list of completely normal things I've never done, or had, or felt. "Now go!"

A moment after we've hung up, I'm pulling my bags out of the trunk, still wondering if someone is going to pop out that front door to shoo me away. When the front door finally swings open, a tiny figure steps out, illuminated by the warm glow of the house from behind.

"Hello!" a sweet voice calls out, then the figure begins walking down the stairs to greet me.

CHAPTER 16

Dax

I'm seriously regretting my life choices. All of them. Becoming a lawyer. Hiring Lila. Allowing Abby to ghost me for a second time. And helping myself to that second helping of parmesan chicken from the now nearly-empty takeout containers around our office conference room.

One plateful would have sufficed.

Perhaps it was the forty-seventh glare in the last twenty-four hours from Lila that put me over the edge, and I found myself stress-eating my way through that second bit since my preferred method of stress relief in L.A. (i.e., Abby Torres) has been put on permanent hiatus.

This whole day has been jinxed.

Considering the look of shock and anger plastered across Abby's face today when I announced to the room that Lila and I, along with a few other sharks from Harper & Associates LLP, were there to represent Davenport Media Group in their bid to acquire The Nile Group, I'm pretty sure Abby would have eaten me for dinner tonight if I'd let her.

There are worse ways to go, I think, chuckling to myself.

Lila breaks her concentration just long enough to glare at me from across the table.

Again.

"Forty-eight," I mutter under my breath, spinning a yellow highlighter through my fingers before catching it again.

"What?" she asks, punctuating her question with another pinched stare.

Forty-nine.

"Nothing," I say, smiling brightly, just to annoy her.

Did I know that it was Abby's enormous, nationwide firm representing the original buyer for The Nile Group?

Yes.

Did I know that it was going to be *her* in that conference room today representing them?

Absolutely not.

I knew her firm's name was on it, but I'd figured if she was the attorney on the deal, she'd have at least reached out to me before flying all the way across the country. Until I saw her behind me at the metal detector, I figured she was in New York, stealing some other guy's lattes off of her friend's coffee counter. Not here in L.A., walking into conference rooms, threatening to take me down with just one look.

Although, I'm one to talk here, aren't I? I didn't exactly call her before I showed up in her city.

Yet, here we are.

Life is funny like that.

Fate is funny like that.

Downright *hilarious*, sometimes.

"Are you going to finish that?" Lila asks, breaking my concentration by pointing her fork at what's left on my plate.

I stare down at the last bite of chicken sitting atop a cold pile of noodles.

"Um, are you?" I ask, shifting my eyes to her fork, hovering menacingly over my plate.

"If you're not, then maybe. Although—" She looks conflicted. "Yeah, no, I probably shouldn't."

"It's all yours if you want it," I tell her, pushing the plate toward her elbows, hoping she'll at least toss it in a nearby bin if she changes her mind.

She sighs, but drops the fork on the table, conceding defeat against my lukewarm, congealed-looking parmesan chicken offer. We're in our fifth hour of poring over these board statements, looking for every last loophole to gain another pound of power if a hostile takeover is where this whole thing is headed, though I know there are at least multiple weeks of document review and in-person negotiations left to wade through for all of us.

"Silas is arriving tomorrow?" she asks. It's more like a question than a confirmation even though she's very aware that Silas is, in fact, arriving tomorrow. That's the plan, anyway, although you never truly know with him. "So, I probably shouldn't," she adds.

She's still staring wistfully at the ugly mass of gelatinous noodles and chicken left on my plate, but I'm not sure how Silas' pending arrival tomorrow has anything to do with her current state of hunger.

The sigh that follows is so loud and tortured that I have to ask.

"What does Silas coming here have to do with whether or not you eat my chicken, Lila?"

I feel the weight of today practically oozing out of my pores. What started out as a chance encounter with the woman I can't seem to shake from my mind, has ended with cold takeout and my moody colleague hemming and hawing over whether or not Silas might notice an extra helping of noodles on her hips that she allowed herself to eat the night prior to his arrival.

"It's not every day I get to meet Silas Davenport," Lila says, raising a brow in my direction like I'm some idiot she's just transported in from the zoo. "What's he like, by the way? Am I his type?"

I blink one, long blink at her as if she's out of her mind for asking me whether or not our top client, and my longtime friend, is her *type*.

Though, given my level of boredom and a solid need for entertainment right now, I decide to egg this on. Lila is one of my favorite people on the planet to give a hard time to, after all. She's more like the work wife I probably should have divorced three years ago since our banter moved from playful — borderline flirty — to mostly tired and all-knowing.

She tosses her fork a bit further from herself, as if to ward off any further notions of consuming additional calories, then leans against the edge of the table, clasping her fists beneath her chin like a child waiting for story time to start.

"Why are you asking whether or not Silas is your type?" I ask. "He's our *client*."

"Just doing my due diligence," she says.

I frown, not bothering to stop a chuckle from escaping my lips.

"Lila, you can't be serious. Finding out whether or not our client is single is hardly due diligence."

"Oh stop, I'm allowed to be curious about him. It's not every day you meet a guy like Silas Davenport, and I just want to do right by him," she says, making a sound in her throat like she knows she's being ridiculous.

"Do right by him, or do right *to* him?" I ask, cracking a grin.

"Can you just answer my question?" she asks. "What's he like?"

I exhale and push myself away from the leftovers, confirming that I'm just bored, not hungry, so finishing that will certainly lead to even more life regret.

"In his younger years, Silas was my favorite of all my friends. Cut from the same cloth that most of us in our friend group were — a little rough around the edges, but always up for a bit of fun. I never even knew the type of family he came from until we were older because he never brought it up. He always wanted to be just another one of the guys. Not a billionaire's son."

Lila's grinning like she shares the same memories of him that I have.

"I would have sung that shit from the rooftops," she says.

I laugh, knowing she's telling the truth.

"I think most people would. Si was just never like that. Not back then, anyway. But we all grew up. Si and another one of our friends, Grant, and his fiancée all went to Boston — Harvard, actually — while I went over to Northwestern." *Where I met Abby, our new opposing counsel,* I want to add, but don't.

"And now he's the life and soul of every party he walks into, right?" Lila says, her eyes hungry for more.

I stare at her, knowing she's in good company, thinking of Silas like that.

"He's a bit different when you know him," I say, feeling the need to defend my friend. "He's been through a lot."

"Well yeah, that was practically plastered across every tabloid cover from here to The Netherlands," she says, like I'm an idiot for stating the obvious. "But as someone who really knows him, what's he like? Is he as charming as the websites make him out to be? Or as wild? Most importantly, is he single?"

I toss my noodley paper plate into a nearby bin and check my phone screen again, noting one missed call from Abby. *So, it finally happened.* She finally called. Six months late. I purse my lips, not sure I'm ready to open up that conversation between us quite yet, especially considering we're going to be meeting in the morning again for more negotiations.

I turn back to answer Lila's line of questions before she adds any more.

"Well, he's incredibly sharp in every sense of the word. Sharp wit, sharp intelligence—"

"Sharp to look at," she injects.

"Interesting due diligence you're doing, Lila," I say.

"Just stating the obvious," she replies, coyly.

"And, yes, he's charming — almost to a fault. But no, he's far less wild than the papers paint him. Part of me thinks those headlines just make for some fairly successful clickbait, given he looks like a Ralph Lauren model with a yearly income that most people wouldn't make across a thousand lifetimes. And the last time I heard from him, yes, he's very much single. Pretty much always single — without any lack of women in his life, if you catch my drift." I rattle through my answers while she licks her lips, ravenously, taking every word in. "And, I'm still your boss," I remind her. "So, if you're going to try to romantically entangle yourself with our biggest client, one who happens to be a very old friend of mine, then it's probably best that you keep that little scandal a secret from me. I don't think I have it in me to read you the ethical rules behind that sort of thing tonight, so please save us both the trouble and don't even go there."

"Oh please," she says, drawing both hands beneath her chin. "I'm just getting some background intel about our client. It's what any responsible attorney would do so I'm not walking into the meeting blind tomorrow."

"Blind? About his relationship status?"

She shrugs like her behavior's completely within the realm of normal. Having been friends with Silas for so long, I've grown used to this line of questioning. Women can't seem to help themselves around him. And why should they? Even without the pool of money at his disposal, he's the sort of guy that most women find attractive. Aloof, charming. But perhaps most interesting of all, he's also loaded to the hilt.

"I don't want to be blind regarding anything to do with him, and if that involves his relationship status, then sure, I'm after that too. There's nothing unethical about doing my due diligence. Besides, Mr. Ethical Standards, you're one to talk."

"What do you mean by that?" I ask, maintaining a well-played expression, the one I've practiced enough times for it to say *fuck off* without being aggressive in the slightest.

"You're. One. To. Talk," she says, more dramatically, as if I need each word enunciated in order to understand what she's telling me.

"I have no interest in Silas Davenport," I tell her, sarcastically, just to rile her up a bit but also to steer the conversation away from where I think she's attempting to go. "However, back to what we're really here to figure out. Have you seen the redaction on page seventy-two? I'm pretty sure it's hiding a—"

"Dear God, you annoy me," she interrupts, rolling her eyes, but her face cracks into another elusive Lila Lancaster grin. My annoying little work wifey. I can't help but smile back.

"But seriously, back to—" I start to say *page seventy-two*, more than ready to move on, but she swiftly cuts me off.

"Abby Torres," she interjects abruptly. "Don't pretend like you guys didn't look like two kids getting caught coming out from the backseat of daddy's car off a dirt road heading straight to love land this morning."

"Interesting picture you paint, there, Lila."

"It was painted *for* me," she says. "By you. You two were practically groping each other outside that conference room when I opened the door. Is she the reason you were running so late?"

I blink heavily, slowly, and *meaningfully* for good measure.

"I don't know what you're referring to, Lila," I say firmly, like I'm beyond bored with this conversation.

She rolls her eyes.

"However, you do win the award for most eye rolls in a night, Lila. I mean, what are we up to now? Fifty-three? Or have we cleared sixty yet?"

She cracks another smile but closes her eyes in an attempt to block the sight of them rolling again.

"Go back to whatever you were saying about Silas' love life," she says, swatting the subject matter away. "Or whatever you were talking about on page seventy-two. Is it where that one line mentions The Nile's interest in only one particular form of AI?"

"You saw that one already?" I ask.

I lean over the stack of documents between us and let the conversation naturally roll over to the real reason we're here working late tonight. There's no reason to let the spotlight sit on Abby any longer than we already have. That ship has sailed. Twice. And the ball between us is still firmly planted right where I left it, nestled snugly on her side of the court.

I stare at the words spanning hundreds of documents between us until all the letters blur together. I'm sure that Abby is poring over the exact same records right now to figure out how her client can leverage them, sweetening their own negotiation power to beat ours tomorrow. I shouldn't be thinking about anything except how to get Silas what he wants out of this. But all I can visualize is how Abby's eyes and hands are likely tracing over the exact same pages as mine right now.

Somewhere in this very same city.

So close, I can practically taste her.

CHAPTER 17

Abby

Olivia was right. But, she's always right. Quinton and Selma's house *granager*, as she introduced herself just now, is like no one else I've ever met.

"House *manager*?" I ask gently, wondering if I'd just heard her wrong as she makes her way down the steps outside.

Starry's laugh is deep and contagious, wrapping itself around me like a gentle hug. "*Gran*-ager," she corrects me, smiling. "Though, I suppose *manager* is what the initial job listing was for. That was so long ago, and I was a lot younger back then. I like to think that I've been upgraded to granager since I started."

She pulls my outstretched hand past her hip, sweeping me into a tight embrace instead of a handshake, the likes of which might rival Dax's. It takes me completely off guard. I've never been much of a hugger when it comes to first-time meetings, but here we go. It's happening.

"I think Quinton started calling me his granager after he had my salted chocolate-chip cookies. Took me a long time to perfect."

"Did you say *salted* chocolate-chip cookies?" I ask, wondering if that's the scent pouring out through the open door, along with the yellow glow of welcoming light.

"The salt gives them a little something," she says, winking as if we've just shared a secret. "I might have stolen that trick from that young celebrity I saw make an appearance on *Iron Chef*— Kendall Fisher, is it?" I chuckle as she laughs that deep, soul-filling laugh again. "Or, honestly, I've been around longer, so maybe it was her who stole that idea from me! Regardless. You've had a long day, honey. Let's get you inside."

She squeezes my hand. I've never felt a hand as weathered as hers. It's like tissue paper that's been stashed away and reused after each gift, soft and lined and somehow familiar. Just as I pull back, she gives me another giddy look that makes my shoulders give way, uncurling from up around my ears. I let out a sigh. Like my entire body has been held in tight formation since running into Dax this morning and I can finally let some of the tension out.

"There now," she says. "Take that deep breath you look like you need. I don't blame you for being tired, sweetheart. Cross-country flights are exhausting. And if you deal with lawyers all day, even though I know you're one too and I'm sure you're a *great* one, honey, but you've got to be practically asleep on your feet by now."

I nod, feeling the weight of the day slough off.

She cups a hand around my shoulder and we both turn, then she matches my stride toward the house, grabbing my bag with her other hand. "I can get that," I say, reaching for my suitcase as we start to go up the stairs.

"Don't be silly." She nudges me forward. "I'm stronger than I look. And besides, you've been lugging it around for two days now, from what I hear. Plus, I could use the extra workout, so you just keep on walking."

She goes up the steps, talking through the silence as if we're old friends with quite a bit to catch up on. It makes my head spin a little.

"Now, Selma and Quinny take most of their house staff with them when they're gone for longer periods of time — Connor, the chef, both their personal trainers, make-up artists, and all the like. It's just Charles — that's the head gardener — and me here with you. We make up the skeleton crew but we manage to do just fine. More than fine, really." She rubs her hand up and down my spine when we reach the last stair, as if to warm me up. "Charles is pretty handy, above and beyond the garden, so I always have my list of things for him to do. He'll be around if you need help with anything. You'll see him hanging around, but he's harmless. At least he should be, considering I married the man."

"You and the gardener are married?" I ask. Olivia hadn't mentioned that.

"Thirty-seven years now," she tells me, stepping over the threshold. "I got lucky marrying a good man for only being twenty-two when I fell for him. Not everyone is that lucky, especially nowadays, from what I hear."

I'm expecting a large entrance room when we pass through the doors and it definitely doesn't disappoint, but the grand foyer of the estate also somehow feels homey and welcoming. The two arched doors are flanked by oversized window seats piled high with cushy, striped cushions beneath towering old-fashioned arched windows that I imagine allow an amazing amount of sunlight to stream in. *What a perfect spot to read a book in, if I am ever to have time for that sort of thing.*

But it's the plants that make me feel like I'm back home. Pots and greenery of every size and shape are spread around like a welcoming crew. I imagine Charles, Starry's husband, tending to them while she looks on.

"Your husband has quite the green thumb," I tell her, spinning on the black-and-white tiled floor to take them all in.

"He does, indeed," she agrees. "Selma and Quinny like being among the living when they're home. All these are *little green friends*, as Selma calls them."

A scurrying fluff ball I'm pretty sure is a cat runs over to rub its flanks against my ankle. I step back, surprised that it seems to like me.

"Oh, don't let her bother you. That's just Millie," she says, attempting to shoo her away. "I pretend to run the house here, but we all know that it's Miss Millie running everything, really."

I bend down to run my fingers through Millie's soft mane, surprised by how tiny her body feels beneath her coat of thick, white fur. She's deliciously cream-colored with a smushed-in nose that makes her look like she's frowning and smiling, both at once, peering up at me with eyes the color of hazy sea glass.

"She actually doesn't bother me at all," I say, as Millie's purr grows louder. She pushes back and forth beneath my hand, like she's anxious I might decide to stop petting her before she's ready for me to go. "I'm just surprised she likes me."

"Well, why wouldn't she, hon?" Starry says, like she has no idea why any cat in the world wouldn't love me.

I don't admit that my own cat seems to want nothing to do with me. Something about the way Starry has welcomed me so genuinely, so comfortably into this wonderful home makes me want to keep that to myself, instead of confessing that I can't even get a cat to welcome me back home like she and this cat that I've never met before just have.

As we walk further into the house, the smell of whatever freshly-baked goods Starry must have in the works grows stronger. When we step inside the warm glow of the kitchen, which is connected to a vast family room, the scent becomes undeniable.

The connecting rooms are sprawling, but designed to be lit only by delicate lamps and intricate wall sconces placed all around. There's even a few tucked into corners of the enormous kitchen so not a single overhead light is turned on. It feels like I've just stepped into the type of home I've only ever fantasized about — something off the pages of a magazine or Pinterest board. Cozy and comfortable. A true hygge-lover's paradise.

An enormous, U-shaped sectional sofa sits around a stone fireplace, looking worn in all the right places, like I could sink down in its soft, supple leather and take a nap after spending all afternoon reading my favorite novel there. All while wood crackles and sizzles in the heat of gently dancing flames.

I don't know what I was expecting when I imagined the inside of a famous movie director and his supermodel wife's home, but it definitely wasn't this.

And then there are the cookies. It smells like a bona fide bakery in here. Three copper cooling racks topped with gooey-looking chocolate-chip cookies are spread out across one of the kitchen islands. I put a hand over my rumbling stomach, starkly aware that it's nearly ten o'clock and I haven't eaten anything more than a browning banana off the office building's snack counter since breakfast.

"Now," Starry says, tutting, "we'll get you fed, sweetheart. Don't you worry. I've already taken care of that. Let me just show you to your room first. We'll grab a cookie on the way, since you're probably dying for a place to put your things down. I wasn't sure what time you'd be arriving so I kept dinner warm for you just in case you hadn't had time to eat yet. I'm right, aren't I — you haven't eaten?" I stare at her, slowly nodding. She made dinner for me. I can't remember the last time someone made me dinner. Myself included. "We'll get your things all settled and then I'll leave it up to you on whether you'd like to come back out to the kitchen for a good meal and some company, or if you'd rather I just brought you a tray so you can eat in peace before letting your head hit the pillow. I hear you're burning the candle at both ends downtown over a big business deal."

"I am," I say, nodding, unsure of how to respond. I've never experienced a house granager, let alone a kind grandmother type of figure before, and the effect of it all is a bit foreign, to say the least. "And thank you for having me. And for all this," I add, waving a hand toward the kitchen.

She crosses the room to grab two melty cookies off the cooling rack, wrapping them both up in a napkin to keep the chocolate from getting on my fingers. When she hands the little makeshift package of cookies to me, it warms my hand.

"You really didn't have to do all this for me," I tell her, feeling a bit embarrassed that this woman I hardly know has gone to all this trouble. "I'm totally fine ordering Uber Eats, really. I do it practically every night back in New York. And by *practically*, let's be honest, I mean *every* night."

She grins, then grabs my bag again.

"Well, consider this a new type of home." She winks so quickly that I nearly miss it. "Here, you don't have to worry about any of those types of things, hon. Like lukewarm meals delivered in a Styrofoam container." She shakes her head, tsk-tsking like me eating Uber Eats every night is a tragedy. "Of course, if you'd prefer takeout, I'm happy to help make the calls for you," she says, a genuine warmth never leaving her. "I'm here to make your life easier, any way I can. But, we can figure out this new arrangement together as we go. For tonight, let's just get you set up in your guest suite. It's just down this hall here."

I feel genuinely speechless. And I'm never speechless. But even if I'm a bit thrown off, I love her energy. I love the whole feel of her. And that's not something I would typically think or say the first time meeting someone.

Starry leads me down a nearby hall, toward what I imagine will be my very own space over the next few weeks.

CHAPTER 18

My brain must think it's seven in the morning, like it is on the east coast, but here in this absurdly comfortable bed, it's only four o'clock in the morning. The sun isn't even up yet.

I roll over, feeling stiff from the tension I carried in my body the last few days. Everything hurts, but most especially my shoulders, which were probably halfway up to my ears most of yesterday.

Yesterday.

I groan into my pillow.

Dax.

Seeing him in that negotiation room felt like a fever dream. The dizzying whirlwind from running into him at the security check to walking down the hall with him, trying to make a plan for later, to realizing that we're on the same deal — or rather, *he's* infringing on *my* deal. The deal that's supposed to make me a partner at the end, if I can pull it off. The same deal that his friend — scratch that, his *client* — the infamous Silas Davenport, is now trying to steal out from under our noses.

Fucking hell.

It's all too much.

Considering how I walked back into the kitchen after settling my bags and ended up discussing this incredibly unfortunate turn of events with Starry well into the night, I really should have slept past four in the morning, me still being on New York time or not. I hadn't meant to stay up so late, but she was so easy to talk to.

"How long until another career-making deal comes along for you to prove yourself?" Starry had asked while I enjoyed her homemade chicken dish. I can't even remember the last time I had a casserole.

"It's not about another one coming along," I said. "It's about not losing my standing with the firm if fraternizing with the opposing counsel ever came to light. None of them can know that Dax and I have ever shared any sort of history."

"Couldn't you just get it out in the open with Brett now?" Charles — or Charlie, as he insisted on me calling him — had asked, after joining us in the kitchen. "Confess before it becomes an issue?"

I mulled that one over all night. But it feels like too risky of a move to tell Brett that Dax and I have history. He would pull me off the deal, then tell the whole partner team back home that I'm incapable of finishing what we've worked on for months. It would set the firm back hugely to have me taken off of this negotiation now. The setback would make our client furious, and the firm would likely have to eat the cost on a good chunk of my billable hours leading up to this point.

It's not an option.

Which leaves only one good option: to just carry on as we are, not letting any history I have with Dax get in the way of what I accomplish in that negotiation room. And never letting anything between us, past or present, come to light. I know I'm capable of doing that.

At the end of the night, Starry gave me a soft pat on my back and told me that I'd better get some good sleep before this morning came too soon. Charlie sent me off with a napkin full of cookies, saying that I might need a little midnight snack if I happen to wake up.

I feel like I've entered some alternate universe where two people living in the same house as me somehow feel like the type of grandparents one might want, but that I've never experienced. Instead of falling asleep to the feeling of gritty liver-flavored toothpaste that wouldn't wash off my gums, like I did all those years ago, last night I fell asleep thinking about what it was like to have someone prepare a plate of warm cookies for me after dinner, plus a glass of something to go with them.

I grab my phone on the nightstand and check to see if I've missed any texts from Dax, but the screen's blank. He ignored my call last night, but I'd told myself that he was probably buried in work, much like me this week, and couldn't find a spare second to call me back.

Right.

He wrote *the ball's in your court* months ago, I remind myself. So . . . if he hasn't answered now, doesn't it mean that I've thrown it back to him?

I should have listened to Olivia and called him before I showed up in his city. But I still think I did us a favor by not even attempting a long-distance type of situationship.

By four fifteen, I give up on falling back asleep and drag myself out of bed. As long as I'm awake, I may as well just get back to work on some of the document review before heading into more meetings today.

But I can't concentrate on my laptop screen, once I get it open.

"You don't have to rush things," Starry had said, topping my glass off the night before. "Sometimes when you're younger, it feels like everything important in your life is rushing toward the ending. Like you want to wrap the complexities of life up with a pretty bow and call them finished as fast as you can. Just to get to the next one. But when you get to be my age, you realize that the *journey* is the fun part."

Fine — maybe I was trying to rush a reconciliation with Dax because we were about to be in the same negotiation for the next couple weeks, but what was wrong with that? I don't want him to feel hurt after what happened after he left New York.

But the whole thing had led to a restless night.

* * *

By the time I walk into the same conference room we were in yesterday, yawning, I realize I've already been awake for more than four hours. I look at the door to see if Dax is making his way in yet, hoping for a natural jolt of adrenaline to hit me once I see his face.

"Morning," Brett says, eyeballing me. "You look like shit, Torres. Get any sleep last night over at your fancy new lodging?"

I bite my tongue so the things I want to say don't come flying out at him, although imagining that my words might have the power to smack him across the face does make my heart feel just a teensy bit lighter.

"Good morning, sunshine," I reply, keeping any bitterness stripped from my voice. "I slept alright, though it looks like you might have been hit by a bit of jet lag. Tossing around a bit last night, were you?" I point up toward his bald scalp. "Your hair's a bit more mussed than usual."

His naturally squinty eyes turn into narrow slits beneath his shiny forehead. He's not finding my jab funny in the slightest.

I stifle a grin.

"Kidding, Brett. You look as spry as ever."

"I slept fine," he says, dryly. "I was up early to go over those pages you sent me — what was it — four thirty this morning? My goddamn phone wouldn't stop dinging with each bloody email you sent."

"Early bird catches the worm though!" I say, brightly. "Or in this case, that extra million or so that my findings just shaved off the top."

I glance toward the door, wondering when Dax and Lila might walk in.

"You're unusually chipper this morning," he says, in his usual growly way. "What's gotten into you?"

"Not enough coffee," I chirp, stepping toward the coffee station at the back of the room. I really don't want to have Brett's attention on me when Dax walks in.

"Want me to grab you more?" I ask, nodding down at his mug.

Brett fingers the same navy-blue Yeti mug that he always has back in New York. He must have brought it with him, which I don't find the least bit surprising. Sometimes I like to imagine that he's just a little boy and that Yeti is his security mug — like a child's blankie, except all hardened metal and full of caffeine. Without it, he might throw a tantrum — even bigger than the ones he regularly tosses my way.

"I got some from the Starbucks on the way in," he says, pinching his lips to the rim. "Better than the nasty stuff they served here yesterday."

"Thanks for offering to grab me one," I joke. "Do you have the barista fill that thing for you?" I nudge his cup with my pinky, knowing it'll rile him. "Or do you get the to-go cup and fill it up yourself?"

He pulls the mug back to his chest, out of my reach, looking as if any contact from me is going to render his special mug unusable.

I smile. I love ribbing this man almost as much as I hate working for him.

He frowns. "They fill it because I ask them to fill it," he says in a monotone.

"Ah, suit yourself."

Without waiting for another word, I make a beeline for the coffee station set up across the back wall.

I've worked under Brett since barely being out of law school. As my supervisor at a top-tier firm, he's treated me like a thorn on the bottom of his pillowy, calfskin loafers since my very first interview, which was the worst interview I've ever had. After asking me to complete a complicated math problem

— something he swore I'd need to be able to do while working in mergers and acquisitions — he tossed a pen across the table at me. His pen bounced off my chest — off my *breasts*, if one is to use more visually clear terminology — and landed squarely on the floor to my left, before skittering to a stop.

The stony silence that followed between us was epic.

He waited, silently, for me to pick it up, and I waited, silently, for him to apologize for such abhorrently disrespectful behavior during an interview.

I should have left the pen on the floor and walked out of the room, since he'd clearly just demonstrated what he would be like to work for. But I didn't. I reached down and picked the pen back up, then finished completing the set of math calculations correctly and calmly, proving to both of us that not only was I skilled enough for the job, but also that my nerves could be unshakable when I needed them to be.

Show, not tell, my law professor had drilled into us during a heady job prep course in my final semester. I'd dealt with situations much worse than having a short, angry man bouncing a pen off my chest, but Brett didn't know that at the time. In fact, most people would never know that. And why would they? All my potential boss needed to know at that moment was that I was stronger than most of the people he would interview that day. The reason *why* I considered myself to be stronger didn't matter.

It should never matter.

I was an underling back then, much more so than I am now. But even back then, I'd learned how to see people for what they really were. I'd learned that skill from a very young age. So what I saw in Brett that day had, in the strangest sort of way, calmed my nerves.

Plenty of people don't show you who they really are for years and years — gaining your trust before letting you down, harshly in the most extreme cases. But other people show you who they are right from the beginning, so you never have to be surprised later. At that moment, Brett showed me that he was the second type of person. Knowing what I was getting into without any niceties or pretenses right from the start was oddly comforting.

The other big firms I interviewed with that week showered me with lavish dinners and the promise of end-of-year bonuses the size of most people's salaries. They were all handshakes and nods, pretending to be unaware of the online reviews by anonymous associates that warned how hard the billable requirements would be, once I was past the fancy dinners and empty promises designed to get me to sign.

Brett's firm had offered me a signing bonus with a clear picture of what my life would be like there. They showed me who they were without any pretense, and I respected them for that.

So when Brett's job offer landed in my inbox the next week, along with four others from, on the face of it, kinder firms, I'd taken the job with Brett. The one that put me within striking distance of that nasty little man every single day. I told myself that once I'd proven my skills and earned a partnership offer, I'd have shown him and myself I could make it through anything. Including another man treating me like dirt — like I was disposable until I'd proven otherwise. And I *would* prove otherwise.

That's the point of all this.

Between my endless working hours, my empty fridge in a mostly empty apartment, and my paying someone else to care for the dozens upon dozens of plants I love to surround myself with, I'm climbing my own personal mountain to slay the demons. To fill the hole I didn't exactly dig myself.

Olivia, Dax — no one understands my reasons behind the long hours or my unshakable work ethic like I do. But even that is just another reason to keep climbing without looking down at how far I've already come. Not every battle is fought for a good reason. Sometimes, it's simply fought to win.

As I turn my back to the room to fill my paper cup with coffee — that comes with black grounds, as it's the very last drop from the carafe — I hear Dax enter the room.

More accurately, I hear his *laugh* enter.

And if I ever forgot that muscle and body memory are a thing, I remember now because my entire body tingles, skin rising with goosebumps as my heart hammers in my chest.

That laugh.

I don't have to look to know that he's here, but I do, since the only thing better than hearing his laugh is seeing the grin stretch across his face while he does it.

I spin around, half-expecting him to be walking in with Silas, since I heard he might be coming in today, and I'm a bit curious to see the man in real life again. We met years ago when Silas came to visit Dax at law school a few times. That was back before he was a known powerhouse or household name, of course. But it's only Lila and Dax walking in. They both look calm — even cheery — with big smiles plastered across their well-rested faces. The whole thing makes me green.

Dax must feel my eyes on him because his carefree demeanor morphs into a smirk, and he excuses himself to get coffee from the machine at the back. The machine I've just taken the last bit of coffee from.

Again? What is it with me stealing this man's caffeine?

"It's out," I say, motioning to the empty coffee pot, forcing myself to appear nonchalant upon seeing him. Like nothing more than a polite greeting between acquaintances running into each other at the coffee maker, as practical strangers might do every now and then. "I was about to make more though."

He should be as concerned as I am that someone here might sniff out any type of romantic history between us. Although I'm not sure his job security is wrapped up in something as trivial as a half-baked romance between him and another attorney, who happens to be here in the conference room today. He is, after all, employed by his mother.

I glance over at Brett to see if he's watching us, which he's not. Instead, he's getting dangerously close to yelling at someone over the phone — something to do with his hotel not offering turn-down service. He's probably talking to his poor assistant back home.

"Thanks," Dax says, motioning to the coffee machine. He takes an empty cup from the stack, as if to let the room know he's only standing beside me for the coffee.

I keep an eye on Brett, making sure he can't hear me while I rub my nose vigorously, attempting to casually hide my mouth from any bored lip readers in the room.

"I called last night," I say into my hand, turning my back toward the room. "And listen, I can't risk someone here knowing that we have" — I lower my voice, whispering the last word out from under my breath — "*history*."

Then I serve up a perfectly raised brow, just to drive my point home.

"No one on my team would care." He shifts his eyes toward Lila, though he doesn't look thoroughly convinced himself. "They know I wouldn't let something like an acquaintance I hooked up with forever ago cloud my judgment on a deal like this."

I stare at him.

"An *acquaintance* you *hooked up* with?" I whisper, feeling more than a little offended. "You can't be serious."

"Is there a term that you'd rather I use when defining our past?" he asks.

I hold my coffee cup up to block my mouth from the room, lowering my voice even more.

"Uh, I'd probably use the term *friends with benefits* before something as removed as *hookup acquaintance*," I say, pointedly. "You make it sound like we weren't even, I don't know . . ."

I narrow my eyes at him, trying to find the right word to describe what he is to me.

"Like we weren't even *friends*?" Dax asks, watching me fill the machine back up with water from a nearby pitcher to make another round of coffee for the room. I'm sure there's staff around somewhere to do this, but it's giving us a reason to talk, in case anyone's watching.

"Well," I say, feeling a bit gutted, "yes."

"I don't know about you, but in my world, friends don't ghost each other for months at a time." He shuts the lid of the machine once it's full.

"Okay." I eye the room in case someone else is coming over. "We can definitely have this conversation, but later. I *want* to have this conversation," I add, quickly. "Just please, for my sake, don't make it obvious that we know each other. Brett would literally take me off the deal the exact second he figured it out. I wanted to explain everything last night but you didn't call back."

He turns around to eye Brett, whose phone is still glued to his ear.

"So that's the asshole who's turned you into a self-isolated robot back in New York?" he asks quietly.

I swallow, watching my boss.

"I can't have this conversation right now. Just pretend you don't know me. At all."

His eyes finally flash to mine and the look in them makes me feel sick. He looks disgusted that I'd even ask such a thing.

"Everything is on the line for me right now," I plead, searching his eyes for any hint of understanding.

"Everything?" he asks. His voice sounds strained.

I shake my head, wishing he'd answered my call last night so we didn't have to whisper our way through this conversation in the back of a crowded room.

"You have to understand. Keep it neutral. We can talk through it once you're ready to take my call—"

"I promise," he interrupts, flashing a tight smile. "You don't have to worry about me blowing your cover by showing that I know you." He pauses. "I mean, that I *knew* you."

The direct alteration from current to past tense plucks a few bricks off the little bridge that I thought we might be rebuilding between us.

"Thank you," I say, softening my jaw.

I keep an eye on Brett, making sure he's still pummeling whoever is on the other end of that phone, instead of paying any attention to me right now. Then I start fiddling with the coffee machine, like I'm still working on making more. Twisting a few knobs here and there, without looking directly at Dax.

"It's this one, right here," he says, placing his hand on mine and moving it to a red button on the other side.

The warmth of his hand threatens to melt my reserve, and for that one split second, I don't even care if anyone notices.

I *need* to make things right between us. I don't know why I ever thought I shouldn't call him after what happened between us in New York. Just being near him again is like fighting the world's strongest magnet, each of us trying to move in the opposite way, when really, all we should be is pressed together. No space left between us whatsoever.

"Can we make time to talk?" I ask, shifting my eyes to his. "Please?"

Thankfully all the attorneys in the room seem to be more interested in the new spread of croissants and bagels being introduced than the overly familiar conversation between the two people at the back.

He wets his lips, but doesn't answer right away.

I allow myself to study him closer and consider how hurt he must have been when I went radio silent a few months ago, following that night. It might be too late to try and make this right.

I infuriate myself to no end.

"Please?" I repeat. "I can call you tonight. Unless . . ." I don't want to say the words out loud, as if it might solidify his need to never speak to me again. *Unless you're really so mad at me that you won't even take my calls now.*

He turns his back to the room, filling the cup he grabbed earlier with fresh drip coffee, then shifts his eyes until they're gazing directly into mine and leans in.

"Let's give it some time," he says, his voice stiff. "Let the newness of seeing you here wear off a little for me. I want — I *need* — to think more clearly when it comes to you."

It's not an outright *no*, but it still stings, like a hornets' nest just unleashed inside my chest, the pain finding my heart a thousand times over. I get why, I really do. I should never have let my fear of falling for him get in the way of reaching out after what happened between us. Even if I wasn't ready, even if I'm possibly still not ready, or possibly never will be. Simply not calling him at all was the wrong thing to do. I see that now. I never meant to hurt him.

"That's fine," I say, turning back to the machine. I twist a random knob, unsure of why, other than giving my hands something to do. "I get it. Totally fair. And yeah, you're right. I'll call you in the next week."

"Make it two," he says, his voice softening. Barely.

"Got it," I say, nodding, and feeling gutted. I'm angry with myself for making him feel like he has to distance himself from me. "You ready to do this, then?"

"Ready." Then he turns to me with a smile that somehow manages to look like an apology.

A few months ago, it was him asking me for a chance to catch up. Not the other way around.

I don't know what I want while I'm here. But I do know that Dax hating me isn't it.

"Alright then," he says briskly, before stalking across the room to call our joint meeting to order.

"Alright then," I repeat to myself, wishing more than anything in the world that I could take back so much of what's unfolded between us already.

CHAPTER 19

Dax

Damn these late nights with Lila and her affinity for Italian takeout. This deal has been kicking my ass. More accurately, Abby Torres has been kicking my ass. And not in the type of sexy ass-kicking way I'd have hoped for after seeing her walk in on that first day.

Ever since I gave Abby the yellow light on calling me two weeks ago, she's been even more aggressive than usual in and out of these meetings. She's denied all the tactics we've deployed to steal The Nile Group out from under her client, while keeping Lila, me, and the rest of the team back at the firm constantly searching for anything we think might prove to be valuable in taking it over. Some of the team members have been pulling forty-eight-hour work benders, not wanting a single advantage to slip through the cracks in the time we have left. It's incredibly unhealthy, and why so many M & A attorneys struggle to get through these huge deals without some type of vice to fall back on.

The temptation to pursue an old vice — Abby, who is skilled in relieving my stress by any means possible — has brought me to where I am now: jogging down the boardwalk near Venice Beach with Ryeson, once again regretting a good chunk of my recent life choices.

Venice Beach is one of our old stomping grounds. Having been roomies at boarding school, Ryeson and I became roommates in undergrad at UCLA. Back then we used to come down here to work out on the weekends — thinking we were hot shit — along with all the ripped bodybuilders on a patch of sand filled with old workout equipment, and lined with open-air beer gardens, any of which were perfect for an after-workout drink together.

Now, we're just a couple of thirty-something professionals who have long since left our ripped, athletic days behind us in favor of long hours spent under fluorescent lights and computer screens. Or at least, that's true for me. Ryeson, on the other hand, is still in way better shape than I am or ever was, even back then.

He's jogging backward in front of me — obnoxiously coaxing me on like a puppy to keep up with him.

"Dude," I say breathlessly as we pound down the pavement, "I'm not as in shape as I was way back then. Whose idea was this anyway?"

"Yours." He grins, looking more like he belongs in the *Top Gun* sequel, playing in the volleyball courts off to our right, than here pounding down the boardwalk of the most eclectic beach in L.A.

Ryeson might not notice the trail of women's eyes he's attracting as he jogs down this particular stretch of the beach, but let's just say he wouldn't be left lonely tonight, if he returned any one of the hungry stares he's sopping up as we go.

"Right," I say, panting. "I forgot."

He slows his pace to jog beside me again.

"You missed your calling as a drill sergeant," I tell him.

"You couldn't pay me enough to be a drill sergeant," he shoots back. "Those days are long behind me."

After UCLA, Ryeson joined the Air Force and eventually became a fighter pilot. Once retired from the service, he flew a few of Silas' private jets for him before establishing his own private aviation business.

"You might want to practice playing one now if I'm going to make it all the way down to the — appropriately named — KillJoy," I say, referring to the beer garden we plan to jog to; that is, if I can make it there before keeling over. "These late nights at the office have been demolishing me."

"Silas riding your ass?" he asks, more as a comment than a question. "Not surprised. I had to send a fleet of pilots his way, since I couldn't keep up with him myself. How's he been doing? I'm worried he's starting to fall back into his old ways with everything I'm seeing online."

I cringe. Si has been canceling his plans to attend our negotiations in favor of these side trips. We don't *need* him there, but it would definitely help his position.

"Yeah, I still worry about him sometimes," I admit. "The media loves to use anything they can to paint him as off-kilter, but I think he's doing alright. Just distracting himself more than usual right now, and who can blame him?"

"He called me last night, asking to fly him to Ibiza next week," Rye says, chuckling, though finally showing signs of panting like me now that the sun has come out in full force. "I told him I would have loved to go if I wasn't so busy running his aviation needs all over the map."

The sun is hanging just overhead, drenching us both in our own sweat.

"I'd give my right arm for a spontaneous, zero-responsibilities trip to Ibiza right now," I tell him. But I had to convince Silas that I wasn't able to take a week-long break from working on *his* deal to join him there, too.

"He also mentioned something about Abby Torres sitting opposite you on this one." Ryeson side-eyes me. "That true?"

"Yep," I say, not really wanting to talk about Abby right now. We haven't spoken personally since I told her to wait longer than a week to call me, but the way she secretly looks at me during breaks on negotiation days has me nearly eating my words. I almost called her myself last night after seeing her show up in a pair of those red-soled heels yesterday, just like the ones she wore on our date in New York. I have a feeling she did that on purpose, just to remind me of what happened the first time I saw her wearing them. I had to bite down on my tongue hard enough to distract myself when we all reconvened during lunch and after I'd spent a full fifteen minutes standing behind her in line at the snack counter down the hall.

"I like your shoes," I said to the back of her hair, not loud enough for anyone else to hear within earshot. I couldn't help myself. "They look a bit familiar."

She looked over her shoulder, just enough for me to see one dimple come out to play, but kept her lashes facing the floor, so anyone watching might miss the interaction between us.

"They'd look even more familiar in the corner of my bedroom," she whispered. "Don't you think?"

Christ.

"How are things between you two now? Is it awkward after what happened in New York? What's going on with her?" Ryeson pauses to nod at a gorgeous blonde who rolls by us, wearing only a thong bikini and a pair of rollerblades. "God bless Venice Beach," he adds under his breath, grinning wickedly at me.

I laugh. This stretch of the boardwalk is known for its vibrant characters, many of whom are legends among locals with well-known nicknames. Venice has always been a place where certain types go to be seen, while the rest of us just enjoy the unique opportunity to watch some of the most interesting people in the city.

"Did I mention we hooked up there a few months back?" I ask, focusing on not breaking my stride. I can see The KillJoy sign coming into view up ahead.

"Like, you had dinner and then went back to her place, yeah," Ryeson says, nearly missing a young hoverboarder who rolls too close to the toe-end of his shoes.

We jog in silence for a beat before he swerves off into the sand to have a stretch.

"Thank God," I mumble, feeling a slight charley horse kick up in my calf, and more than happy for the break.

We face toward the ocean as we stretch our calves, watching the waves kick up onto the shore and catching a breeze rolling off the water.

A few surfers are out, in wetsuits, but it's still a bit too cold to be swimming without one. Most of the beach crowd is just sunbathers and families, looking for a day of fresh air and sun.

"What the hell happened after that?" he asks. "You sleep together in New York, then she shows up at your conference table in L.A. What are the odds of all that happening?"

I shrug. "Slim to none. There wasn't much to tell after New York. though," I say. "I left the ball in her court, literally, and she never called me. Then she turns up here, going after the same company as Si and me. You should see her though. She's a force in that negotiation room."

I shake my head, recalling every detail of her arguments yesterday. The way she stood up in front of the room, her white blouse barely hiding the nude bra underneath, tucking her hair behind her ears, long nails brushing stray bangs back from her eyes, and how she licked her lip, biting the bottom one between her teeth between each important point she made, darting her eyes at me each time. I remember every detail of her speech, except the words coming out of her mouth. Lila had to give me a summary of it an hour later when we took a quick lunch break together.

"Having her in that negotiation room is killing me, man. I feel like an idiot for putting her off another week. The tension between us is like a fucking volcano. I feel like I might need to meet up with her just to be able to concentrate on the rest of what we need to do."

"What's her deal, anyhow?" Rye asks, pulling his foot up behind his thigh to stretch out his quads. "I always liked her.

You know that. I was hoping things would work out after you two graduated."

"I tried," I remind him. "She ran. Then, after New York—"

"She ran again," he says, finishing my sentence. "Are you expecting anything different this time?"

I shift my stance to brace my toes up against a guard rail and straighten my leg, stretching the back of my calf out. The slight cramp is disappearing, thankfully.

"I told you, I'm not really looking for meaningless hookups with women anymore," I say. It might sound stupid to say that out loud to certain guys, but I know that if anyone will get it, it's going to be Ryeson.

"No, I get that," he says, nodding, shifting to stretch out the other leg. He looks as if he might be ready to start jogging again. Thankfully, the place we're heading is just another half a mile or so down this stretch. "I always felt like you two were kind of meant to be together or something. She wasn't anything to me, but I still think about her sometimes."

I shoot him a look.

"No, not like that. But for you. I haven't liked any of the other women you've dated half as much."

"Well, that's wonderful," I say, dimly. "Considering that Abby was never really in a relationship with me. It was always just a physical thing on her end. She told me she hasn't even dated in New York. For a girl that looks like her — how is that even possible?"

"Some people have real demons," he says, stepping back out on the pavement again, after waiting for a man with a huge blue and yellow parrot on his shoulder to walk by. "Doesn't mean they're not worth killing those demons for, in the end. Has she said anything about wanting a second chance?"

"You mean a third?" I ask, correcting him. "We're opposing each other on this deal right now. It wouldn't be okay if her boss found out."

"Silas wouldn't care if you two hooked up while working on this deal, would he?" he asks.

I imagine Silas' reaction to finding out that Abby and I had reconciled while working on this deal.

"I actually think he wishes that we would hook up again just to weaken their stance, which of course isn't even ethical."

Rye laughs. "Shocker!"

Silas has been asking repeatedly when I'm going to *tap that* again, ever since finding out Abby was on the opposing side. I'm hoping when he does make it to one of these meetings, he doesn't slip and say the wrong thing, making it awkward for all of us, especially Abby. But even as his legal counsel, I have about as much control over Silas as I do the wind, which means none at all.

"Then what's the hold up?" Rye asks, jogging beside me once again. I wish we'd just walk the rest of the way. We're almost there, but he's turning it into a final push sprint.

"*I'm* the holdup," I tell him, breathing harder. "I want something more meaningful for my future. I don't know if Abby will ever be ready for something like that. Or would even want it, to be honest. But she deserves a hell of a lot more than what she's allowing herself to have."

"I'm not sure how often two people have the type of thing that the pair of you have," Rye says, pumping his arms to give this last stretch his all. I fight beside him to keep up. "All I know is that if I ever find that type of thing you two have, I'm not going to give up that easily."

I stay silent, mostly because I'm not sure what else to say, and also because I'm getting completely out of breath. I don't think anything about giving her up has been easy for me.

"If she doesn't date, who does she have in her life?" he asks. "Friends? Is she close to her family?"

"Her best friend, Olivia," I huff. "But she's off in Hawaii."

"Who else?" he asks. "Parents? Siblings? Anyone?"

I keep the pace beside Ryeson, mentally rolling back through every conversation I can ever remember having with Abby about the inner workings of our lives. Plans for upcoming holidays, me going home for a long Easter weekend,

Parents' Weekend at the law school when she'd told me she was heading out of town instead of having anyone come see her, even Christmas spent in New York each year — something about reaching her firm's billable hour requirement at the end of the year, even though we both know she was probably well over that requirement before Thanksgiving.

I think of every single time I've brought up pending plans regarding my family, who would probably rather die than have me skip various holidays and events at their house. Of New Year's rituals at the dinner table or Valentine's Day packages sent to my dorm room with balloons and chocolates — things I used to find somewhat annoying as a teenager, then came to depend on the older I got, recognizing that not everyone has these types of family tradition in their lives.

All those things I've talked about with Abby and yet, I can't recall a single time that she's chimed in with her own plans. Her own funny family traditions. Memories as a kid. Instead, she listened to snippets from my life with thinly veiled fascination.

I stop running, nearly getting slammed into by a kid on a bike with training wheels. Thankfully, her parents manage to steer her around me.

"Sorry!" I say after them, breathing hard. The dad nods at me as they go.

Ryeson stops, but is smart enough to step off the pavement before someone slams into the back of him, too, then shifts his eyes back to me, looking confused as to why I've suddenly stopped again when our bar is coming up.

"I'm not sure she has anyone," I say, now fully convinced of it.

"Well, that's a problem, man," he says, stepping out of the way of a woman pulling a wagon behind her with a big, blown-up globe nestled inside.

"Peace," she says, smiling seductively at Ryeson while pointing two fingers up toward the sky.

"Peace," Rye says, looking gobsmacked by that smile, but holding up a matching peace sign.

I'm an alright-looking guy, but any time I'm beside Ryeson, I may as well be invisible. His inherent charm never fails, and I find it wildly entertaining.

"I think I need to talk to Abby," I say. "Like really talk to her."

"Why don't you just give her a call? No shame in breaking that silence first," he says.

"No." I know somehow that calling her first would be the wrong move right now. I need to let this breathe. "That's got to be part of it. She's got to be the one to pick that ball back up and make the next move."

"Well, don't wait around too long, bro," he says. "Some things are worth waiting for, but other things are just worth having, without any wait at all."

CHAPTER 20

Abby

Brett and I are in the middle of another drawn-out mediation on this deal. Our fourth one this week. Today's endeavor is an all-day affair that keeps us locked in a conference room together and, more than anything, I wish Dax was sharing this room with me instead of the bulldog.

What makes it almost worse is that Dax and his team are in a separate conference room next door, while I sit here with Brett, and The Nile Group team is somewhere else in the building, waiting for the mediator to act as the middleman and travel back and forth between all the rooms with points and offers and contracts, attempting to get everyone to sign and end this whole thing. However, it's not going smoothly for any of us. We've been gridlocked for the last ten days. All to be expected in this monstrosity of a deal, but it feels like we're stuck in the eye of the storm, where eventually one of the parties is going to get desperate enough to start throwing more capital on the table to get it done. Davenport Media, I'm guessing, will go first.

This particular phase involves a lot of waiting and strategizing, which I personally love, but in this deal, it also involves not seeing the other teams for days. So even though Dax and I have had a professional wall up between us this whole time, making it impossible for us to act familiar with one another, I was getting kind of used to waking up and seeing him here. I began missing him the first morning we went into separate rooms, the pit in my stomach only growing deeper as the days piled up.

After six hours in this room, Brett is starting to pace while clutching his phone, trolling the crew back in New York, even though it's well after ten p.m. on the east coast. They've been running through every detail of our potential next move, while I've been tasked with handling the Uber Eats order for both of our dinners. Thai curry for me, and a burger for him.

I'm pulling open the food delivery app, thankful for a slight break from document review, when a text from Dax pops up on my phone. Just seeing his name on my screen sends my stomach spiraling. We haven't spoken since the conversation at the coffee machine, where he asked me to give him space and time. It's been killing me not to reach out since then, but I can understand him wanting space.

I look across the room at Brett to make sure his phone is still pressed to his ear, my paranoia running high. But the text from Dax breaks the pit in my gut wide open.

Who do you spend Christmas with?

I knit my brows together. What does Christmas have to do with anything?

I think of how to respond before deciding on the truth:

Sometimes Olivia's family. Why?

His response is nearly immediate.

Why not yours?

Blood pounds in my ears and I set my phone back on the table, face down, wondering what brought this on. Feeling a wave of frustration, even though it's all innocent enough, I pick it back up again and punch in a reply.

They're not really big on holidays. Why?

Three dots appear, then disappear. I watch the phone until I feel Brett's eyes on my face, when I glance up.

"Make sure they don't put mustard on mine," he growls, eyes narrowed. "And sweet potato fries if they have them. Barbeque sauce to dip. None of that ketchup shit."

I squint my eyes and nod, logging the request somewhere in my brain, which is still forming thoughts.

I type another text to Dax and hit send.

Who do you spend Christmas with?

He writes back right away, showing that he isn't too distracted to respond after all.

My parents.

Then he adds,

How come yours never came for the family weekends at law school?

My breathing speeds up. We just went from innocent to pointed. This is a completely random family-centered interrogation. I glance at Brett. Where the hell is he getting these questions from? Could Brett have mentioned something offhand to him? Dax and I haven't spoken in nearly two weeks, and this is his opening line? Before I can rein in my unnecessary anger, I respond,

Why the sudden interrogation about my family?

146

I set the phone back down and focus on slowing my heart rate with deep breaths, then pick it back up to start placing our food order, while trying and failing to convince myself that I really don't care that he's asking any of this. I don't need to answer any questions about my family from Dax. I don't even know why he'd start questioning anything to do with my history. He never has before. What would make him start now?

Just as I'm typing *no ketchup* into the special directions box, Brett snaps at me from across the room. "Torres, go to the supply room and grab the document from the printer that Kelly just sent through."

I glance up from my phone.

"Kelly's sent it to the printer? Here?"

Kelly, his PA, is sitting back in New York.

He looks at me as if a bug is making its way down my forehead and he's too annoyed to flick it off for me. Then he parts his teeth and allows himself one long blink before holding my eyes with his.

I really hate this man.

"No, I just printed them from my phone." He holds his phone up in front of his face to really drive his point home.

I suck in my top lip to stop anything from coming out. I'm even more exhausted by his attitude than usual. Having not had any other staffers to distract him here these past few weeks, Brett Bowen's wrath has been suffocating me since we arrived.

"Where's the supply room?" I ask.

"Down the hall. On the left." He points out the door without looking up from his phone.

Fabulous. I rise from my chair, thankful to get a moment to breathe out of this room. Alone.

"It's one hundred and twenty-seven pages. Count them before you come back. Not a page missing, Torres," he adds.

I drop my chin to stop myself from glaring at him, and instead glare at the floor.

"So, I shouldn't hand a couple pages out to strangers on the way back?" I ask, under my breath.

"What?"

"I said I'll be right back," I say louder, more innocently.

I slink down the hall, wondering what came over Dax to throw all those questions out at me in a string of texts. Questions about my family, the holidays, weekends in which I was the only person I knew whose family didn't travel in for Parents' Weekend or family football game days. I always hid out in my apartment during those weekends to avoid questions about why no one from my life had bothered making it over.

I turn into the last room after hearing a commercial-size printer pushing out page after page, but there's already someone standing in front of it.

Dax turns around, just as I come to a halt, barely two feet into the room.

He gives me half a smile, then turns back to the printer, as if he doesn't even know me. Which, I remind myself, was my idea.

I clear my throat, then slide up beside him, both of us staring down at the pages being spit out of the machine, our backs to the open door.

"Hi," I say, glancing sideways at him. This document must be his, and mine will likely start printing after his is done, which buys us more time to stand here awkwardly like we didn't have incredible sex just months ago, and two years before that.

"Hey," he says, crossing his arms.

We stand in silence, the sketchy, mechanical sounds of the printer filling the air. I hate this.

He leans over, just enough that our sides brush against each other, then he tips back, spine straightening again. I look over my shoulder to see if anyone else has made their way inside this same room, or could possibly be standing outside the door to see what happens next.

This is the first time we've been truly alone since I got to L.A., and this is how we're going to spend the few minutes we have?

Absolutely not.

Without giving myself time to change my mind, I spin around and shut the door to the supply room, turning the lock once the latch is in place.

Dax turns, startled. He lowers his eyes to the lock. "Well, that's one way to make an entrance," he says, ironically.

I step toward him, lowering my voice.

"So, you're finally ready to talk, I take it?" I ask, holding up my phone. The text thread between us lights up the screen.

"It's been a few weeks. If this deal ends soon, I would have hated not getting the chance to do it in person."

I frown. Do it in person?

He explains, waving one hand between us. "Talk. Talk in person. Not do it in person." He laughs, but I'm not totally ready to join in yet.

"What was that text string about?" I hiss louder, unsure of how soundproof these walls are. "All those random questions about my family. What's with the sudden interrogation? What did Brett tell you about me?"

"What do you mean, *interrogation*? And what does Brett have to do with anything? I was just curious about you," he says. He shifts on his feet.

"Curious about me? Or my family?"

"Why would either option make you this upset?" He studies me.

I fold and unfold my arms. "It doesn't," I say, flicking my hair back. "I just don't know why you'd wait nearly two weeks to reach back out to me, and the first thing you want to know is who I spend holidays with?"

"Admittedly weird," he says, nodding up at the ceiling as if he hadn't thought of that. "It's just something that's been on my mind lately."

"What, Christmas with my parents?" I say, deadpan.

"No, *you*," he says.

I clench my jaw. "What about me?"

"Christ, Abby. *Everything* about you." He moves a step closer. "Seeing you in New York, spending all that time catching up, I realized I knew close to nothing about you. I mean, I know a lot about you, don't get me wrong, but—"

"Oh, yeah?" I interrupt, wanting to steer the conversation elsewhere. Away from my family. "What do you know about me, Dax?" I hate how defensive my voice sounds. I hate it. I hate this. But those questions, while innocent to most, have me on edge. There are certain parts of my life that I don't like anyone to know about. I'm an expert at brushing intrusive questions aside, questions most people would welcome as a sign that someone wants to get to know them better, but it's hard to hide from his direct line of fire.

"What do I know about you?" Dax repeats my question. His shoulders slump in the middle, like just me asking is an insult.

I shrug, my eyes softening. "Well?"

He licks his lower lip, eyes darkening. Then it all comes tumbling out.

"Abby, I know that you're one of the most complicated women I've ever met. And that even though all the signs point toward you having very little interest in this outside a bedroom, I know that would never be enough. Not for me or you."

I inhale sharply, my heart pounding. Not sure how to respond.

He keeps going. "I know that you bite your lip — just like that." He points to my mouth and I release my lip from my teeth. "Almost like a distraction tactic when you don't know what else to say. And it usually works because all I can think about for at least ten minutes afterward is how much I want to be the one biting that lip instead of you." I laugh, feeling seen. "I know that when you laugh, your nose scrunches up and your eyes crinkle at the sides in the most stupidly adorable way, and that I'll do almost anything to see it again and again when I'm around you." He pauses to swallow and study me harder before going on, lowering his voice a shade. "I also know that painting in your apartment was somehow painted by you, and that you have a hell of a lot more than just work going on in that head of yours. No matter how hard you try to convince yourself otherwise."

I feel like the wind has just gotten knocked out of me.

"But what does any of that have to do with questions about my family?" I ask, in nearly a whisper.

"Because it's one more piece of the Abby puzzle that's missing. I know we're fucking amazing in the bedroom together, but I want to be fucking amazing outside of it, too. And if I'm ever going to get a clear picture of you, I need to know all of you. Not just the parts you're okay with."

I feel like I'm standing under a spotlight. And while my heart is darting around the circle of light, looking for somewhere to hide, I know there isn't one, this time.

"I saw your place in New York, Abs. Living in that office prison cell with a futon, paying someone else to live your life — feed your cat, water your plants. Do you even see the way you've chosen to live? Your entire apartment was bubbling over, brimming to the top with *actual life* while you don't even keep crumbs of it in your fridge to feed yourself. There's this deeply creative, passionate side of you, locked up in here," — he presses his finger into my chest, just ribs and skin and muscle left between him and my heart — "that you're afraid to show other people." He shakes his head. "But why? You've gotta tell me. Because coming from someone who's tried to break your walls down after seeing glimpses of what's behind them, you've built a whole damn fortress up around yourself. And I can't, for the life of me, figure out why the hell you think you need it."

I feel breathless. Like I've just run a gauntlet and come out the other side.

I nearly turn back to unlock the door, intending to run down the hall and avoid this whole conversation that I, admittedly, just opened . . . But something in me keeps my feet planted right where they are. At least for one split second longer.

CHAPTER 21

Abby closes the gap between us, running right into me, the force of her knocking me back until the lower half of my body is pressed up against the office supply counter beside the printer. It's covered in staplers and paperclips, extra reams of paper and folders. She reaches behind me, grabbing me by the belt, then spins us both around until it's *her* back pressed up against the counter.

She hoists herself up onto it after clearing the papers off the top with one swipe, then wraps her legs around my waist, pulling my face down to kiss her.

And I let her.

More than let her.

I kiss her back, gently and hard all at once, forcing the anger I felt toward her out of my mind. Trading it for the quiet distraction of her lips, desperate against mine, doing the complete opposite of what she asked me to do here a few weeks ago.

She arches her spine, pressing the front of herself into me, her breasts straining against her shirt, hips flush against mine. I pull her buttons apart as she untucks the hem of my shirt, undoing the buckle of my belt before I can wrap my head around where this is going.

She unzips my pants, but before she can get her hand wrapped around my cock, I take a step back, gasping for air, putting my hands up between us, like I'm surrendering in a battle I'd rather die in.

We're both completely out of breath.

She swallows, blinking at me. Confused.

I turn to tuck in my shirt, forcing my head to come to terms with what's just happened, before spinning around to face her again.

She's buttoning her blouse back up, sitting on the countertop, eyes burning. Searching for an answer as to why I just stopped us from doing something we both so clearly wanted to do.

"I'm sorry," she says, her chest still heaving. "You wanted space but everything you said, I . . ." She pauses, looking more bewildered. Embarrassed. "God, I don't know why I just did that. It's like your superpower. You drain every bit of self-control I have. It happens every time we're alone, doesn't it? I have a lot of self-control, but not around you."

I knead my temples, wishing so damn bad that I wasn't still mad about how things ended between us in New York. Wishing I didn't actually want more from this woman than what she's apparently willing to give. It would make everything so much easier between us.

"You still want to talk about what happened after New York," she says, nodding. "And, you're right. We should."

I run a hand through my hair. "Ah, yeah, about that . . ."

The printer beeps loudly, signaling that my print job is done.

We stare at each other, slowing our breathing, until the printer starts shuffling through another job. This one must be Abby's.

"One hundred and twenty-seven pages," she says, nodding toward the machine. "That's how long we have until Brett starts wondering where I went. Possibly less, since yours took so damn long."

She shoots me half a grin, then flattens her hair back down on top of her head from where I must have just pushed it out of place while we were . . .

Christ.

I force myself not to go there right now.

"Right. So we have one hundred and twenty-seven pages to lead this elephant out of the room real quick, don't we?"

She looks past me at the locked door. "Unless he comes looking for me sooner than that."

I stare at her, hoping she takes the reins on this one. I've said enough as it is until I hear where her head is at. I clear my throat.

Your turn, Abs.

"Everything you just said about me? You're right," she begins, "about all of it. I hope you can forgive me for being an emotionally stunted idiot. Your assessment of me is spot on."

I wait for her to go on, but that seems to be all she's got.

"Is there more of an explanation behind that apology? Or a suggestion of how to go about this . . ." I ask, giving her another chance to explain.

"Whatever this is between us is already so foreign to me. I don't really know how else to say it."

"Then say whatever you feel or think right now. Even if it sounds wrong," I tell her.

"Nothing I say is going to sound like what you want to hear." She shrugs. "I'm impossible. Even when I want something, I convince myself that I don't. It's like this bomb goes off in me whenever something feels like an emotional risk."

I laugh a little harshly. "I'm the emotional risk?" I ask.

No matter how much I want her, how much I've always wanted her, I'm over her half-baked excuses. This time, it's all or nothing.

She starts again. "I'm not sure how else to say it—"

But I stop her. "Abby." She looks up. "I don't want a perfect rebuttal from you. I want the ugly one. I want the horribly ugly reason why you only seem to run." I wonder if any of this is getting absorbed by her, or if it's just bouncing off her ears like a hailstorm.

"Everything you're saying is fair."

I study her face, wondering if maybe I'm just more invested in all this than she is. Maybe I always have been. Second chances, Fate, and all that idiocy can be wildly confusing when it only leads to another dead end. Some things are just impossible to push into working, and I'm starting to realize that Abby may be one of them.

I don't know if it's frustration from the last near-decade streaming out of my mouth, but whatever it is grabs ahold of me and it just starts pouring out, right here in the supply room.

"What if I'm just blind when it comes to you?" I ask, holding my arms out to my sides. "Maybe things between us — things that feel so fucking *right* to me — have always been one-sided. Me and only me believing that there's something magnetic between us. Something I've never felt when I'm around anyone else in my entire life, because no matter how hard I try to stay away from you, we're like a pair of bookends with a whole lot of story left to play out before we get to be rightly smushed up against each other again. With nothing left in the middle to keep us apart. Whether either one of us likes it or not, the world just keeps shoving us back into each other's lives, Abby. And maybe this is me being naive, or stupid, or honestly just completely insane to want to see what's still left to read between us. Whatever it is, whatever block there is in your mind, I wish you'd just try."

I'm spent by the time I get to the end of my tirade, but I had to say it.

I'd never been sure what Abby's life might look like behind closed doors. What this girl was like when no one else was around to see her. But going to her place for the first time — seeing the way her home was overflowing with life, but none of it coming from her, just existing around her — made me realize something I'd never thought about before.

She has a wall up that I've never been able to break through, sure, that's the part I've always known. However, what I didn't know for sure until recently — having experienced what I saw and heard that night, and thinking through my conversation with Ryeson about who she may or may not have in her life — is that Abby's walls have absolutely nothing to do with me.

Those walls have everything to do with whatever it is that she's gone through in her life. And I care too much about her to let her go without at least trying to help break them all down.

If not for me in the long run, then for her.

And if I'm not the one to help her do it, then who?

I tighten the hinge of my jaw, forcing the silence to linger, refusing to add another word from my end, until finally, she clears her throat.

"Am I the head side or the tail?" she asks, sniffing lightly.

"What?" I ask. Annoyed that she isn't responding to anything I've just said.

She talks louder. "Am I the head of this bookend or the tail side? As you were talking, I was imagining us as a pair of bookends with all these adventures and stories left unread between us. Though, in order to be two incomplete sides, we'd have to be some type of body-based pair — maybe a horse, or a fish, or a tiger — something that needs both ends back together in order to make any sense, right?"

I frown, wondering if I'm hearing her correctly.

"I think, given the circumstances between us, that I can safely call dibs on the head-portion of our bookend metaphor, sweetheart," I say, allowing my voice to become soft.

She snorts out a laugh, her face brightening.

"That's fair." She nods, grinning. "Which makes me the ass portion, I suppose. Fitting."

I purse my lips, trying not to laugh.

"Your words, not mine," I tell her. "We can call you the tail portion, though. Maybe it's a horse-shaped bookend or something. With the ears and nose on one end and the tail and back hooves on the other. Jumping through a mess of books and stories in the middle, or something ridiculous."

"I think that suits us pretty well," she says, smiling as if she knows this entire metaphor is a little more than absurd, if not deeply fitting. "I may not embody the most poetic end of the whole thing, but as you said, given our history, I admit that I deserve to be the fairly blind back side of it all, sure."

She begins to laugh, quietly at first, but before long, the sound fills up the whole room. I wonder whether anyone outside can hear us, but a bigger part of me has already stopped caring.

I love that laugh so much that I laugh, too. Aware that regardless of the outcome of this, I'm still going to have to face this woman in a conference room for the biggest deal of either of our careers, with the future of hers on the line.

Still, I wait for a beat to see if I can hear anyone coming down the hall, then I decide to go for broke.

"I'm crazy about you, Abby. But I'm not at a point in my life where I want to chase my tail any longer than I already have. I want . . ."

I pause, trying to take this whole notion out of our horse bookend metaphor, and put it as plainly as possible. But, before I can finish, she does it for me.

"You want someone who will run along beside you, not have you spinning in circles anymore," she says, nodding. "I get that, I really do."

"Getting it and being it are two entirely different things," I say, gently.

We pause, hearing someone walk outside the room. Just when I think they've passed, the handle on the door starts to jiggle.

I look at Abby as the color drains from her face.

"Fuck," she hisses, looking around for somewhere to hide.

I pull open a closet door beside the counter. It's full of cleaning buckets, extra boxes of office supplies, and a vacuum.

I pull her into me by the waist, then give her a quick peck on the lips, wishing I could just drag her in with me.

"This isn't over," I say, lightly.

"No, it isn't," she says, before pushing me inside. Then she closes me in.

The closet is pitch black, but I can hear the sound of her heels tapping across the floor, then the door to the main supply room swinging open.

"What the fuck is taking so long? And why is that door locked?"

It's Brett's muffled voice.

Christ. That was close.

"Oh, the handle must have been locked before I shut the door," I hear Abby saying. "Didn't want the other team peeking over my shoulder at these pages."

A stack of papers gets shuffled off the print deck.

"Damn straight, Torres, but you're taking forever in here. I shouldn't have to come babysit you in the supply room. Get back in there. You've been distracted as fuck since you got back to L.A."

"No, I—" Abby stutters.

Back to L.A.?

Brett's voice gets louder, not giving her a chance to answer.

"Don't tell me the idea of spending time in your sad little hometown has gotten you all up in your head, because I can get someone else from the New York team to replace you out here in under twenty-four hours if you can't handle being back."

Back? Hometown? I thought Abby was from New York.

"That's ridiculous, Brett," Abby says, her voice growing farther away, like she's leading him out of the room. "Of course I can handle it."

"Good. You better get your head in the game, because I don't give a shit what happened here before you—"

The supply room door closes heavily behind them.

Two pairs of footsteps set off, while Brett's voice grows more muffled until I can't hear them anymore. But, instead of freeing myself from the tiny closet, I press my forehead into the door, needing just another minute to myself.

CHAPTER 22

Abby

It's after ten o'clock when I finally sneak back into the house. I don't know why I'm sneaking, other than it just feels like I'm breaking some late-night curfew at a house that isn't really mine. Starry and Charlie have been beyond welcoming since I arrived, but I haven't been able to shake the feeling that they aren't really here for me. They're paid by someone else to keep an eye on everything — including me — while I'm here. It's as simple as that.

Millie greets me at the door and I pick her up, immediately feeling the slow roll of her purr beneath my fingers, even before she's pressed against my chest. This cat, on the other hand, has decided to enjoy my company based purely on her own free will.

I tuck her soft ears under my chin and we make our way to the kitchen. We round the corner just in time to see Starry pulling a dish from the oven.

She looks up. "Ah, I thought you might make it home soon," she says, beaming happily at us.

Whatever is under that tin foil in her hands smells divine.

Brett's burger order had arrived with both ketchup *and* mustard on it, but sans the barbeque sauce I'd requested for him. He'd complained so vehemently after manhandling the bun that I'd just shoved my curry across the table for him to eat instead of dealing with his hangry attitude the rest of the evening. So, it just happens that I'm starving.

After what Brett had mentioned off-handedly in the supply room, I was too mad to hear him complain about something as miniscule as mustard on a burger, and spent the rest of our day in silence with AirPods stuck in my ears unless the mediator was back in our room to talk. He's my boss, sure, but shutting him out felt warranted.

Brett is privy to more information about me than most, based on two unfortunate events.

The first was when he asked an array of unprofessional, prying questions about my past life during my second interview, which I answered based solely on a steady rush of nerves.

The second occurred on Christmas three years ago when he'd rushed into the office that evening for a quick client emergency and found me half-drunk at my desk, shedding a few tears over the fact that my aunt and uncle had left for a cruise with their children a day before I arrived home to spend the holiday with them. I thought they'd just run off to a store to finish holiday shopping until I sent them a text asking where everyone was. My aunt responded with a photo of them all on the ship's deck in their swimsuits.

Hence the alcohol and tear-fest that followed.

However, Brett had never brought any of that stuff up in the way he had today. The stress of this deal must be bothering him even more than usual since I'd always assumed he was at least decent enough to keep his mouth shut about everything he knew about me.

Until today. And of course Dax was hiding in the closet when he broke that invisible barrier.

I eye the dish in Starry's hands. "Does that happen to have something edible in it?"

"I should think so," she says, laughing, placing it on the center island in front of one of the barstools. She pats the counter beside it, inviting me over.

I take a seat and lift the foil off, releasing a pillow of steam from what looks like a ground-up pile of meat and potatoes.

"I hope you like meatloaf, hon," she says. Then she picks a bottle out of the nearby wine fridge and pours two glasses, handing one to me. She settles down with her wine glass opposite me. "How are things going with the deal? And that Dax fellow? Have you two sorted things out yet?"

I stare at her over the top of the meatloaf as she talks. It's not that I don't want her to stick around, I do. I really do. After everything that happened today, I want to talk to someone — and Liv is on a flight to Tokyo right now with Dom, so I can't call to get her perspective on any of it. Even beyond all that, I enjoy talking to Starry — more than most people, actually. But I assume she's ready to officially end her workday and head to bed, not stay up late talking to her house guest, i.e. *me*, yet again.

"You don't have to stay," I tell her, gently. "I totally get it if you're ready to clock off for the day. It's pretty late."

I nod like I understand, but she looks a little taken aback.

"End my workday?" she asks, then she starts to stand, looking embarrassed that she'd planned to stay up with me, chatting. "Oh, I'm sorry." She grabs her glass off the counter. "I should have asked if you wanted company before I sat down."

"What time do you normally get off work?" I glance at the clock on the wall. "Tell you what, I'll start ordering dinner to pick up on the way home for myself so you don't have to wait up like this. I did order some curry tonight during the meeting, but Brett's burger had ketchup on it and—" I pause when I notice a new look in her eyes. She looks embarrassed, which was definitely not my intent. "I'm sorry, I don't know why I'm wasting your time with all these details. You're probably exhausted from a long day of work, which I totally understand, and thank you so much for the dinner. It smells amazing."

I smile wider while she studies me.

I don't know if it's the subtly sad look on her face, or the fact that I feel like she can see right through me, but after everything that's unfolded today, my eyes do the most uncharacteristic thing. They tear up. My eyes almost never tear up. Especially in front of someone else — someone I hardly know.

I blink a few more times, clearing out the onslaught.

Lord, it's been a long day.

She tilts her head to the side then sets down her glass.

"I'm happy to trudge off to bed, sweetheart, but I do want to let you know that I don't stay up with dinner for you because I *have* to. I stay up to see you when you get back home because I *want* to."

I sniff. I can't do more emotions today. I simply cannot.

"You what?"

She tilts her jaw, then sits back down lightly on her chair. "This is my job, sure, but I enjoy taking care of people. I enjoy taking care of you. None of it feels like work to me."

I blink and spin a little back and forth on the stool.

"Right," I say, frowning. "But, you're also paid to, which I appreciate. And your days seem awfully long — you're up to make breakfast, and then still waiting for me this late at night. It's really not fair to you."

She laughs that twinkly sort of laugh, like she can't believe I'm making this assumption. "I thank my lucky stars every day that this is my job, because it never, not once, has felt like one. Of course, I take it seriously — making sure everyone under this roof has exactly what they need." She reaches across the table to pat my hand, squeezing gently before letting her palm slide off. "But make no mistake, I don't stay up for you while you're here because I'm paid to. I could just leave the food in the warmer, if that's what I thought you needed."

"Then why?" My voice nearly cracks but I keep it together.

"Well, I make sure I'm up to say goodnight before turning in because I know how much nicer it is to come home to a warm kitchen and a listening ear, at least most of the time.

And if I get to add that to your day, then I've done what I was put here to do. And I don't mean by Quinny and Selma."

I lean back, noticing how her eyes shine in the soft light of the kitchen. In a way, she reminds me of someone. Someone I haven't seen in a very long time.

"I think you're actually being serious," I admit.

Her laughter rings through the kitchen and I finally crack a real smile.

"Of course I'm being serious," she says, shaking her head as if I'm ridiculous. And maybe I *am* being ridiculous. "Honey, I didn't grow up in a house like this." She twirls her wrists around over her head, gesturing around the room. "One filled with this much comfort, like Quinny and Selma have. But, I swore to myself that one day I'd create the type of home I always wanted to live in. Take control of how my future turned out. I'm just happy that this, right here, is where I landed."

"You didn't grow up in a nice home?" I ask, startled that someone this robust and warm didn't grow up in a place just like this one.

"No." She shakes her head.

"So how did you learn to create this?" I lean against the counter. "This type of — *feeling* — you have here?"

"Honey, I took a good hard look at how I grew up. Everything I felt, everything the people around me did, and I decided that I wanted the exact opposite. So that's exactly what I did."

I tilt my head to the side. "Just like that?"

"The proof is in the pudding, isn't it?" she asks, winking.

"I suppose it is," I say, suddenly seeing her in a whole new light. To think that all this could be *learned* instead of inherited, like blue eyes or a face full of freckles. It's something I'd never even considered.

"Do you think that might work for anybody?" I wonder aloud — more to myself than to her.

The lines around her eyes deepen as she leans in to grasp my hand. Then she holds it for a minute before saying, "We can make our lives out to be exactly what we want them to be. Personally, I just had to wake up one day and take a good hard look at where I came from and choose to run the other way. Carve a new path without a map."

"You make it sound easy," I mumble, wondering how much about me she might recognize in herself.

"You'll figure it out," she says, passing a fork across the island. "Now eat up before it gets cold."

I shift on my chair, pushing a square of roasted potato onto my fork. "How — how would you know that I have something to figure out?" I ask, quietly.

"Because everyone has something to figure out, hon." Her voice is firm, leaving no room for error. Then she gently adds, "And now that you know I'm off the clock, I can leave you here to enjoy that, if you'd like."

She smiles like she understands if I'd rather eat alone, and starts to stand, but I hold my hand out to stop her.

"No, don't," I blurt. Then I straighten my spine and swallow. "I mean, I would love the company. If you don't mind."

Her grin grows and she rests her elbows on the counter between us.

I lower my voice and raise a brow. "Do you want to hear what happened in the supply room today?"

She throws her head back to laugh, nodding. Then she hops up and bustles across the kitchen to grab a plate of brownies from the cupboard. "Dessert when you're done. Now, tell me everything. I've got all the time in the world."

I take a bite of the meatloaf and grab a brownie for good measure. Then, I do. I start at the very beginning and tell her everything.

CHAPTER 23

Dax

I've just started drifting into an almost dreamlike state when my phone buzzes on the nightstand beside me. My eyes are so sore from the eyestrain of reading hundreds of pages of documents the past few days that even the LED glow of my phone screen sends them into a swell all over again. After everything that happened between Abby and I in the supply room today, I'm hoping it's her. I'd sent her a text afterward to ask what Brett had meant as they were walking out, offering to talk more, but she hadn't written back yet.

I grab my phone off the desk, but it's Silas' name I see. He was supposed to fly in last night to join the flurry of offers today, but much to Lila's trepidation, his arrival was pushed back a few more days.

Again.

He's now expected to arrive on Monday in time for next week's run of meetings. Something about a sailing race in Spain, or something of the sort, delaying his arrival. God only knows when it comes to that guy.

I slide the circle over on my phone and clear my throat, preparing myself to sound alert and ready for a chat.

"Si, hey man, what's up?" I speak as if it's the most normal thing in the world for him to call his buddy-slash-attorney at this hour after I've already worked a fourteen-hour day for him.

"Hey man, sorry it's late," he says on the other line. "Just had to let you know that I won't be making it next week after all. The swells over in Belize are, like, way too good to miss at the moment. But you and Lancaster are still fine handling everything without me around, yeah?"

I rub my eyes.

"Of course. We're going in even stronger than . . ." I pause, feeling like I shouldn't call Abby's side out. "Everyone else."

"Is there anything else I can answer for you before you head off to Belize?" I hope this conversation with Silas is short. Like, thirty seconds or less kind of short.

"Nah. I just wanted to see if you were up. I just left Majorca this morning and the time difference there is a beast, man. I was going to see if you and Ryeson were up for a—"

I stop him before he can get the words out, glad he can't see my reaction to anything that resembles an invitation to anything but sleep right now. "You want me in top shape tomorrow so I can continue digging into this, Si. Primed and ready to win for you," I say.

"Right. No, yeah, you're right," he says, brushing the hope from his voice.

I clamp my mouth shut to stop any snarky responses from coming out and rub my eyes even harder, glad he can't see my face right now. He's been so lonely since Grant died.

"Hey, did you see Jules is selling Grant's nonprofit, over in Boston?" he asks. I note the control in his voice.

"Yeah, I've actually been handling the sale for her."

I let a thick silence fill the line. That's probably the real reason he's calling right now. He must have just seen news of the sale.

"I'm sorry, Si," I say. "I should have told you, man. Client confidentiality and all that, though."

"Yeah, no, I . . . I understand. It's wild, man. Wild."

I close my eyes, wishing I could make some of this easier on him.

"Si? You still there?"

He sucks in a breath, but doesn't follow it up with any more words about Grant or Jules.

"Yeah, no, totally. Sorry, man. I'll let you go. I know it's late. I just, yeah, thank you for working so hard on this. I'm lucky to have you, as always, but you already know that. Glad you know what you're doing with all this." He laughs awkwardly.

Christ, Si.

"Of course. Besides, you're paying me handsomely to do it," I remind him, forcing a light laugh to coast through the line.

"Highly deserved." He sounds proud. "Goodnight, man. See you and Lancaster at some point. Looking forward to meeting her. Till then, carry on. Keep me posted."

I say goodnight and place my phone back on the charger, then roll over and push a second pillow up over my head. I hate what all the loss has done to him. But I shake it off the best I can and just as I'm about to slip off into dreamland, my phone buzzes on the nightstand for a second time. I groan and press it to my ear without even bothering to confirm his name on the screen.

"We've got it from here, Si, I swear to God," I mumble to him.

"Funny, I swore the same thing to God earlier tonight, too," Abby's voice streams into my ear.

I pull the phone screen back in front of my eyes to make sure I'm not dreaming just yet.

Sure enough, it says *Abby Torres.* Clear as day.

I sit up.

"Abby?" I'm now fully awake. "Are you okay? You're calling" — I glance at the clock — "late. You're calling *really* late." *Booty-call levels of late*, I want to add.

"Yeah, sorry about what time it is. I just really didn't want to wait until tomorrow to call you. I couldn't sleep." She sounds a bit off. "By the way, have you ever tried yoga?"

I cover my face with my palm.

"You're not high, are you?" I ask. "While legal, Cali grass is different from New York's — or at least that's what I hear, so tread lightly if that's what you've been up to tonight. Do you need a ride home or something?"

She laughs.

"I don't think so, no. Not unless Starry happened to put something in those double chocolate brownies. She put a little stack of them *on my pillow*, Dax, in case I woke up hungry later. I swear I've gained fourteen pounds since I got here, but I can't resist. I think she gets the eggs from the chicken coop out back."

I click on the lamp beside me.

"Okay, yeah, you've definitely ingested some special brownies from whoever the hell Starry is. Sounds sus, Abs, if you're finding random food on your pillow. And you don't need to be taking a ride-share alone right now. Send me the address of wherever this chicken coop is, unless you plan on having that asshat pick you up?"

"Asshat?" She chuckles. "You mean Brett?"

"Sure."

"That's a great name for him," she says, and I know she's smiling through the line. "But, no, I'm not high. Starry's not some random person, she's the house granager at the place I'm staying."

I wince. If not high, then maybe drunk, considering she can't even get the word *manager* out right. I rack my brain for why Abby would have a house manager in L.A. making her baked goods from scratch with eggs plucked straight from a chicken coop at this time of night.

Better yet, why is she calling me so late to tell me this type of thing? I'm guessing our little fling in the closet today threw her for as much of a loop as it did me, but I didn't see her calling me drunk, or whatever she is doing, this late.

I take the bait anyway, too curious not to.

"Why do you have a house manager?" I ask, settling back, giving in to the idea of getting no real sleep tonight.

My phone buzzes against my cheek, even though she's already on the line.

I look down at the phone, wondering who else is calling me this late.

"Are you trying to FaceTime me?" I ask, her invitation flashing across the screen.

"Just accept it," she says.

I hit the green button and the screen goes black, only to be replaced by a live image of a pink satin pillowcase with what looks like three chocolate bricks piled up on top of a red plate.

"Can you believe this?" she asks. I still can't see her face.

"I mean, I was kind of hoping for an entirely different view when I accepted that FaceTime request, but yeah," I say, vaguely wondering what I'm looking at. "Are those the *special* brownies?"

She snickers. "The only thing special about them is that they're made with fresh eggs and that they were left *on my pillow*."

I nod, acutely aware that she has a view of me while I'm still looking at a plate.

"I've just finished some questionable takeout that was not fresh, nor was it delicious, so unless you're planning to deliver those to me right now, with the promise that you're not high or drunk before driving, then I'm having a hard time figuring this call out . . ."

"I'm sure Starry wouldn't mind me bringing you a few," she says, thoughtfully. "Which means that I hope you're up for an in-person visit these days. I'd rather talk face-to-face without the thrill of Brett nearly walking in."

"Starry, the house manager?" I clarify, trying to keep up.

She corrects me, "The house *granager*."

Silence.

"Abby, where are you?" I finally ask.

"That's what I've been trying to show you," she says.

"Can you turn the FaceTime screen on you now? I need to see if your eyes are dilating properly."

I can hear her mumbling sarcastically, something about me being high-maintenance, but once the camera's flipped around, Abby's nose fills the screen.

"Whoa, hold on," she says, pushing the zoom out until her face comes into view, dimples deepening on either side of her pillowy lips.

Just looking at her face, especially her face outside work, makes me feel at ease, and I'm suddenly not sure how anyone survived without FaceTime before this moment.

"Hi," I say quietly, unable to stop a smile from filling my face.

"Hi," she says, matching my expression.

"Did you call just to let me know that you're considering marrying whoever this Starry person is tonight for her baking skills and that you need a witness? Or was it really just to show me that pile of allegedly drug-free brownies?"

"Mmm, both?" she answers.

"Well, in that case, I'll be over in twenty. Though, I only take cash when called to be a formal witness."

"To a marriage?"

"To anything," I tell her. "Don't tell Baldy, but I'm easily bought."

She laughs.

We sit in silence then, grinning at each other.

"Thank you for answering," she finally says. "I know today was a bit . . . confusing, to say the least."

"I'm glad you called," I say, my voice deepening. Even through the phone screen, I can see her cheeks turning a sweet shade of pink.

"I want to ask you something." She looks more serious.

My heart rate picks up. "Shoot."

"I've been staying at Quinton Rockwell and Selma Hatfield's estate since I arrived," she admits, like it's some type of confession.

"Okay." Having lived in L.A. most of my life, random run-ins with celebrities rarely surprise me anymore, though this admission is a bit bigger than most. "I'm sure there's more to this story, but now that whole house-manager-slash-special-brownie thing does make more sense . . ."

"Right," she rushes to say. "Staying here is all part of what I'm about to tell you. The house granager-slash-manager and I have kind of become . . . friends." She pauses to smile. "She's like the resident grandma of the house. She takes care of everyone Quinton and Selma have here, including me."

I imagine Abby walking into a warm kitchen with a little grandma figure there to bake brownies and put them on her pillow at night. It sounds amazing.

She pauses and I wait.

Then she takes a deep breath like she wants to say something, before letting all the air inside her fizzle back out. Two more times this happens, before she finally finds the words to express the issue that seems to be plaguing her.

"Obviously, you heard what Brett said in the supply room." She narrows her eyes as anxiety fills her face, she's looking more nervous now than she's looked over the past few weeks of billion-dollar negotiations. "Your text asked if I wanted to talk about it."

"Something about how being back in L.A. might be getting to you based on something that happened here?" I say, studying her eyes as I do.

She nods, then puts a hand over her chest. "God, my heart is beating out of my chest right now."

"What did he mean by that?" I ask, slowly. "I thought you'd never been to L.A."

She chuckles harshly, then looks apologetic, blinking at me through the screen like she's not sure what to say.

"Abby, I meant what I said earlier." Christ, if I could teleport to her instead of telepathically hug her right now, I would. "There's really nothing you can say that'll scare me off."

"In that case . . ." She suddenly looks amused.

"Okay," I go on, "short of you telling me you're into lighting me on fire or something. But other than that, I'm game for whatever it is that you look so nervous about telling me right now."

She tucks her lips between her teeth, then tilts her chin up and mumbles "fuck it" toward the ceiling. "I swore I'd never do what I'm asking you to do," she finally says, looking back at me.

"I'm game," I announce.

She laughs. "You don't even know what I'm going to ask."

"Doesn't matter."

I return a lopsided grin, but her face shifts to serious, like she's made her final decision about whatever this is about.

"Will you go somewhere with me tomorrow?"

I laugh. "Like in the daylight?" I ask, fishing for more reassurance that I'm not about to get swept up in the Abby train again.

"Yes. In the morning. I know you're just as swamped as I am with work, but tomorrow is Saturday, so I thought that maybe you could take a little time off to go see something with me. Something that might be better at explaining some things. Better than my attempt right now, anyway."

I'm supposed to meet Lila at ten thirty tomorrow morning to run through our next steps of the deal, which, unbeknownst to Abby, is going to be turning into a hostile takeover sooner than we'd have liked. Regardless of his continued absence, Silas' business manager wants the deal done and is pushing to have it finished before the month is out. Abby has next to no idea that Lila and I are burning the midnight oil trying to get in position to push a hostile takeover forward before The Nile Group has the time to give itself over to her side.

"Yes, I'll go," I tell her without doubting my decision. Lila can take on a day of document review and fill me in later. She and the other eighteen attorneys we have working around

the clock back at the firm this weekend. I won't be missed.
"What time?"

"I'll pick you up first thing in the morning," she says. "Text me your address."

CHAPTER 24

Bright and early next morning, I'm already outside — sitting on the front porch admiring my view of the city and wondering why I don't come out here more often — when Abby's car rolls to a stop. I've already met two neighbors, and got to pet a very nice golden retriever rescue mix named Sasha that lives down the street.

When Abby parks her car — SUV? No, definitely car — I go sauntering down the driveway to rest my forearms on its open window frame.

"You didn't tell me you were driving a toaster around L.A.," I say through the window of her rental, which looks more like it'd toast my bread than take us out on an adventure. Maybe it can do both.

Chuckling, she hands me a Starbucks cup through the window that already has a faint, berry-pink lip stain around the hole in the rim.

"Your matcha latte is growing on me," she says, nodding toward the cup.

Her lips are filled with the same berry color she wore that day in New York, like strawberries ground up in a mortar and pressed deeply into her skin. I fight the urge to taste them, just to see if they taste as sweet as they look, and settle on sipping the frothy green tea from the place her lips have just been.

"You added vanilla," I say, licking the sweetness of the tea mixed with the taste of her lips off of mine before taking a second sip to confirm my suspicion.

"I did." She grins. "Carrie mentioned it helps the flavor."

"Tastes good." I smile, and I don't just mean the tea.

"You're welcome," she says, watching me. I can tell she's thinking about that morning in New York, just as much as me. And then everything it led to later that night.

She starts turning a light shade of pink before nodding toward the empty passenger seat beside her. "Now, get in before I lose my cool here and have to drive away."

I squeeze her shoulder through the open window before it begins sliding shut, wanting to ask where she's taking me that has her looking so nervous.

She hands me a small plate wrapped in aluminum foil when I climb in beside her. There are two brownies sitting underneath the silvery cover when I peel it back.

"Courtesy of Starry," she says, but she's staring out the window. "Is this where you live?"

I nod, sniffing a brownie for any special ingredients before biting into it.

"You own it?"

I nod again and then I can't help it. My eyes roll back and I let out a long groan.

"Oh my God, you were right. These are pretty special. But not, like *special*."

She laughs.

"Not in the way you initially thought last night," she says, watching me take another bite. "You never told me you live in a place with that kind of front porch," she adds, eyeing the long, raw wood-plank porch filled with two white rocking chairs, before pulling the toaster-slash-car out onto the road.

"You've never asked about my porch style," I point out. "But in case you're wondering, yes, I live in a house with a wraparound front porch. And if those two rockers didn't already turn you on, there's three more around the other side that you just can't see from the road."

She grips the steering wheel a bit harder, and bites her lip, though it does nothing to hide her amusement. "You stop that sexy talk right now before I turn this car back around," she says, through a laugh.

"If that porch does it for you, you should see my back patio."

She erupts into nervous laughter and I manage to get another sip of matcha through my lips without spilling it out the side as we race down the road to wherever Abby has decided we're going.

"Seriously, though. Who are all those rocking chairs for?" she asks, a more serious tone taking over from the one she had just a moment ago. "Are you hiding a whole wife and kids inside?"

"One day, I hope."

Her eyes dart over to mine, narrowing, before drifting back to the road.

"Your future wife likes rocking on those?" she asks, forcing her brows together. "Chatting with neighbors that are out on their evening walks. That type of thing?"

"In my head, sure," I say. "I mean, I haven't exactly drafted it out, but back when I had the house built, I had the contractor position the house on this hill so the porch has a perfect view of the sun setting over the Pacific. My future wife and I plan to watch it every night."

Her lips curl up in a smile.

"Like melted butter over a shimmering stack of diamonds," I add, lowering my voice; that's what my dad used to say whenever we watched the sun setting over my parents' panoramic view above Sunset Boulevard. We only ever did that a handful of times together, since both of them were stringent workaholics, but the way he described it like that each time always stuck out in my memory.

"I can't imagine having a life like that here," she says, wistfully. "L.A. is so different from New York. Similar in some ways, and yet so polar opposite when it comes to others."

"I hear some people even call it the *best* coast," I joke, looking out the passenger window so she can't see the sarcastic smirk stretched across my face.

"I'm not sure we're ever going to agree on that." She gives my elbow a gentle nudge. "I haven't been able to find a decent bagel since I got back here."

"*Back* here again?" I ask, catching the word that sticks out from the rest. "Before yesterday, I thought this was your first time visiting."

Her hands silently wring the leather covering the steering wheel like it's a wet towel before she answers.

"I've actually spent a lot of time here," she says. "But you're right. It's like another planet to me."

"You never mentioned spending any time in L.A. before. When I offered you that job at the firm here after law school, you acted like L.A. was a different planet — and one you had no interest in seeing."

"I didn't. Not again."

She swallows, then pushes her tongue along her top teeth. Finally, she looks at me, but her face holds a new type of vulnerability, her eyes raw, like there's nowhere to run.

"Where are we going today, Abs?" I ask, wrapping my arm around the back of her headrest.

Her eyes darken, like clouds shifting shape when a storm is coming in. I wait for her to answer.

"Just some place I didn't want to go alone, but felt too important to miss while I'm here. Things are starting to wrap up with The Nile, from what I can tell, so I didn't want to wait any longer. Then after yesterday with you, and Brett, I figured now was as good of a time as any."

I nod toward the windshield, wondering where on earth she could possibly be taking me, but I keep my eyes turned toward the road that's peeling away beneath us.

"So," — I pat the window frame on my side of the car — "did you pick out this traveling toaster here? Or was this just part of your and Starry's elopement registry? Or . . ."

She snorts, then braces one hand over her stomach, like it might settle down whatever nerves are coursing through her as we continue down the road. I wish I could lighten her mood, but I have a sense that she's the only one capable of doing that right now.

"I really want you to meet her," she says. "Starry, I mean. And not because I am completely enamored with her, but because I'm pretty sure that everyone on the planet should meet someone like her at some point in their life."

Meet someone in Abby's world? Other than Olivia, I've never even heard her discuss anyone in her life except Brett, and he hardly counts.

She chews her lip, a fresh set of nerves evidently rolling in.

"I'd love to meet her," I say, grabbing her knee before sliding my hand off and back over the top of her headrest.

"Here Comes the Sun" by The Beatles comes coursing through the speakers and Abby reaches to turn the volume up. I can't tell if it's a ploy to change the subject, or if this is really some favorite old song that she loves.

But it doesn't matter.

Because once Abby starts singing along, tapping her thumb on the steering wheel to the beat, I don't care whether she's trying to distract me or herself with the song.

If she wants to talk, we'll talk. Otherwise, I'm happy to play passenger princess to whatever adventure we're on this morning.

The beach?

The pier?

Does it matter?

For maybe the first time ever, Abby's initiated something outside of a closed-door rendezvous, and there's no other place I'd rather be than right here, waiting to find out where the hell she feels the need to take me.

* * *

Nearly an hour later, we're inching down a street lined with trash bags overflowing into the gutters, replacing the manicured sidewalks we left behind long ago. Chain-link fences and a little pack of off-leash dogs meander past my window. I'm starting to wonder if Abby got lost after exiting the freeway. But, she's checking the map on her phone religiously, still humming "Here Comes the Sun" to herself while injecting whispered street names, and making tiny sighs under her breath.

"Are you kidding me? Mrs. Perry is still at that place?" she says, more to herself than me as we pass a tiny, brittle-looking woman sitting on a worn-out chair that looks like it was painted orange at one point, but is now fully rusted out. Paint is peeling off every inch, like a snake shedding its skin, while the woman blankly stares out toward the road.

"Oh, God, that place really went downhill, wow," she mutters, looking out of her window at a barely-standing pile of plywood and bricks. Graffiti-covered boards cover whatever is left of the windows and door.

"I think this might be—" She slows, nearly to a stop. "No wait, not yet. God, it's been forever."

She drives a bit further, until finally, we pull off to the side of the road in front of a line of what should be identical row houses, but each one is worn in its own way, making each one of them somehow stick out like a sore thumb. One more torn up than the next. All in some state of disrepair. One with two missing windows, covered with black garbage bags stretched over the otherwise large gaping holes, billowing in the wind.

One of the plastic covers is pulled back, and a little girl with dark brown pigtails peeks out from behind the hanging garbage sack, her pale skin a stark contrast to her hair and the bag behind her.

She watches us intensely, but instead of ducking back into the house when she and I make eye contact, the little girl smiles and sticks a hand up beside her face, waving at us as we roll along the curb and come to a stop right in front of her house.

My stomach spirals, wondering what Abby could possibly need on a street like this, with a little girl like that behind a missing window.

But Abby's watching the little girl, too, except, unlike me, she's already waving back, smiling shyly.

Abby mouths the word, *hi*, and the little girl grins.

"Do you know her?" I ask, gently, watching the way her eyes study the figure in the window.

Abby shakes her head, her eyes shining.

"Not in the way you might think," she says, shifting the car's gear to park.

As quickly as she appeared, the little girl vanishes behind the black trash bag, and I watch it flutter in the wind, waiting for her to reappear, wondering why in the world her parents have her living in a place like this. Wondering, too, if we've somehow come here to help her.

What could we possibly be doing here, Abs? I want to ask, but I don't.

Not yet.

"Do you know her parents?" I try next, taking a stab at why we've driven all the way across town and stopped here on this particular street.

I'm well aware that there are some neighborhoods around here that you just don't go to unless you're lost and wind up there by accident. And this, right here where we've just parked, is one of them.

"Does this have anything to do with the negotiation over The Nile?" I ask, wondering what other reason the chic, put-together, always laughing, Abby might have to bring me here.

She shakes her head again.

"Nothing about today has anything to do with work," she says, lightly. "Or anything else you already know about me."

Then she opens her door and gets out of the car.

CHAPTER 25

Abby

I shut the door behind me and walk across the road, turning around to make sure Dax hasn't chickened out when it comes to following me, but he's directly on my heels. I grab his hand and we set off together down the road.

Part of me is mortified that I decided to bring him here today, but if there's anything I've realized, it's that I won't do this alone. I don't want to. And besides, it's too late for all that right now. We're already here, aren't we?

The smell of trash permeates the air since the sanitation department hasn't been down this road yet today. Most of the houses here just put their trash bags out at the curb all week though, instead of waiting for the city's official trash day. It's easier to keep the dogs and raccoons and whatever else away from the doors and windows of the houses that way. I know all too well that horrible things on this street always find a way in, no matter how much you try to prevent them. And not all of them will leave nicely when asked.

When we arrive at the front of it, my feet won't move any more. I couldn't breeze past this place, even if I wanted to — which, right now, I do. In fact, everything in me wants to breeze past this house now that I'm here.

It's more gray than I remember. More dingy and worn, since most of the yellow paint has peeled off, leaving only a hint of that lemony color my dad started painting it one summer — even if he only got half of the front wall done before giving up on the rest. The door on the front is a different color than I remember. It used to be thick, brown-painted wood, but it's been covered with a tawny green color that looks out of place among the yellow-gray hues surrounding it.

The yard looks the exact same though. As if whoever lives here now enjoys yard work about as much as my parents did. Weeds as high as my hips, with a dead flower box hanging off the wall beneath one of the windows.

The window that used to be mine.

The flower box was a gift for my seventh birthday. The last birthday I ever had here.

I fix my eyes on the house, afraid of what I'll see written all over Dax's if I turn to face him.

Out of the corner of my eye, I can tell that Dax is watching me closely — me, not the house — and it's making me feel uneasy.

"Do you know who lives here?" he asks.

I bite my lip, then pull it out harshly, feeling my skin swell beneath the pressure of my teeth.

"I used to," I tell him, forcing my eyes to meet his, for only one second, before pulling them away again. "But I don't think I know whoever lives here now. At least, I'd be surprised to know that . . ."

To know that they're still alive.

I can't finish that sentence. It's been too long and they were in such a sorry state when I left them. In fact, I'm somewhat surprised to see that this place is still standing here at all, and that it does actually exist in the world. It isn't just a figment of my imagination.

I've filled so many holes within my childhood memories. Sometimes filling the blanks with happier, made-up moments of holiday traditions and things that other kids in class always talked about having, that I never did.

But standing here now, I know that this part of my childhood memory is undeniably real.

I *lived* here.

"That little girl in the window," he says, slowly. "You knew her?"

I turn to face him, and though I have no idea what look is stretched across my face, it must be a doozy because Dax stops talking and takes a small step toward me, brushing a stray wisp of hair behind my ear.

"I only know her in theory because I used to *be* her," I say, admitting it out loud to both him and myself in the same breath. Then I turn back to the little yellow-gray house with the ugly green door. "Not *her*, exactly, but I was someone just like her. This was my home, growing up."

He turns to look — really *look* — at the little house we've stopped in front of.

"This was my street. This" — I smile, looking directly at him — "was the coast I grew up on. The *best* coast, as you like to say." I clear my throat before going on, trying to stay composed. "I don't know why I had to come back here, but I guess I did. Something about putting things out into the universe so they stop having so much power over you." I blink, remembering something Starry said last night while we talked, hoping with everything in me that it's true. "And thank you for coming, I mean I just couldn't . . ."

I stop talking. My brain won't work properly anymore because that rickety little handle on the green door is turning over from the inside.

It suddenly swings open. I feel like I might faint.

An angry, tired looking man steps out.

For one blinding moment, my eyes trick me into thinking it's someone else — he reminds me of my father, but horribly aged. Rabid, completely bedraggled, and high, stepping out to call me back home once the streetlights have turned on.

I blink, and he's gone. Replaced by a man I've never seen before.

He narrows his eyes sharply toward Dax, then me.

Dax swings his head toward the man, then back at me, and I can tell he's probably wondering if there's anything he should be doing at this moment. Or if that's my father we're looking at.

Just be here with me, I want to tell him.

"Can I help you?" the man calls out, his voice completely unfamiliar and unsteady. "You waiting on the one eighteen? Haven't seen you two around here before."

The one eighteen. Just hearing that number makes my stomach take a nosedive. Even the bus routes haven't changed around here.

I shake my head.

"No," I call back, and I feel Dax let out a little sigh of relief. "I used to live here. Just came back to see how the old place is holding up."

"Ah," he says, eyeing us both up and down like we might be here to fleece him. "You're not wanting to come in, are ya?"

"No," I quickly call out. Although I wouldn't say it out loud to the man, wild horses couldn't drag me back into that place. Not ever again.

"Thanks!" Dax calls out next, waving a hand above his head.

We *should* keep moving down the sidewalk, but my feet stay firmly planted.

Dax's feet stay rooted next to mine, too.

He takes my hand and holds it tightly while I bring myself to inspect the exterior of the home I spent seven long years living in.

"Do you mind if I just take a look from here?" I call out to the man.

He watches me for another moment, then tosses one hand out toward us, as if he doesn't care anymore.

"Free country, suit yourself," he grumbles. "Though I wouldn't stay out here too long. You two look like you're lost."

The door slams behind him and I let out a sigh of relief once he's gone back inside.

Then I take it all in, knowing I will never, ever be back.

Battered shutters hang at the front window — torn off now on one side. Tall grass and weeds growing every which way, as if not a day has passed. Two concrete steps on the front are still cracked down the middle, right where I tripped up them one day after school, splitting my lip on the doorknob so badly that I vowed never to try and skip up them again. The roof, which has possibly never been replaced, is still sagging between the chimney stack and what I know to be the kitchen toward the back of the house. The same kitchen where I used to watch my parents mix their potions and cocktails, never thinking whether their little girl might be wondering when they might use that stove to make something for her, too.

I wonder if the wall my mom used to chart my height a few times still shows the thin lines where she'd hold a book over my head, then mark where my hair met the book's edge with a pen. I still marked my height every birthday myself, since after the first few years, she'd forgotten to do it. My lines were wobbly and imperfect above her straighter ones, a visible reminder of when everything went wrong.

Once I feel certain that I will never again question the realness of this place, or its power, I turn away, toward Dax, afraid of what I might see etched across his face, now that he knows the truth about where I came from. But instead of disgust, or even surprise, I'm met with understanding. And acceptance.

"So, this is it?" he asks, squeezing my hand. "I had no idea you were originally from L.A."

I shrug, ready to explain why I brought him all the way out here when the whooshing sound of a city bus exhaust muffler shoots a stream of ice straight through my veins.

"Oh my God!" I say, spinning around. I saw the bus stop sign still standing when we walked up — it's covered in red spray paint now — but the odds of the one eighteen showing up while we stand here right now are slim to none.

And yet . . .

The doors of the bus creak open and people start spilling out onto the sidewalk all around us.

My heart thumps in my chest, threatening to send me into cardiac arrest when I look up at the driver.

"Catalpa Street!" The woman's voice carries to the back of the bus, loud enough to wake anyone who might have fallen asleep on her route. A few sleepy passengers stand, then make their wobbly way down the steps that carry them outside.

I stare up at her face, more aged now than I remember, but still proudly wearing that same, tired bus driver's hat — the one with the gold medallion pinned across the front. The exact same one she'd let me wear sometimes when I was having an especially hard day, when we rode around her whole route together. She'd pepper me with questions. Questions that no one had asked me before.

What're you gonna do when you get out of this town one day, Miss Abby?

How'd you score on that reading test last week with your teacher Miss Johnson?

What's your mama up to today, honey? Was she awake before you left?

Did you water those seeds I gave you last week for your new flower box out front?

When I woke up this morning, I knew that I'd be seeing my old house today, but nothing could have prepared me for seeing her, too.

She pats a few of the passengers on the back as they make their way out, calling niceties over their shoulders, along with what I imagine to be a few inside jokes, too.

"See you tomorrow, Miss Candi!" an elderly man in a bowler hat says brightly, as he steps off the stairs. He rushes past me, bumping into me gently as he does.

And when the crowd has cleared, I'm left with only the sound of my heart drumming loudly in my chest.

Blood coursing through my hands and fingertips.

I feel every inch of my body pulsing when I look up at this woman. I stare up into her eyes, feeling just like I did at seven years old, about to ride around town with the only friend I had in the whole world.

Miss Candi smiles down at me, as if about to welcome some new faces onboard.

"Miss Candice?" I say, barely above a whisper, hoping she remembers. Hoping, against all odds, that she shares the same fond memories from my childhood, the ones I've tucked away in some last part of my mind reserved for happier things from this particular era of my life. Things I know I experienced as a child, in her presence, that were everything a kid should have.

Kindness.

Warmth.

Love. Or at least something that felt a lot like love to me, or as close as I ever got to it, anyway. Something — I realize now — that felt a lot like someone caring for me.

I see the exact moment that my face, though much older now, registers in Miss Candi's memory — when her face suddenly drains of all its color.

It's then that I finally smile, letting her know that it's okay. I understand why she did what she did.

Tears sting my eyes, so quickly that I have to blink them away.

Her forehead wrinkles into a tight little V beneath the rim of the hat as if she's staring straight into the past, the ghost of the girl she'd once helped.

Helped, Miss Candi. You helped me. And I understand that. I didn't. But I do, now.

The words won't come out.

"Honey?" she says, a whisper. It sounds like a memory. "Abby, honey, is that you? What on earth are you doing here?"

Her eyes shift toward my house.

"They don't live there anymore, do they?" I ask, confirming what I already know.

She shakes her head.

Dax clears his throat a few inches behind me. I don't have the words to explain any of this to him right now. I will. But I can barely take the shock of running into her, unplanned like this, myself.

I stare, afraid to blink. Afraid that if my lids close, even for one second, this impossible mirage will disappear.

She looks more weathered than the last time I saw her, sitting in that very same seat, at this very same bus stop right outside my front door. Smaller, somehow. Like either she must have shrunk, or I must have grown. Of course, it's me that's grown, but the memory of her is one of the few I've grasped hold of with an iron fist, and it's hard to change the image of someone you once loved so dearly as now just a human, not a superhero. Scars, wrinkles, exhausted eyes and all.

"I . . . I wasn't expecting to see you," I stammer. "I just came back to see this old street."

She shoves the gear on the dash into park and rushes down the stairs, folding me into the tightest embrace.

Every single thing comes flooding back.

Sitting alone in the front seat of bus one eighteen.

Riding right behind Miss Candi like I did most afternoons.

Passing the hours of her bus route together, probably boring her with all the smallest details of my day, reveling in how wonderfully well she'd listen to me.

How Rowan Sanderson always seemed to have the prettiest hair-dos in class, each with a bow that matched another new outfit that day, a never-ending collection, I'd tell her.

How I wished my mother would wash and brush my hair like Rowan's mother must have done.

How I wished my mother would look at me at all.

Did you fall asleep during your lessons again, honey?
What'd you have for lunch today?
You hungry?

She'd pass a Kudos bar back to me from the box she kept hidden beneath her seat, usually before I'd pass out somewhere along the route, usually just after we passed through Collier Drive.

Some days, I didn't just pretend that Miss Candi was my real mom, spending time with me every afternoon after school like I always wanted — I'd started fantasizing about asking her to *be* my mother, for real. To take me home with her, so I'd never have to go back to that little gray-yellow house again.

The last time I saw Miss Candi, I'd been standing at the bus stop waiting for her to come pick me up like I would on any other day. With a picture I'd drawn for her, rolled carefully and held softly in my fist so it wouldn't be at all creased when I climbed up the stairs and unrolled it for her. The drawing was of the bus. Our bus. But I'd made it look more like a house than a city vehicle, permanently parked in front of a sea of purple flowers with Miss Candi and me standing in the front of it, holding hands.

Smiling.

I'd been planning to ask if she could be my mom that day. Maybe I could just stay on the bus with her that night. Get donuts in the morning, or go to that milkshake place I always dreamed of going, the one with the black-and-white checkered floor and the waitresses who dressed like they worked at a fifties diner. The one we always passed on her route, and I'd beg her to pull over just one time.

Miss Candi had driven up like usual that afternoon, and after all the familiar passengers tumbled out, I started unrolling the sheet of paper so I could board the bus with it outstretched in front of me, imagining the joy crossing her face when I asked the question I'd never been brave enough to ask her before.

But when I looked up, beaming, with my drawing unraveled across my chest, two suited passengers — a man and a woman — exited the bus. They stopped me when I tried to go up the steps.

"Are you Abby? Which house is yours?"

"We heard from Miss Candice that you might need some help."

"Are your mom and dad home now, by chance?"

I tried explaining to them that I lived in that little gray-yellow house behind me, but that I needed to get on the bus like I did every other afternoon. They stepped in front of me, blocking the way up.

Miss Candice and I have plans.

I have an important question to ask her.

"It's that one, there," I said, pointing.

Their eyes followed my finger.

And for the first time, I saw it all through someone else's perspective. The overgrown exterior with the broken chain-link fence in the front, two men — who I didn't know but had seen on my porch more than once — passed out in the old, rusty lawn chairs. Mom and Dad probably inside like that, too. Flies buzzing in the empty kitchen. Stale scraps of tomato paste crust and beer cans, powders and packages I wouldn't understand until later in life. But otherwise empty.

Always empty.

"We just have a few questions for you, Abby," the woman said. "Could you walk down to the house with us for a little bit?"

I looked up the stairs to Miss Candi for help.

Why are these strangers — strangers who know my name — coming out of our *bus?*

But Miss Candi already had tears rolling down her cheeks.

"I had to, baby." The last words she ever said to me back then. "I'm so sorry. You're going to live a better life than this."

I tried to push past them, tried to show her my drawing anyway. Unrolling it again as they held my shoulders back.

But of course, I never got up the stairs.

She just nodded, looking pained when they asked her to continue on down the road. Get on with her route.

"It'll be easier this way," the man said. "Once she can't see you anymore, she might not fight us as much."

Within the week, I'd been placed with an aunt and uncle I didn't know I had out in New York.

And until now, I had never seen Miss Candi's face again.

CHAPTER 26

Dax

The driver of the bus comes tumbling down the stairs toward us, wrapping Abby up in a long hug, rocking her back and forth, holding her like a child tucked safely between her arms.

The woman pulls her back, only long enough to study Abby's tear-stained face, then squeezes her in again, repeating, "I'm sorry . . . I'm sorry . . . I'm sorry." And finally, "I had to. You know I had to. I hope you did what I always told you to do. I hope you got out of there and never looked back, baby."

"I did," Abby answers, nodding. "And I know you had to do what you did. I didn't at the time, but I do now. Thank you. I know now, I promise. Thank you . . . thank you . . . thank you."

CHAPTER 27

I take the wheel when we get back to Abby's car, and silently drive us back to the main stretch of road, away from that awful line of houses, until we come upon a little burger joint, the sign out front boasting *best milkshakes in the west*.

Abby suddenly asks if we can pull in.

I don't question her. Instead, I grab a hold of her knee, and don't let go until we roll to a stop near the front of the building.

She looks up at the sign, staring at the old burger joint as if she's just seen a ghost. Her second or third ghost of the day. "Best in the west," she mutters, reading the sign. There's a faint smile on her face when she turns to me. "Can we go in?"

"You're hungry?" I ask, surprised that the visit to her old neighborhood didn't just destroy her appetite.

She grins wider. "Something like that."

When we walk inside the checkered floor diner, a waitress greets us. She's wearing a folded paper hat, like we've just stepped back in time to the 1950's.

"Two of your biggest strawberry milkshakes. Extra sprinkles," Abby says when the young waitress asks for our order. "Do you want anything else?" she asks, turning to me.

"Ah, just the biggest pile of fries you have, to go with them," I add.

"Excellent choice," Abby says, bumping into me.

"I hadn't pegged you as the *extra sprinkles* type of girl." I bump her back.

"I am damn near full of surprises today." She tilts her face up to smile at me, knowing everything we've done today has come out of left field.

We walk to a table in the back. I slide in across from her in the blue vinyl booth and push two paper straws through the plastic lids of the water cups the waitress hands us. Folding the wrappers up into tiny accordions, I wait for Abby to speak.

I drop the paper accordions and gently nudge her leg under the table with my knee, keeping it pressed up against hers, wondering if I should be sitting next to her instead of across from her, if only to hold her upright after everything that just happened.

"I wasn't expecting a home tour today," I finally say, letting her off the hook as the one to break the silence. "I'm really glad you took me with you."

"I'm not totally sure whether I'm glad I took you or not," she says, smiling faintly. "It's been so long. I wasn't sure what to expect when I went back there. But I've been feeling like I should. Seeing Miss Candi there was completely unexpected. I definitely feel shook at seeing her like that, but I'm really happy I did."

"I can tell." I hold her hand, then I let it slip away. "Do you want to talk about it? Or—"

"She's the person who called CPS on my parents," she says, looking firmly into my eyes. "She started the whole process that got me adopted by my aunt and uncle over in New York."

Christ. My stomach drops out. I could tell something major had happened between them, but I couldn't have guessed that. I wait for more, still wondering how a bus driver could have had that much impact on her life, or knew that whatever waited for her in New York was going to be better than whatever was happening in that house. Or what Abby would have had to go through to get to that point.

"Bus one eighteen was like a mobile daycare to me," she says, somehow looking fond of the memory. "I'd sat in front of my house for who knows how many days, watching that bus come and go, the happy-looking people getting off, orderly lines waiting in front of it. Miss Candi, as I later came to call her, was always welcoming people onto that bus with a big ol' smile. I never knew where any of them were going, but I always knew that she just looked happy to have them there with her. So one day, instead of sitting out in front of my house, waiting for my parents to come home with — hopefully — something to put in the fridge after being gone for a few days, I got on."

"Your parents left you without any food for *days at a time?*" I can't imagine this version of Abby.

She nods. "But Miss Candi let me on the bus that day and changed everything for me."

"She let you on the bus? All alone as a kid?"

"She did," she says, wistfully. "And every day after that, too. She'd welcome me on that bus of hers with a big smile. Didn't even make me pay. I'd ride around with her for a few hours most days, until her shift ended. Sometimes I'd sleep, sometimes we'd just talk about kid stuff that I didn't have anyone else to talk to about — school, other kids in my class, that kind of thing. And then she'd let me back off in front of my house, promising me I could ride again with her the next day. She started bringing extra food for me to have on the rides, so I knew that I could eat at least once a day with her, as long as I got on that bus."

"Christ," I whisper, shaking my head. I had no idea. "What happened . . . to your parents?"

"I'm not totally sure," she says. "My aunt and uncle never talked about them, and I eventually stopped asking."

"And how were they?"

"My aunt and uncle?" I nod. "Better than my parents, but they'd already raised a few kids of their own and had zero interest in having me there. They stopped short of sticking me in a closet under the stairs, but I was basically invisible to them. I think I reminded my aunt of her brother — my dad — so I was probably fairly painful for her to have around. But I had food and a clean home, so that was a step up. I graduated from high school early just to get out of there. So, I guess it all worked out better in the end. When I first got to New York, I'd dream about getting through school faster, just to go back to L.A. and find Miss Candi so she could be my real mom, even after all that had happened. But instead, I just went off to college once I graduated. You know, life took over."

I shake my head, trying to imagine this version of Abby. The one who pushed herself to excel, even after everything. Closing herself off from relationships along the way, though now I can definitely see why.

"I can't imagine growing up like that," I tell her, wishing I was sitting next to her instead of across the table so I could hug her, hold her. Kiss her.

"Everyone has a past," she says, smiling reluctantly. "And now, I suppose, you know mine."

The waitress places our order down on the table, along with a bucket heaped with hot fries. I grab one of the long ones off the top and shove it down into my milkshake before popping the whole thing in my mouth. I'm not sure if I'm at all hungry, or mostly just unsure of what to say.

"You dip your french fries in your milkshake?" Abby asks, watching me grab another.

"Don't tell me you don't?"

She grabs a long fry off the top and scoops up a heap of melty pink shake with it before taking a bite.

"Mmm . . . k," she says, chewing. "Better than I thought."

I drag another fry through my shake.

"I always wanted to come here," she says, looking around like she's taking it all in. "This place was on Miss Candi's route. Fun fact — that sign out front has never changed. I always told her I wanted to try the best milkshakes in the west. Almost every day I'd beg her to stop here." She laughs. "Of course, she couldn't stop her bus route to grab me one, but I always thought we'd come here one day."

I try to picture a tiny, seven-year-old Abby sitting on a big bus seat, nose pressed to the window, dreaming of the day she could sit right here with a big strawberry milkshake, just like she is today. It makes me feel dizzy, trying to imagine what it must be like for her now, sitting here in the exact place she always asked the driver to go.

"What else did you want to do back then?" I ask, wishing I could give her the type of childhood that every kid deserves. One with giggly sleepovers and rainbow sprinkles on her shake, or at the very least a childhood with parents that love her and a fridge full of food.

"Oh, gosh, everything," she says, grinning wistfully. "I heard about all the fun stuff from my classmates, but I never really got to go further than wherever Miss Candi's bus route went. My parents didn't own a car, and they certainly didn't take me with them wherever they went when disappearing for days at a time."

I can't imagine.

"They'd disappear for days at a time?" I ask.

"I could never decide if it was worse having them home, or having them disappear. Both had their downsides."

"Where did you want to visit as a kid that you never got to go?" I ask, watching her eyes brighten at the idea of visiting some of these places.

"The pier," she says. "I haven't seen it, but I hear there's a big Ferris wheel there."

"The Santa Monica Pier?" I ask.

"I think so," she says. "A girl in my class brought a picture of her and her family there to school at the beginning of the year once. I stared at that picture for probably a solid five minutes, wondering how that was close to our house and yet I'd never even known it existed."

"I can't imagine how you must have felt when you learned that Disneyland was also a few miles away!"

She laughs, then shakes her head. "You have no idea how much that one hurt." She manages to grin.

"What else?" I ask, my heart breaking even more.

"The beach," she says. "The Pacific."

"You never got to go to the beach as a kid?"

"Not once."

I'm already making a mental checklist in my head of all the places we need to go to while she's here.

"Anywhere else?" I ask, using a fry to wipe a long drip up the side of my shake cup.

"The Hollywood sign," she says. "These are all just typical little kid dreams, you know? All the silly places I heard about from the radio or my classmates, mostly Rowan Sanderson, really. She was always doing fun stuff with her family. I always kind of hated her for it."

"Then let's check some of these things off your bucket list, before you go back. I mean, as long as you're here for a few more days."

"Or weeks?" she asks. Her eyes meet mine and she shifts in her seat. "Don't answer that." She grins, knowing her time here in L.A. hinges on the deal we're both embroiled in, outside of all this. "I know today feels like a step in the right direction, but I'm still not going to be a pro at this."

She waves her hands between us, over the surface of the table.

"Not the best at dipping fries in your shake? No, it's terribly messy," I say, pointing to all the drops she's left between her cup and the table. "But you'll get the hang of it. And then you'll never go back to just ordering fries again."

"No." She laughs, nudging her knee against mine beneath the table, but she leaves it there, pressed up against mine. "*This*." Her eyes find mine again. "If you're even still interested in me after knowing more about me."

"Abs," I say, my voice softening. I run my hand across the table until I find hers. "Knowing more about you just makes me fall harder for you. There is nothing you've shown me today that scares me off, not even in the slightest."

"I just don't want you to see me as some victim of my circumstances from earlier in life. I don't like it when people pity me when they find out. Teachers, friends, social workers when I was a kid. Always the same pitying look, like everything I've gone through defines me, when it doesn't. It's why I try to hide it as much as I have. I hate when—"

"Abby," I interrupt, squeezing her hand until she looks at me. "Pay attention when I tell you this, so you never have to question it when it comes to me." I lean in and push the food aside. "I don't pity you for what you've gone through. I am in awe of you for what you've endured and become."

Her brows knit together, eyes glossy. "You're not . . ." She pauses to find the words, swallowing hard. "You're not *weirded out* now? Knowing that . . . I don't know . . . my own parents didn't even want me around?"

Her voice is so quiet, it comes out just above a whisper, cracking at the end.

"I don't know the entirety of what your parents had going on. But I get the sense that drugs and probably alcohol played a part in it."

"From what I understand and remember, yeah."

"Then I don't think them wanting you or *not* wanting you had much to do with the circumstances that you were in."

Her lips turn up at the corners.

"I never thought of it that way."

"Then believe it," I tell her, squeezing her hand afresh. "Not everyone who has kids can care for them. But that's never — and I do mean *never* — the kids' fault. Their problems had nothing to do with you. And Miss Candi . . . What she did? I don't know her, but I can tell from her reaction today that making that call damn near killed her. That's how much she loved you. That's how much she cared and wanted better for you."

A lone tear slides down Abby's cheek, and I swipe it away before going on.

"But your aunt and uncle can suck it," I say, before I can stop myself. "They should have done better."

She snorts, then manages to laugh.

"I owe a lot to them. They did the best they could. It's not my fault they were done raising kids by the time I came to live with them. They had their own lives, their own issues. But they fed me, sheltered me . . ."

"Loved you?" I ask, searching her eyes.

She blinks, then looks down at the checkered floor.

"Honestly, I don't know. Once I moved out, we kind of lost touch. I used to come home for holidays and whatnot, until one year I went home for Christmas and the house was empty. They'd left for a cruise in Florida with their real kids and hadn't even bothered telling me."

"The apple doesn't fall far from the tree in that family," I tell her, wishing I'd known about all this years ago so I could have been taking Abby back home for holidays with me. Even if it was as nothing more than friends. Whatever she could have handled, as long as she wasn't alone in New York. Especially ever since Olivia, who is clearly her chosen family, had decided to stay in Hawaii. A decision that must have been impossibly hard for her, too.

"Do you think it's possible for an apple to fall farther away from the tree?" Abby asks, bringing her eyes back to mine. "Or do you think I'm going to be incapable of loving someone — of being loved by someone — always? Like it's hereditary or something?"

"Not if I have anything to do with it," I tell her. Then, I stand out of my seat and slide into the booth next to her, pulling her in for a kiss.

CHAPTER 28

Abby

I can see the Ferris wheel from here. The little yellow and red bucket seats perched under each matching umbrella spin slowly, nearly stretching out above the whitecap waves beneath the pier. There's a bright yellow roller coaster and what looks like a Tilt-A-Whirl beneath the structure, but I only have eyes for the towering, circular wheel. I've wanted to see this thing in person since Rowan Sanderson brought in that photo in first grade.

I smile, my nose nearly pressed to the car window. Dax grabs my knee over the console between us and I take his hand in mine, grinning over at him.

"Let me just park the toaster real quick," Dax says, throwing the car into reverse to try and fit into a tiny parking spot near the sandy boardwalk.

I turn back toward the beach, sand as far as I can see in each direction, with a wood-plank pier stretching out into the water. At some point, someone somehow fit a whole amusement park on an enormous wooden pier that reaches out over the waves. It all looks a bit intimidating now that we're here, but I am determined to ride the wheel before we go back home.

"I can't believe I'm here," I say, once Dax gets the car in the spot and turns off the engine. He insisted on coming here after we finished our milkshakes at the diner. We've both taken the rest of the day off from work. It *is* Saturday after all, and we deserve a break. "I wish I had a swimsuit. How warm is the water?"

"Chilly, I'm guessing. Do you want to grab a bathing suit from a shop and try it out though? There's plenty of kiosks that sell them down on the boardwalk." He eyes the nearest souvenir shop lined with flowy kaftans and bikinis.

"Not today," I tell him, smiling. "Let's save the ocean for our next date."

He turns toward me.

"Date?" he repeats, locking his eyes on mine. "Excuse me, Abs, but did you just use *the D word*?"

"I did," I say, laughing. "Granted, this isn't nearly as fancy as that Michelin Star restaurant in New York." I glance out the window one more time, feeling like I've somehow stepped out of a nightmare and into one of my childhood dreams, which is now coming true. "But honestly, this is so much better. For so many reasons."

We get out of the car and pay for parking, then make our way toward the ticket booth at the entrance to the pier. I can already hear the sound of children shrieking on rides as we're surrounded by families and parents corralling excited young kids while we wait our turn to buy a wristband for the rides.

I watch the little girl in front of us reach up to hold her mother's hand while we wait in line. The mom squeezes her daughter's hand ever so slightly, as if she's done it a thousand times, and smiles down at her before stepping up to the counter.

My heart suddenly tightens, as if caught in a vice.

I feel Dax's eyes on me, and when I turn, he slips his own hand into mine, gently tightening his grip. Like he knows I can feel the emptiness of my hand while watching what could and should have been part of my own memory. I lean into him and rest my head on his shoulder, then close my eyes, breathing in the smells of sweet cotton candy and buttery popcorn mixed with the salt of the sea.

"I love it here already," I tell him, my eyes still closed as we wait for our turn. "It's every bit as chaotic and wonderful as I imagined."

"Just wait until you see the view from the top." He kisses the crown of my head.

As soon as we have our wristbands, Dax begins leading us toward the Ferris wheel. When we get to its base I look up, seeing couples and families, groups of teenagers, and girlfriends taking selfies filling the seats. I watch them for a moment, imagining what the view of the ocean might be like from way up there.

"Is it okay if we save this one for last?" I ask. "I want the full pier experience, and I feel like that one might be the icing on top of the cake. Like the grand finale at the very end. I want to look forward to it for just a bit longer."

Dax laughs. "Of course. Whatever you want. What do you want to do first?"

"Definitely not that," I say, turning to the Scrambler. It's like an egg beater, swinging little tubs full of people around its center. "I think I might see that milkshake again if we go on that."

"How about the roller coaster then?" he asks, pointing toward the yellow track that's laced throughout the park. It doesn't look intimidating at all.

"I love that idea," I tell him.

As we walk toward the line, he pulls me into him, wrapping an arm around my shoulders. I turn and tuck both arms around his waist, like a mid-walk hug, and squeeze into him as close as I can get.

"Thank you for taking me here," I tell him. "It's like a palate cleanser after seeing my old house today." He kisses me again. "Did you come here often as a kid?"

"Me?" He laughs, thinking back. "I believe I came here twice. My parents are workaholics. We didn't do much together when I was a kid. Hell, we still don't do much together as adults."

I look for any sign of residual hurt on his face, but he doesn't look sad about it at all.

"Did that ever upset you?" I ask, wondering if he has any regret left over from his childhood, too.

"No. I don't have any siblings. I think it happens with only children sometimes, where the parents kind of treat you like one of them instead of just a kid. Sometimes I wish my parents had treated me more like a kid, taken me to do this type of thing more, but I can't hold any of that against them. They were — they *are* — remarkable people. They just weren't the warmest parents to grow up with. But that's alright. My mother taught me to argue, to win, to run her firm after she retires. I think that was her way of showing me love. I think I'm a lot like her."

I smile, trying to imagine an older, battleax version of Dax in the courtroom.

"She sounds like she might be intimidating," I say.

"Nah. The thing about my parents is that they like whoever I like. Eventually, anyway." He squeezes me closer. "Maybe you'll meet them sometime. Maybe over the holidays, if you need a place to go."

"I can't imagine." I'm trying to imagine a Harper & Associates Christmas with two of the managing partners and a tech legend, Dax's father, all sitting together at a glittering table set for Christmas dinner. "Big tree, lots of traditions, that kind of thing?" I ask. It sounds like a Hallmark movie waiting to happen.

"You might have to find out," he says casually, as if there isn't the weight of a future in that statement — a future in which Dax and I share holidays together with his family. My stomach drops, but in a good way, and we aren't even on the roller coaster yet.

We step in line and it moves quicker than I'd have guessed. Before we know it, we're stepping into the tiny, car-shaped coasters secured safely to the track.

Smushed together, Dax tucks an arm around me again and kisses my temple.

"You ready for a wild ride?" he asks, grinning at me as a worker swings her arm in between us to check that the bar is tight over our laps.

I smile and nod, knowing the ride, at least for me, has already begun.

CHAPTER 29

Dax

Abby holds up the giant fuchsia dog, looking concerned. It's nearly as tall as she is, and I paid fifty-two dollars to throw baseballs at a tower of wooden milk bottles — in a game that I'm pretty sure was rigged — for ten whole minutes to win it. But, the look on Abby's face when the guy handed it over instantly made the damn thing priceless. I'll have it shipped back to New York myself if it means that a piece of me gets to go back with her.

I have no idea if it'll even fit in the back seat of the toaster-shaped car we drove here in, let alone this Ferris wheel we're climbing into.

"Is it going to fit?" Abby asks, looking panicked as we step into the swinging bucket seat.

"You can leave it at the kiosk with me and grab it after," the ride operator suggests, holding out a hand to take it for her.

Abby wistfully watches him take it away, then scoots in closer to me, eyes twinkling. The whole pier is settling into a golden twilight glow, the first rays of a cotton-candy-colored sunset shooting out over the horizon across the waves of the Pacific.

"Did you have a preference for the red or the yellow? Which color did you ride, in all your fantasies about this place?" I ask, pointing out the seats before and after us. By now we've ridden every ride here at least twice, with the Ferris wheel and Scrambler being the only exceptions, taking breaks to sample all the best-looking food stands and to play games. Abby insisted on trying cotton candy for the first time, finding the way that it melted in her mouth magically addicting, and buying a second bag to take home with her for Starry.

Now, the sunset is starting to match the pink stain of her lips, sweetened from the soft sugar floss. I look back out over the horizon. We've managed to time our final ride just right. The view will be incredible once we get to the top.

"Zero preference on seat color," she says, as we wait for the other riders behind us to be seated before the wheel starts to turn. "I just wanted to ride it. How's the view from the top? And now that we're on, I hope there isn't an earthquake."

I turn to her, gaping.

"Why on earth would you say that?" I ask, feigning panic.

She laughs. "I have no idea! I take it back," she yelps up at the sky. "No earthquakes for the next ten minutes, world!" She grimaces, shrinking back in the seat. "Sorry."

I laugh.

"So, let's say there's no earthquakes and we make it up to the top. Can we see Liv waving from Hawaii up there?" She grins.

"I wouldn't know about the view," I tell her. "I imagine it's going to be stunning with the sunset though."

She swivels her head to look at me, thoroughly confused. "I thought you said you've been here?"

"My parents are both afraid of heights. So if I wanted to ride anything that went too high, I had to do it on my own. I was too afraid to do this one alone as a kid, so I always skipped it."

"You're kidding." She snuggles in closer to me, then rests her head against my chest. I breathe in the smell of her, still pinching myself that today has unfolded the way it has. "We both get to do this one for the first time, together?"

I nod. "Yep."

"Then I'm *glad* I never rode it as a kid," she says. Her eyes are shining. "This is so much better."

My chest tightens. Watching Abby today, it's like whatever effect the secrets of her past had on her has been lifted. I've never seen her so carefree. It's like the little girl in her has come to the surface, getting to live out an experience she always dreamed of.

"I hope no one from work is at the pier today," she says, suddenly, looking around.

"My entire team is definitely trapped at the office doing doc review today. What about yours?"

"Honestly, if I saw Brett at a place like this, I wouldn't have to worry about being barred from the office because of you. Instead, I'd die of shock the moment I saw him with a candied apple in his hand."

I laugh, trying to picture it.

The final riders get secured in and the operator returns to his control box, sitting beside Abby's pink dog. Then the wheel creaks to life, pushing our bucket seat out toward the front of the wheel ever so slowly to start. Abby gasps, then leans closer in to me, grabbing my hand.

I settle back against the seat and decide to watch her expression instead of the view slowly coming into focus as we ascend, rising out of the crowd below. I can tell that everything she's seeing right now, the view of the ocean as our seat rises above the pier, is stunning her.

I can get back on this wheel to see it all for myself another time. The view I have of Abby right now — of her eyes as she takes it all in for the very first time — *that's* the view I'll never get to experience again, and that's the one I want to remember.

I smile, soaking her in. The way her mouth is open just slightly, tiny gasps escaping through her lips as more and more of the ocean reveals itself, stretching out across the horizon to take up the whole sky. It feels like we're flying above it all, our feet swallowed up by the pinks and golds now painted beneath us.

Abby's skin and eyes are bathed in rose gold and sunbeams. A fringe of dark lashes flutters, like she's blinking back the whole experience of being here while I take it in. Watching as she closes her eyes, for only a moment, then inhales the sticky, salty air before turning to look at me.

She catches me watching her instead of what's unfolding in front of us and immediately flushes pink, like the sky. Then she nods her head toward the melting rays of light, a thousand tiny diamonds shimmering across the edge of the world. Her eyes beam playfully at mine, as bright as the flecks of light bobbing out on the water.

"You're missing it," she whispers, her lips curling up at the edge.

"Would you believe I already have the better view?" I ask.

"No." She laughs.

"Maybe this is the one I want to remember more," I tell her. Then I lean in and kiss her, just once, so she doesn't miss the view she's waited a whole lifetime to see.

Her cheeks flush as the sky bends around us.

"Dax Harper," she says, nudging my shoulder. "You never change, do you?"

I laugh and kiss her one more time. "Some things are better left unchanged," I tell her.

"And some things can only get better when they do," she answers, a whole wealth of meaning in her eyes.

Our seat is nearly at the peak of the ride, traveling backward now toward the apex of the wheel.

"You know," she says, grinning, "what's the point of being on a Ferris wheel if you're not going to make out with someone at the top?"

She smiles and I lean in, pulling her face into mine, gently cupping the tender line of her jaw when our lips finally meet. She tastes of cotton candy melted in the heat of the sun, and her lips open to me, pulling us into a kiss that somehow feels more meaningful than every other kiss we've shared before.

***

I'm driving us back to my house, still high on our time at the pier, when my phone rings. An eighties ballad from Def Leppard blasts through the car.

"That's your ringtone?" Abby laughs, side-eyeing me. "I hadn't pegged you for a sappy eighties love ballad kind of guy."

I side-eye her back. "You're not the only one with a closet full of secrets," I tell her, chuckling.

I hand her my phone since I'm the one driving us down the freeway back toward my house. She glances at the screen, then at the clock on the dashboard. It's nearly nine p.m.

"It's Lila," she says, pressing her lips together. "Do you — I can — uh, do you want to answer it?"

"No," I tell her, taking the phone and putting it in the cup holder between us. "There's nothing work wise that can't wait until tomorrow."

Almost as soon as I press the side button to reject the call, it starts ringing again.

Abby glances at the phone screen.

"Lila," she says, sighing quietly. We both know where this is probably heading — which, if Lila gets her way, is probably not back to my place like Abby and I are planning. "You should probably answer it, otherwise she'll keep calling until you do."

I groan and hit the side button to reject it again, hoping she gets the hint that whatever she needs to tell me can wait.

The car is silent for a moment, until it starts ringing a third time.

"Is it about work?" Abby asks, narrowing her eyes at me. We both know we have an ethical wall up between us to keep work separate from our relationship. "Or . . . are you guys, like, I mean, either way, you can answer it. I'll just cover my ears."

"Are Lila and I . . . ?" I look at Abby and she raises her brows like she doesn't want to fill in the blank for me. "Christ, no! Lila is like my work wife, twice divorced and bitterly awkward."

Abby snorts. "Okay, then answer it. I'll cover my ears so there's no way for me to hear whatever it is that she needs to tell you."

I press my phone to my ear.

"Who's dying, Lila?" I bark, deadpan, into the phone.

"You, if you hadn't answered." She sounds annoyed already. "Why didn't you answer?"

"I have a life outside work, Li," I remind her.

"Since when?" she asks.

I groan, glancing over at Abby, who has both hands pressed to her ears, humming my phone's ringtone softly to herself. I stifle a laugh. This girl is hardcore when it comes to following rules.

"What is it?"

"You'll never believe what Trudy uncovered in the twenty-seventeen Hicks file. There's notes from the president of—"

"Lila, stop." I clear my throat, now concerned that Abby might be able to hear Lila through the phone somehow. Christ. "Can we talk about it tomorrow?"

"Absolutely not. If we're going to have this run through and approved by the Davenport Media team by Saturday morning so they have it ready when negotiations pick back up on Monday, we're both going to be pulling an all-nighter tonight and working all the way through tomorrow. I'll take a nitro cold brew, thanks, if you're planning to stop for coffee on the way in."

I groan. "Lila, you've been at this nearly as long as I have. There's no way you need me in there tonight. You and the rest of the team—"

"Dax, I'm telling you. Silas' assistant said he's truly planning to make it in person by Monday, and whether that happens or not, this is big enough that it's all hands on deck. I'll see you when you get here."

She hangs up.

I pass the phone back to Abby and she takes her hands down from her ears, then looks over. I shake my head.

"Fuck," she whispers. "You can't be serious. What is it?"

"You know I can't answer that." I blow all the air out of my lungs, which isn't the only thing that suddenly feels annoyingly deflated.

"I get it. The marginal life of a M & A attorney, I know. I understand. You don't have to explain," she says, grabbing my hand and squeezing. "Want me to drop you off at the office?" she asks, looking out of the darkened window.

"If you wouldn't mind," I say. "Everyone will just assume I took an Uber if they're near a window. It's too dark to see inside the car."

She nods, then glances over.

"It was still the perfect day," she says, smiling.

"Well, not all of it." I squeeze her hand back. "But I'm glad it ended better than it began. Although it could have ended a whole hell of a lot better . . ."

"No," she says, "I think I needed to experience all of it. Even better that I got to experience it all with you." She grins. "And don't worry about tonight. I have a lot to process anyway and it sounds like you do, too."

"You're not mad?"

"I swear, I'm not anything but happy," she says, as we race down the freeway.

CHAPTER 30

Abby

I start jumping up and down when I finally see her coming through the airport terminal, though it'd be quite hard to miss Olivia in that bright yellow sundress, set against the darkest tan I've ever seen on her, which is bringing her cobalt blue eyes out like glowing saucers, even from all the way over here. I'd be surprised if she was still recognized as frequently as she used to be while hosting *The Good Day Show*. Her entire demeanor has changed since she made Hawaii her home.

"There she is," I yelp, leaning back against Dax, loving the way he squeezes me into him from behind, gripping my hips in both hands, before he lets me go so I can bound across the airport terminal to hug her. Both Dax and I have the rest of today off, as well as tomorrow, while our clients review everything one more time before final deliberations begin on Monday. Once I'd told Olivia that I had roughly 48 hours off work, she booked the next flight to L.A., never mind the fact that she'd just returned from Japan. She wanted to see me, but she said that, even more, she just wanted to hug me after hearing about my chance meeting with Miss Candi.

Liv squeals so loud that at least four people turn around to see where the noise came from. She sets off toward me, pulling her Barbie-pink luggage behind her like she's dragging an eight-ton rock on wheels.

We meet somewhere in the middle, instantly smashing together in a hug, and then rock each other back and forth until we're both heads back, laughing.

She smells like sunscreen and coconuts and I've missed her so, so much.

"You made it!" I'm buoyant to have her right here in the flesh.

"And you thought I shouldn't even bother coming at all with all the script stuff going on back home, but I couldn't *not* take advantage of you being just a six-hour flight away!"

"You even flew commercial," I muse, giving her a grin. "How incredibly down to earth of you."

Her fiancé, Dom, owns a few private airliners, but Liv insisted on just flying here on a regular commercial flight since he was already on a business trip to Lisbon this week. Though I do know that she flew in first class.

"Oh gosh, I would have felt silly taking one of those huge, hulking things with just me inside," she says, sheepishly.

Then she looks past me.

"Oh my God, there he is!" she exclaims as Dax makes his way over to us. She gives him an enthusiastic hug next, eyeing me brazenly over his shoulder.

"I forgot how fucking cute he is!" she mouths.

"Yes, he is," I say.

"Yes, he is *what*?" Dax asks when Liv finally lets him go.

"So fucking cute," I say, smiling up at him.

"Ah." He looks around like he's not sure how to respond. Then he slips both hands into his pockets, grinning. His smile heats me from the inside out. I zone in on his mouth, the way his lips widen each time he talks or smiles — sometimes I don't even hear the words that come out of them anymore. It's like every move he makes is akin to foreplay, especially since we've both been so swamped with the deal since Lila's interruption that night that we haven't been able to spend much time together.

Each time I've seen him since then, whether sitting in a conference room or taking an elevator upstairs together, my body has responded like I'm actually beneath him, muscles contracting and ready to twist and turn around him.

We were silently filling our coffee cups this morning when our arms brushed and I could think of nothing else but him pushing me against the conference room wall, not caring if we had a whole room of people watching, as long as he made me forget that anyone was there. With no secrets left between us now, I want *nothing left between us*. Clothes, words, whatever it is, he can have it. I want him — all of him — more than I ever have. And while I love that Olivia is here for a quick weekend trip, it might actually take every last ounce of willpower I have left in me not to pounce on him the second she takes a moment too long in the ladies' room, or we have to wait on her to order our next meal. I feel like a loaded gun, ready to fire, with a hair trigger the only thing keeping me contained.

"Now that your girls' weekend has officially begun, I should probably just leave you two to it. Want me to drop you off back at your place, or do you have somewhere else you'd like a ride to?" Dax asks. He offered to help me pick Olivia up after we finished work this morning, knowing what a zoo the LAX terminals can be on a Saturday. He's used to it, whereas I'm out of practice due to my total lack of driving in New York.

"No!" Liv says, grabbing her suitcase handle again so the three of us can make our way through the airport and out to the parking garage. "This is a girls' weekend, *plus* Dax Harper."

"Oh, is it?" He glances over at me. "I hadn't heard that."

He grabs the handle of her suitcase for her, his forearm flexing as he begins to roll it through the terminal.

"Now you have," Liv says, linking her arm through our elbows, planting herself in the middle of us. "And thank you for grabbing that suitcase. Damn thing nearly broke my shoulder already, heaving it off the luggage claim thingy."

Dax looks over the top of her head at me, grinning. I smile back. We are both taller than Liv and I wish I could kiss him over the top of her head without making it completely awkward. Dax and Liv met a few times back in law school when Olivia came to visit me and they got along famously.

As soon as I told her that I took Dax over to see the house I grew up in, and how we'd run into Miss Candi while there, she insisted on coming out to see me immediately.

"This is huge," she said a few days ago over FaceTime while looking up flights to book for the coming weekend. "You're, like, transitioning into a butterfly there, babe. There's no way I'm missing this." I could hear the clacking of her nails on a laptop keyboard. "I can be in L.A. by Saturday morning."

"*Transitioning into a butterfly?*" I asked, rubbing my eyes — which were still burning from all the never-ending doc review Brett and I were slogging through almost every night after meetings were done.

"What's the plan today?" she asks, squeezing us in closer to her.

"First, we're going to a brunch spot over in Balboa," I say. "A beach Dax mentioned is one of his favorites is just down the road from the brunch spot, right? You said Corona del Mar is one of the more calm stretches?"

We still haven't made our way over for a beach day yet, and I'm dying to go. Visiting a place I'd always wanted to see as a kid with both Liv and Dax beside me now truly would be a dream come true.

"Oh, Dom loves Corona," Liv pipes up. "And Balboa. I haven't been to either, which means we need a seasoned tour guide." She fixes her eyes on Dax. "Dax?"

He glances at me, his face melting into a smile.

"Sure, I'll join you," he says, relenting. "The huevos rancheros there are the best in the city. And I know you'll both like the mimosa menu."

"Yes!" Liv squeals.

"Thank you," I say to Dax, squeezing his arm.

He reaches around the enormous suitcase to kiss me — just once, but it's enough to tide me over until later, and I'm really hoping there's a *later*.

"Plus, we need to get reacquainted!" Liv calls to us, making it clear that she's still listening, even if she did just miss that peck. "I need to find out more about the guy that's gotten my girl to crawl out of her office more than fifteen minutes a day!"

I roll my eyes but smile, knowing it's true.

* * *

By the time we get there, the restaurant is well into the brunch hour, and the mimosa crowd is getting a bit rowdy, but happy. One whole wall of the restaurant opens up to yachts and boats sitting in the channel that branches out toward the Pacific coastline to our left.

Long, yellow sunbeams filter into the room, along with a soft breeze through open windows. The women are a sea of colorful sundresses and the men wear linen shorts or seersucker trousers with boat shoes.

Life is good in L.A., I realize. The vibe, the weather — all more relaxed and warm than what I'm used to back home.

"God, it's been ages since I had a good brunch out," Liv says, plopping down in the booth beside me. Dax slides in opposite us as she continues, "You two getting brunch together a lot? Or . . . ?"

The meaning behind her question is clear. Dax chokes on the water he's just sipped while I smile. Olivia holds nothing back, and I love her for it.

"Ah, nope," he says, dabbing some water off his lip with a napkin. I want to kiss it off. "No brunch yet."

"Well, don't miss the opportunity on my account if it arises this weekend," she says, winking right at him. She grins. "I'm perfectly happy hanging out with Starry and Charlie back at the house in the case of any unscheduled absence by my girl, here."

Dax tucks his lip in before peering over at me, then bursts out laughing. Liv smiles happily, and picks up the menu as if she hasn't just very much suggested that Dax and I take the opportunity to sleep together, should the opportunity arise.

I shrug, grinning.

"You have no idea how much I've missed you," I say, pressing my arm up against hers.

She drops her head to my shoulder, resting it there for just a moment, before popping back up again when something on the menu catches her eye.

"Lavender orange mimosas!" she exclaims. "Love those!"

"Me too," I say, leaning in to read over her shoulder.

"Oh, but the pineapple jalapeno sounds good too," she muses.

"Look at the raspberry sparkle one," I tell her, pointing to the photo at the bottom. The cocktail glass has edible glitter along the rim.

"Ah, and the pear basil," she adds, pressing the side of her head to mine as we peruse the menu together.

"You two are like sisters," Dax says, nudging my bare ankle under the table. I stop looking at the menu with Olivia long enough to peer up at him. He's watching us across the table with a funny look on his face. "Maybe even better than sisters. Are you sure you're not related?"

I grin at Olivia, so ridiculously happy to have her sitting right beside me, instead of on the phone screen like she's been for so long now.

"I actually did that Ancestry.com thing, hoping we'd show up as long, lost cousins once," Liv says, stifling a laugh behind her fist.

"You did not!" I say, pulling her hand down to see her full-on smile.

"I swear it," she says, slapping her hand to the edge of the table, before using it to cover her eyes like she's embarrassed. "I never had a sister, and all my cousins were older, and honestly just the worst, plus I figured we were both from around New York, so there had to at least be the slightest chance. Although, that was before I knew you weren't from the east coast at all!"

We both burst into full-on, gut-spinning laughter — mostly because Olivia's cackling laugh is one of the most contagious I've ever encountered, but also because I feel so relieved to see her here in the flesh. Ever since we met in undergrad and became roommates, she's been my family. Our bond was instantaneous, like we'd known each other in a past life or something and just had to pick up where we'd left off. I don't know what it was about her that drew me in, or made me feel safe with her right from the get-go, but it stuck. This is the longest we've ever gone without being around each other in real life and I don't think I realized how much of me went missing the day she moved away.

"I think she's better than a sister," I say to Dax, pulling her into a tight side-hug since we're already wedged between a table and the firm booth behind us. "The bond between friends is sometimes thicker than blood anyway."

He raises a brow, as if surprised by my words, but his face quickly morphs into warmth and understanding. He draws his foot against my ankle again, grinning across the table at us.

"Aw, babe!" Liv squeals, pressing her cheek into mine. "I've really missed you."

CHAPTER 31

Dax

We left the brunch spot a few hours ago, after they'd had three mimosas each, finding a clear spot on the shore of Corona del Mar.

"I'm starting to rethink this whole west coast thing," Abby had said after setting eyes on the Pacific once we got here, her toes dug into the hot sand.

"If you like this, then you need to come see me in Hawaii, babe," Liv had answered. "Like, stat. This ocean might be the same one here but it's literally turquoise when you're standing on the beach where I live. When is this deal supposed to be done — so we can plan a trip out?"

The deal.

They'd carried on, making plans for Abby to visit Liv on the North Shore, while I pinched myself, remembering that Abby and I are butting heads in the conference room nearly every day of the week, and through email too, plus over the phone when all else fails, on behalf of our clients. It's hard to believe that the girl that I admire for her tenacity in that negotiation space is the very same one here this morning. Wild and free, now down by the water with Olivia, piling up a little mound of sand between them.

They were talking about God knows what, out of earshot, when I went to go find us a few waters and another bottle of sunscreen from the shop down the way.

There are other beaches I could've recommended, ones that are longer or whiter or softer, but I like the way the cliffs jut out along this one. They give it a rugged feeling, regardless of the luxe neighborhood it borders. It can be reasonably quiet here, a harbor really, tucked in among the multi-million-dollar mansions that line the cliffs above. I've often seen celebrities walking their dogs, or hiding on a blanket beneath the rim of a sunhat with giant sunglasses so they, too, can enjoy it in peace.

If I could have cleared the whole beach for her to have it as it should be, quiet and soul-cleansing, I'd have done that. However, this way — with her best friend and three mimosas down beforehand — is pretty great, too.

Now that I'm back, waters and sunscreen in hand, they've peeled off their sundresses in favor of bikinis, even though the water is still chilly, and are now holding their arms side by side, comparing hues, laughing about the way Abby's skin tone is more like a vampire's than a human's.

Abby has always been beautiful, but this particular version of her is the very best version I've ever seen. She's let her hair down out here. Figuratively and literally — pulling it down from that dark top knot she favors, to let it spill out, thick and wavy, nearly reaching past her elbows, blowing out behind her in the breeze. Her amber eyes glow, somehow absorbing each ray of sunshine before pushing that ray back out again. I'm almost glad she forgot her sunglasses today because it means I don't miss anything beaming out of her eyes. The joy, the carefree way laughter radiates from her — head thrown back, laughing with her closest friend.

She and Liv marched their way down the beach when we got here, holding hands, giggling with their heads pressed together, talking the whole way as they walked. I stayed back, letting them have their moment. Knowing how excited Liv must be to get Abby to join her near her beloved Pacific, and Abby having her chosen 'sister' here to encourage her to experience yet another thing she's wanted to do since she was a kid.

I had my boarding school brothers from the time I was thirteen, my own pseudo family while away from home — a band of brothers, never bonded by blood, but by choice. We each missed our families, but having that safety net gave us the courage to grow together while away. I know how important such formed-by-chance relationships can be to shaping a story, and a life.

After spending just one morning with them, it's clear to me that Olivia is Abby's family. It's easy, when you have both biological and chosen family or friends, to see how both can exist and each be just as special as the other. How friendships can live alongside family bonds, flourishing so strongly that friendship becomes nearly as important as family relationships. Sometimes, even more important.

Abby doesn't need her family to be loved. She has Olivia. And, if she continues to let me in, she'll have me, too.

"How is your skin only showing signs of a tan instead of a burn?" Olivia asks, pressing a finger into Abby's shoulder. "You should be red as a tomato by now."

We've reconvened on the sand together, away from the water's edge. The girls are wrapped in a couple of thick towels that I keep in my car for spontaneous jaunts to the beach while the three of us are sitting on a blanket, watching a family of four build an intricate sand castle a few yards away between us and the waves.

Abby presses a finger to her chest, watching her skin change color when she releases it.

"I have no idea. Good genes, I guess?" she says.

Olivia chuckles, but I stop watching the family to look right at Abby. That's possibly the first and last time I'll ever hear Abby refer to herself as having *good genes*.

"My mom might have had skin that tanned well. I think, from what I remember, anyway," Abby says, inspecting her skin. "I could be wrong about that, but I know that I inherited my hair from her. That's one of the things I remember. I used to braid her hair for her whenever she'd pass out on the couch. I'd watch TV and brush it, braid it. It was thick and coarse, just like mine. Dark as mine, too."

Liv stares at her, then shifts her eyes to mine and raises her brows before moving her gaze back to Abby, who's missed the looks on both of our faces. Instead, she's watching the family play, intently.

"I've never heard you say a word about your mom," Liv says, quietly, letting a handful of sand run through her fingers.

"I haven't thought much of her until this trip. Does that sound awful?" She winces, suddenly searching our eyes for any judgment, though I know she won't see any there, from either of us. "Like I blocked them out until now."

We shake our heads in unison. I frown, wondering what it must be like to never think of your parents.

"I keep thinking I see them here. A woman with a dark head of hair, or a grungy-looking guy in a Lakers T-shirt or something, will walk by and I'll do a triple take, like it might be them. I never did that back in New York. Ever since we went to the house . . . it somehow solidified that everything was, or is, real, or something. I think I'd convinced myself that maybe I'd imagined how bad my childhood here was. But *everything was real*. All of it."

I squeeze her hand, wishing I could take the worst of the memories away from her. Wishing we could go back and erase whatever horrors she experienced as a kid. Sure, it made her into the unassailable force that she is today, but there must be easier ways to make a diamond than squeezing a lump from a coal mine.

"I don't want that stuff to define how you see me, though," she says, staring at both of us, her eyes scolding us for something we haven't yet done. "I've tried pretty hard to keep my past away from who I am now, but there's been something about being back here and being taken care of by Starry and Charlie, and" — she brushes her cheek against my shoulder, smiling — "no offense, having *you* totally reject me unless I got out of my own way." She shakes her head. "I don't want it to hold any more power over me than it has for all these years. My parents weren't perfect, my life was far from perfect, but I shouldn't have to hide it, right?"

"Never," Liv says, drawing Abby into a sitting hug. "I don't think you should ever feel like your past gets to define who you are. Growing up with two normal parents — although, really what's *normal* anyway? — doesn't make me more worthy of a single thing. Just like growing up with abnormal parents doesn't make you any less worthy of being surrounded by people that love you. I've been trying to tell you that for years, Abs."

"No, I know that now," Abby says, squeezing her back.

A cheer from the castle-building family in front of us catches our attention. The little girl can't be more than five or six, while her older brother must be closer to ten. They're working to fill a blue bucket with waterlogged sand, repeatedly flipping it onto the beach to create a wall for their castle. Each time the boy lets the girl pull the bucket off, a bit of the castle wall crumbles. She looks toward her parents, who clap and cheer when it stays mostly standing. Her older brother beams at her, pushing the broken bits back up the wall, patting them into place whenever needed, patiently showing her how the wetter sand compacts better than the dry. The parents watch their kids, holding hands over a worn, denim blanket stretched beneath them.

Abby continues watching, a faint smile on her lips, making me wonder if building a sandcastle at the beach with her parents was another thing she always dreamed of doing. I'm sure it was.

"I'm starting to feel like I want some of those things," she says, nodding toward them.

"Want that?" Liv asks, pointing toward the family. She widens her eyes. "Kids?"

Abby laughs. "Slow down, tiger," she says, holding up her hands. "What I mean is that I'm starting to feel like, at the very least, I want a life outside my office."

I smile. I've seen this side of her coming out more and more since our trip down memory lane, but I'm happy to hear her say it.

"Not to scare you," Olivia says, pausing dramatically, "but I think you're already succeeding at that here." She winks at me, but Abby is too busy watching the little girl carry a sloppy bucket of water and sand over to her parents to notice. The mom screeches when it almost lands on her lap, and we all laugh.

Olivia holds my eye and smiles, no longer studying the family in front of us like Abby, but me instead.

"Thank you," she mouths silently.

I smile back, not sure what the thanks is for, but feeling like it has to do with a lot more than just taking them to the beach today.

CHAPTER 32

Abby

Back at the house, Starry has prepared a five-star feast, as Charlie calls it, for the three of us.

"I'll get the food all situated for you if you'd all like to go and freshen up first," she says, welcoming us each with a hug, as if we've all joined her for dinner here a thousand times. I can tell that Starry and Charlie are as fond of Liv as I am, as they pepper her with questions about her and Dom while beaming at her replies.

Charlie shakes Dax's hand warmly, exchanging words of how much they've already heard about one another from me.

Then Dax turns to Starry.

"You've created a beautiful home," he says appreciatively. "And I hear you've been taking good care of Abby while she's here."

"Ah, a house is just a house," Stary replies, smiling. "It's the heart that turns it into a home."

Dax smiles at me after that.

"Now, you two can use a few of the rooms down here to freshen up," Starry says, leading Dax and Liv from the kitchen area down the long hallway of spare rooms, winking at me over her shoulder as they disappear.

***

When we're all gathered back in the dining room, there's a roasted bird in the middle of the table, surrounded with mashed potatoes, broccoli salad with little bits of bacon and grapes, homemade dinner rolls — which I've never tried until now — crystal goblets of red wine from the wine cellar in the lower level of the house, and probably something baking in the oven for later, since the house smells both sweet and savory.

Starry's set the dining room with three place settings, but Olivia and I insist that she and Charlie join us for dinner, and grab two more.

"I haven't seen either of you in months!" Liv says to Starry and Charlie, when we've all sat down together. "Dom is sad not to be here."

"Speaking of, did he pick that out himself?" Starry asks, passing a carafe of wine around the table, nodding toward the enormous engagement ring sitting on Liv's finger.

I smile at her while she nods at Starry, beaming.

"He's perfect," Liv says, sighing happily, then digs into the wooden bowl of palm-sized rolls nearby. They're still warm from the oven. "I wasn't sure what it would be like to stay over there, away from everything I knew back home, but I can't picture my life without him anymore. He makes anywhere feel like home."

Dax catches my eye and smiles when she says this, and I feel myself redden. "I know the feeling," he says quietly.

My heartbeat picks up the pace. I'm loving everything about today, but I'm dying for a moment alone with him, too.

After far too much food and laughter around the dining table, we've all helped clear the table and are gathered in the kitchen. Liv and I are working through the pile of dishes near the sink when she announces that she and Starry have a lot to catch up on and that I should make sure Dax arrives home alright.

"I think I just got kicked out," Dax whispers into my ear, sending a tingle down my spine.

"I'm kicking you *both* out," Liv announces louder. "I mean, I'm sure you're *both* welcome to stay here but you might enjoy some privacy at the end of a long day . . ."

"What are you talking about?" I ask, leaning into her by the sink. Even though Starry insisted that we don't touch the mess, Liv and I are making quick work of them to thank her for preparing such a feast for dinner.

"It's literally my job, girls," Starry says, shuffling around us like a mother hen while we bump her away with our hips.

The sink is wide enough for both Liv and I to stand at the edges, passing dishes between us, then placing them in the double dishwashers on either side.

"You're going to put me out of a job if you keep this up," Starry insists, finally stepping back. She holds her palms up in front of her like she's giving up.

"Consider it our thanks," Liv says to her. "Besides, I know Abby's going to fight me on what I just suggested, so this will at least make her feel like she's done something nice for us before she goes. What she doesn't know is that I'm totally jet-lagged and must get some sleep the second we're done here."

"But the time change goes the opposite way," I muse. "It's only four in the afternoon where you live—"

"Shhh," she says, grinning. "Details, details. Just get out of here!"

When Dax heads to the door to leave, Liv shuffles me out the door with him.

"I'll see you tomorrow," she insists. "Love you, bye."

She gives me air kisses on either side then grins before shutting the door with a thud. I know she's just trying to pass me off to Dax with as little awkwardness as possible, but she's failing miserably. Dax is watching the whole exchange from the bottom of the stairs in front of the house near his car.

"Pretty sure you're quite well-versed in finding your way home," I say, eyeing him shyly. Now that the time might be coming for me to venture off with him I'm suddenly feeling a little reserved.

"It's always a good idea to have a riding partner." He shoves his hands into his pockets.

I hear the bolt slide across the door behind me. Olivia's just locked us both outside.

"She is ridiculous," I tell him, laughing. "I am well aware of how capable you are of arriving home safely in this very sturdy-looking car."

"Oh, I don't know about that," he says, lingering on the last step. "I've been known to get a little off-track when left on my own. Especially when my thoughts are elsewhere."

He shifts his weight, then grins up at me and I allow his eyes to meet mine, noticing something familiar come to the surface.

"Do you *want* me to come with you?" I ask, feeling nervous, afraid he might reject me since I have a feeling that if I get in that car with him, it'll be the first time we get past kissing since I got to L.A. What if he's still feeling hesitant after New York?

"Only if you want to," he says, his gaze not leaving my eyes. He grins.

I walk down the steps, meeting him at the bottom, loving the way his arms envelop me the second I make it onto the same step as him. It strikes me that there's really no other place I'd rather be than right here with his arms wrapped around me.

He watches my face.

"I think this goes without saying, but I am absolutely mad about you." He brushes a strand of hair back from my forehead, but leaves his palm pressed against my cheek.

"I don't think it's much of a problem," I tell him. I swallow down the butterflies threatening to consume me. "I meant what I said on the beach earlier today. I do want a life outside of work, one that holds more meaning than a pending partnership offer, or proving to myself that I can handle someone like Brett breathing down my neck every day without it breaking me. But" — I force myself to keep my eyes on his instead of turning away — "I meant what I said at that burger joint, too. I can't promise that I'll be *good* at any of this."

"Oh, I disagree," he says.

"How would you know?"

"Because you already are." His voice lowers and it feels like we're the only two people in the world right now. "All I ask is that when you start to feel scared or nervous or, heaven forbid, real feelings for me, that you tell me. You don't run."

He searches my eyes until I take a breath.

"I won't run," I tell him. "I swear I won't, this time."

He leans in closer, and I think he might finally kiss me, but he stops just as I start to feel his warmth pour into my waiting lips.

"Good," he says, "because you deserve to have it all. The chemistry, the heat, the *feeling* behind something that doesn't have to end the second the sun comes up."

"Who said anything about the sun coming up?" I tease him, closing my eyes so he can, please, *for the love of God*, kiss me. "If I go back home with you, you can't mistake the cold shoulder I'll be forced to give you at the office as anything other than me maintaining my job until this deal is done."

"Is that a yes?" he asks.

His smile brushes against my lips and he pulls me in with his arms laced around my back.

I grab onto his belt and pull him into me so our bodies are tight against each other, and his rock-hard intentions are clear. I see sparklers behind my eyelids by the time we draw back from the kiss, and I tuck my bottom lip in, just to keep tasting him.

"Should we forget the ride and go back inside?" I ask with my eyes still closed. Just the thought of what the group inside might do if we try to sneak past them to hide out in my room makes me laugh.

"With all of *them*?" he asks. His voice goes up an octave and he widens his eyes, as if I've just suggested a cold shower instead of a closer bedroom. "And get potentially swept away in a riling game of canasta or something even longer, heaven forbid, like Monopoly?" I laugh. "I love them, I do, and I'd love to do that another time, but tonight? Not a goddamn chance. I'm taking you home with me."

Then he kisses me deeply, like we have all the time in the world.

CHAPTER 33

Dax

By the time we race up to my door after making out at every stoplight all the way home, I'm ready to push Abby up against the wall, right there against the front of my house.

She spent most of the drive rubbing my throbbing cock through my pants in the dark. It took everything in me not to pull over and take her right there in the car. Breathless moans escaped her lips as I fought to keep my hands off of her.

But when there was traffic on the 101, I failed miserably.

At one point, I had my hand shoved up beneath the hem of her sundress, clutching onto the rim of her panties, running my thumb back and forth along that soft center of hers over the fabric, feeling how ready she was for me through the thin cotton.

Now, she's watching me try to get the front door unlocked but the key isn't going in.

"Never seen you have trouble getting anything in before," she says, pulling me into her, kissing me harder after my third failed attempt.

I continue trying to shove the key into the door with my hands wrapped behind her back, while she's kissing me, but the lack of success eventually makes her laugh.

"Fuck," I breathe out, pulling away so I can get us in the door.

I hold the key up to the porch light and realize I've been trying to shove my office key into my own front door lock this whole time. *How long have I lived here?*

"It's okay, Mr. Harper," she whispers, wrapping herself around me from behind so I can see what I'm doing.

She slips one hand down the front of my pants, clasping onto my cock, coiling her hand around me while I try to concentrate on finding the correct key.

It's impossible.

I close my eyes and brace myself against the door.

"You have to stop," I say, grabbing her hand, forcing it not to move another inch. "I want your entire body but if you keep doing that . . ." I trail off.

She laughs and holds her arms out to the side, like she's about to get searched, still pressing against me from behind.

"Your wish is my command. But you'd better get this thing open or your neighbors are about to get a show."

Two years. That's how long I've lived here and that's how long it feels it's taken before I get the door open and grab her around the waist to get us both inside. I slam the door shut and immediately push her up against it, not even bothering to turn the lights on.

She wrings my shirt in her fists, kissing me like it's the first time we've ever done this and she's starved for me. I pull Abby's dress up over her head and toss it to the floor behind us, then start working my way down her body with my tongue, tasting every inch of her skin. The salt and sun of the ocean are still ripe on my tongue, tangy and sweet.

"I wish I had time to shower," she says between groans.

"You're not fucking showering right now," I growl into her neck. "You're not going anywhere. I want you exactly how you are."

She moans gently when I unclasp her bra, letting her breasts spill out into my hands. I take one in my mouth while kneading the tip of the other between my fingers.

"You taste fucking amazing," I tell her, wrapping my mouth around her nipple, before returning to her lips.

She tilts her head back against the door, eyes closed, smiling.

"Funny, I could say the same for you," she says, breathlessly.

My cock throbs in response and I press myself against her.

"You have no idea how bad I want you," I tell her, pulling her panties off.

The fabric hits the floor, and I take a step back, fully aware that I've just undressed her without removing a single thread of clothing from myself.

"Take me wherever you want," she says, arching her back off the door, pulling my lips back into hers.

She grabs my hands and wraps them around her waist, planting them firmly on her ass. I squeeze the flesh, pushing my hard cock along the front of her, needing her more than ever before.

"Bedroom?" she asks.

"Too far," I say, wrapping my teeth across her collarbone, biting down slightly.

She gasps but pushes closer into me, a full body shiver rocking her. Goosebumps spring up on her skin.

"Here then," she asks, unbuckling my belt.

I slide my jeans off to the floor, my boxers and tee still hanging on — but just barely. I want nothing but skin between us.

"Condom," she says, finding a spot of flesh beneath my ear. The place she knows I love.

It's nearly impossible to stop myself once she starts doing that, but I have to.

"In my bedroom," I say, stepping back. I hold one finger up in front of her. "Don't you dare move."

I take another step away and can see her standing; can see her from head to toe. Her black mane nearly covers her breasts, while the curve of her hips is leading me to the promised land.

I wrap an arm around her waist and pull her away from the door, holding her face between my palms, telling myself to go get what we need, but finding it impossible to walk away from this. She grasps onto my forearms, kissing me harder, then pulls my shirt up over my head.

"You are fucking gorgeous," I say into her mouth, holding her face between my palms.

Then I reach a hand between her legs. She moans into my ear when I slide two fingers up into her, finding her clit with my thumb, and groan into her neck. She's never been more ready. She widens her legs to make room for me, and as much as I want to slip these boxers off and push the rest of me into her, I know I have to stop.

"Don't move," I say.

I walk away, wishing to heaven I already had a condom in my pocket . . .

But when I come back to the foyer, she's gone.

"Abby?" I call out, the house still dark except for a yellow glow coming from the kitchen.

When I walk in, she's sitting on the counter top, one knee crossed over the other with a glass of water in one hand, her hair spilling across her shoulders and chest.

She smiles.

"Thirsty?" I ask, leaning against the entry, grinning at the sight of Abby sitting naked in my kitchen.

"You have no idea how thirsty a girl can get," she says, taking another sip.

Then she uncrosses her knees, and spreads them a few inches apart, arching her back. My eyes drink in the sight of her, no longer thinking about anything but my tongue and all the things I want to do to her with it right now.

"What about you?" she asks.

"Wider," I say, staying where I am.

Her knees slide apart farther. Everything I've been missing since New York comes into view. She puts the glass down between her thighs so my view of her is suddenly blocked.

Then she gives me a challenging look, arching a brow while holding back a smile, as if silently asking me to come move it.

"Move the glass," I tell her. Then I step toward her.

Her eyes darken, but she moves the glass, placing it beside her, then widens her knees even more, leaning back on one hand.

"You have no idea what I've wanted to do to you since you got here," I tell her, closing the gap between us, not yet wanting this image of Abby sitting here like this to be over, but not sure how long I can keep my hands to myself.

"Show me, then," she says, draping her eyes across mine. "And don't be shy about it."

CHAPTER 34

Abby

When Dax gets to me, he pulls my knees until I'm sitting at the very edge of the counter, then he steps between my legs, pressing the length of him up against me.

I wrap my arms around his neck, pushing myself as close to him as I can. He kisses me, and everything in my body springs to life, blood rushing to the smallest parts of my body, everything arching up toward him.

He takes one of my nipples in his mouth again, but starts fishing around my water glass with one hand.

I pull back to see what he's doing.

He's grinning mischievously, an ice cube in hand.

"Up for a little fun?" he says, holding it up.

I narrow my eyes at him, curious where he thinks that ice cube is going to go.

"Trust me," he says, lodging the ice between his front teeth.

Too curious not to, I nod, trusting him. Knowing I've always trusted him.

His mouth finds my neck and he starts running the ice cube down my skin, past my collar bones, to the flat stretch above my chest. The sensation of his hot lips wrapped around the ice burns deliciously with raised goosebumps left behind on every inch of skin he passes.

Drops of ice water roll down my chest, making their way past my navel, cascading between my legs. It feels amazing.

He passes the ice over one nipple and I shudder, pressing my hands behind me so I can arch my back and push myself into him more. He brings his hands to my sides, hot and warming from within.

He takes the ice from his mouth.

"You like that?" he asks, holding the ice in his hand.

I inhale sharply, about to say yes, when he takes the cube and drags it slowly down my thighs with his fingers, kissing me on the mouth. His lips are cold and hot at the same time. I gasp, feeling the droplets trickle down my open thighs, off the counter, and down to my toes. He spreads my knees wider, then steps in between them, so he can drag the ice slowly up my leg, watching my lips and eyes closely as he does.

A breath catches in my throat when he reaches the apex of my thighs. He drags the ice slowly until it crosses the tip of my clit, and I inhale sharply. Barely a flutter across the top, before he's dragging it back down the other leg.

"You do like that," he says, appreciatively, kissing me as he does it again.

This time, he lingers longer in the middle between my legs, running his fingers against my clit with the ice until I'm gasping away from his kiss. The mixture of ice cold, warmed immediately by his hand once he circles again, feels incredible. A new sensation I've not yet experienced, and I love it.

"That feels unreal," I groan into his mouth as he circles the ice once more.

"There's a better way to do this," he says, drawing the ice back up to his teeth.

He runs it down the front of me, dipping into my navel, but moving past that, back to the sensitive zone between my legs.

I close my eyes and dip my head back, breathing deeply while I wait for him to make contact with—

That.
Right there.
I exhale and shudder.

Wrapped around the ice, his lips create a pocket of warmth around the cold as he traces my skin, melted water dripping between each fold. The feeling is erotic, bringing every sensitivity to life. Then he finally drops the ice to the floor, kicking it to the side, before wrapping his lips around me, pushing his tongue inside.

The heat of his mouth while my skin is so sensitive nearly sends me over the edge, lapping deeply at the peaks and valleys of my most intimate spaces. Then he presses his tongue harder, bringing a rush of blood pumping, muscles contracting against him.

"Dax!" I moan, arching my back more, pushing him deeper inside.

My breath becomes shorter, as I nearly come to the edge, losing control.

I hear the rip of a condom wrapper, then Dax puts it on, and pulls me off the counter, right over the top of him. He slides into me, and after all that heat and ice, the sensation of his throbbing depth inside me pushes me straight over.

"I'm coming already," I moan into his ear, as he thrusts into me, the counter bracing my body against him now. I wrap myself around him, biting his neck, his shoulder. "Dax!" I moan.

"I'm not going to last either," he says. "Fuck, I've wanted to do this since I saw you here in L.A."

He pushes harder, faster into me, then bites down on my shoulder, and I unravel. Earth-bending waves of pleasure course through my body, radiating out my fingers and toes, like red-hot lightning bolts shooting down every limb.

I kiss him desperately, tasting myself on his lips, then pushing my cheek into the crook of his neck, breathing all of him in, loving everything about this moment. Each time he thrusts, it sends another wave of pleasure through me.

"Don't stop," I tell him. "Never fucking stop."

His body shudders in mine as he begins to swell. He groans against my neck, a shock of pleasure coursing down my spine. I hold him tighter, until his body pulses too.

"Don't let go," I whisper into his ear, wrapping myself tighter around him. Wishing I could just live my life out like this, Dax and I dissolving into one.

He lifts me from the counter and carries me across the room.

A moment later, he lays me gently across his bed, then climbs over me. He pulls a heavy comforter up over our shoulders, and presses his body into mine, the feeling of him deliciously warm and cozy. The glow of the moon through the window near the bed illuminates his face, hovering near mine. He pushes my hair back from my cheeks, drawing my eyes up to meet his. One arm draped behind my head so we're just two shadows cast beneath the blanket of a full moon.

"I want you to stay," he whispers through the moonlight. "I want to wake up next to you, Abs. I want you to sit beside me in one of those empty rocking chairs on the porch when the sun comes up tomorrow. And I want to bring you coffee in this bed, my bed, without having you second-guess any of this."

I smile at him, surprising myself by feeling okay with what he's proposing. Dare I say . . . feeling unafraid.

"That sounds awfully early," I tease. "Does it have to be the sunrise?"

He smiles, and nearly kisses me again, but stops just before he gets there.

"I will take nothing less than a sunrise, and at least one cup of coffee before you go back home."

"Make it two," I tell him, brushing my smile across his parted lips. "You drive a hard bargain, Mr. Harper, but I think you might have won this round."

"Two then," he says, kissing the corner of my lips. "And a sunrise."

"Deal," I say, sealing it with a kiss.

CHAPTER 35

Dax

She's not here. Abby's not beside me in bed when I wake up. Before I can even roll over, I curse myself for being naive enough to fall asleep, like I should have stayed up all night in front of the door so she couldn't bolt.

But when I start to get up, there's a note on the nightstand, propped up against a hot mug of coffee. I feel like I'm having déjà vu in reverse. My stomach plummets toward the mattress and I grab it, forcing myself to read her note, for better or for worse.

> *Dax,*
> *Come join me outside before you miss it. And consider this your personal invitation to play ball.*
> *P.S. Thanks for not giving up on me.*

I breathe a sigh of relief that feels like I've been holding onto it since that first morning I saw her in New York. The door in the corner of my bedroom leading out to the wraparound porch is already open a crack, so I throw on a pair of sweats and walk over to push it the rest of the way open.

The most beautiful girl in the world is wrapped up in my blanket, sitting on one of the white rocking chairs outside. Her cheeks are bathed in amber sunbeams, which are just starting to make their way up over the skyline.

She turns, and although I've stared into that face more times than I can count, it's as if I'm seeing her for the first time. The liquid gold in her eyes, like honey in the warmth of the early morning light. Her thick, dark hair, normally piled high on her head, is now wavy and down, encircling her chin, falling against her cheekbones and shoulders, still mussed from my hands running through it for most of last night. She smiles, and my whole future flashes with it. One that includes twenty-five-thousand mornings just like this stretched out before us, enough for us both to reach at least a hundred years old. Which might not even be enough, if every one of our days begins just like this.

"Hi," she says, giving me a lopsided grin. "I was about to wake you. I wanted to let you sleep as long as possible, but I also wasn't going to let you miss this. You woke up just in time."

She turns her gaze to the rising sun, but I keep my eyes on her, knowing the better view is the one right in front of me. I slide into the chair beside her, but it doesn't feel close enough, so I grab her hand, holding it in the space between us.

"I've never done this," she says, closing her eyes against the sunbeams. The melted pat of butter rises on the horizon, tucked between the buildings with bright rose-colored rays and canary-yellow fragments of light shooting out all around the towering cityscape.

I squeeze her hand, already aware that she's never allowed herself to stay longer than it takes to open her eyes and bolt from the bed. That is, if she allowed her eyes to close at all the night before.

"I know," I whisper.

"No, I mean I've never watched the sunrise. With anyone," she says, tightening her grip on my hand without looking over. "I didn't even realize that it should be on my L.A. bucket list, but now I don't want to miss a single second of it."

I love the way she eats up every new experience as if it'll be her last. It feels like a dream. Sitting on my wraparound porch with a girl I've imagined having here dozens of times. Wondering what it might be like to see her face as the sun fills the sky, doing exactly what we're doing right now.

"I'm glad you stayed," I tell her.

She turns to look at me. "Want to hear something wild?" she asks.

"Always."

"I've never had someone waiting for me when I get home. Other than Liv, of course, when we were in college, but I mean someone who's there wanting to take care of me."

Oof. That spot in my chest that ached for two days after Abby took me to her childhood neighborhood suddenly twists open again.

She tightens the blanket up around her shoulders, still bare underneath.

"How is that possible?"

"When I got to L.A., I was dreading what it would be like to live somewhere with a house manager and a gardener — all these people in *my space*. I knew it'd be better than staying anywhere near Brett, but I thought I'd be hiding out in my room and counting down the days until I got back into my empty apartment back home." She chuckles, like she can't believe she's saying that now. "But it's going to be the second thing I miss the most after I get back." She grins at me and I think, from her face, that I'm the first. "How have I gotten to be thirty years old without having experienced that?"

"Most people have never experienced living with a house manager," I tease, knowing it goes so much deeper.

She laughs, and I lightly tug her arm, pulling her up onto my lap. She settles in against me, tucking her head just below my chin. I tighten my arms around her, no space between us.

"I don't mean that I've missed out on having a house staff." She laughs, gently pressing her elbow against my ribs.

"Then what have you been missing?" I mutter into her hair.

"Feeling what it's like to come home."

I kiss the top of her head, wishing I could make any of this easier on her. Hoping I already have.

She goes on. "I've never come home at the end of the day to see someone who's genuinely excited to see me." I look down at her as she stares into the rising sun. "It's like pulling back the curtain on the type of life I've never even allowed myself to think about."

"And you've had that here," I say.

"Every single day."

She sniffs and takes a sip of her coffee, setting the mug down on the table beside us.

"I've spent my whole life not knowing how wonderful it could be if I let someone in."

It feels as though my chest splits straight down the middle. How can anything I say fix the heartbreak she's been caught up in for her entire life? Or the realizations of a life that could have been?

She smiles up at me, as if embarrassed, then adds, "You want to know the worst part of this, now that I've finally found someone that I like saying good morning to?"

I nod, but I think I already know the answer.

"That I'll be leaving you here when I head back to New York at the end of all this."

It feels like a gut punch, hearing what I already knew come out of her mouth. "We can cross that bridge when we come to it," I tell her, pressing my lips into her, breathing in the sweet scent of her hair, already feeling the weight of missing her. The truth is that even though my parents were wonderful parents, I've never come home day-after-day to anyone who has missed me, either.

All this is making me realize that some voids in life can't be felt — it's not until they've already been filled that you realize the hole was there all along.

"How ironic is it that we had all that time in law school, where we lived on the same campus, and I waited all this time to finally date you?"

I laugh.

"It was hardly wasted time," I remind her.

"But it could have been so much more meaningful."

"Maybe we needed it to happen this way so we could appreciate each other more by the time we got here."

She pulls back then kisses me, slowly, and if she's trying to make her lips do the talking for her, helping me recognize everything she's feeling in this moment, she's doing a pretty good job of it. By the time she pulls away, I never want her to stop.

"I don't know how I got lucky enough for you to give me a second chance," she says, settling back against my chest.

"Third," I remind her.

She laughs.

"Third. I don't know how I got lucky enough for you to give me a third chance," she repeats correctly.

"Some things are worth having," I tell her. "Even if it takes a few tries."

Then we finish watching the sun rise, until the entire sky is as bright as I've ever seen it.

CHAPTER 36

Dax

As it turns out, maybe some things *do* change. Maybe second — or third — chances have the power to change everything.

CHAPTER 37

Abby

Starry, Charlie, and Olivia are sitting at the kitchen island with a sizable stack of blueberry pancakes between them when I walk in. There are two empty plates — for me, and I'm guessing Dax, if he had decided to come back with me. But he walked me up to the door, leaving me with a kiss and the promise of a call later.

It's nearly eleven, so it's pretty much exactly what I was expecting to see when I walk in. Coffee and the sunrise turned into another round of making love, this time in the shower. Which then turned into a second round, that time in his bed, before Dax turned me loose for the morning so I can spend more time with Liv before she heads back home tomorrow.

It's a quick trip, but I'm so glad she made it.

Charlie eyes Starry when I walk in, and they both quietly excuse themselves to go run some errands. Starry gives me a hug before turning toward the door.

"Good morning," I say, smiling, turning a bit red, like I'm returning home to my parents the morning after being out late for prom. "You don't have to run out of here."

"I'm going to take care of some errands in town with Charlie first, to give you some time alone with Olivia. She's been keeping us in stitches all morning with stories about her and Dom. You two have a lot to catch up on." She winks.

"Are you hungry?" Liv asks, grabbing the stack of pancakes off the counter after Starry and her husband have headed out. "Let's go outside. It's too nice out to be sitting in here any longer."

We walk out to the pool deck and settle into two lounge chairs, picking bites of pancake off the plate while taking in Quinton and Selma's incredible view.

"Spill. Everything," she says, facing me.

I don't know what type of smile comes across my face next but Liv immediately rolls onto her back and starts laughing.

"Never mind, you don't even have to say it out loud. I can see it written all over your face. You and Dax *made* fucking *love*, didn't you?" she yells into the view, like she's announcing it to the world. "When you didn't come back last night, I knew it. You always come back home right after you've been with him, but here you are. It's late morning, Abs, and you're just barely walking back in. I feel like I need to throw you a party for losing your virginity or something."

I roll onto my back, smiling up at the black-and-white striped umbrella canopy stretched over our heads.

"I definitely didn't just lose my virginity." I throw her a look.

"In a way," she shoots back, grinning. "The I-didn't-run-away-from-meaningful-sex-last-night virginity counts, too. Possibly even more than the other kind."

I laugh, then relent, considering the wisdom in Olivia's words. "Fair," I say, stealing a warm blueberry off the top of the stack. It tastes like it was sprinkled in cinnamon.

"You like him," she says, pointing a finger at me.

"Of course I like him." That should be obvious.

"No, I mean you *really* like him, Abby. You aren't even the same person around him anymore. The woman I left behind in New York last year, and the woman you are right now are two very different women," she says, wistfully. "It's like you've blossomed from love."

"Oh my gosh!" I roll my eyes at her, genuinely feeling so happy that she's here with me, especially to hash through all this. "When did you suddenly become a poet?"

"Love makes everyone a poet," she says, dreamily, grabbing my hand. "When's the wedding? Can we make it a double?"

"Oh my gosh, stop!" I laugh, rolling back over.

She laughs happily. "I'm kidding about the double wedding thing though. Of course I'm kidding! We each need our own. Just promise you'll get married at Dom's estate over in Hawaii. You have to come see it first."

"Liv, please," I say, quieting my laugh. "Let's just slow it down here."

"Fair enough. How are you feeling about everything?"

"Excited. Happy. Everything about last night felt exactly right." I sigh, remembering the moment we rolled over in bed together to fall asleep, Dax wrapped around me, pillows propped up beneath our heads. It was perfect. Then I knit my brows, adding, "But also a little nervous."

"That's completely normal," she says, nodding.

"Normal?"

"To be nervous at the start of a relationship? Hell yes, that's normal. No one wants to get hurt, especially after opening themselves up."

I eye her, wondering how much of my anxiety is normal.

"Abby, whatever level of nervousness you feel right now is going to be normal for you. Stop trying to analyze it, and just enjoy it. Imagine the start of a relationship where you didn't feel any butterflies at all. It'd be disappointing. This feeling you have right now? It can be the most delicious part."

I smile, absorbing her reassurance that just because I'm feeling a bit jittery doesn't mean that Dax and I are doomed to failure.

"Okay, if you insist. I'm going to trust the process," I tell her.

"I wouldn't say this about many men, but I trust Dax when it comes to how he's going to treat you. It's been six or seven years since I last saw you guys together and I only had what you told me to go off regarding how he felt about you. Even then, I felt like he was a good catch. But after seeing him around you this weekend? Abby, he's the real deal. I swear."

I smile.

"You think?" I ask, still grinning.

"I do." She nods happily. "I really, really do." Then she frowns and smiles all at once, as if it's taking all her effort to hold some silly tears back. "I'm sorry," she says, fanning her face. She blinks and one falls out. "I'm just stupidly happy for you."

I laugh and shake my head, watching her get sappy while absolutely loving everything about it.

"We watched the sunrise out on this huge porch he has. It's, like, long and full of rocking chairs facing the skyline. I don't know why, but I always envisioned myself having a porch like that."

"Because it's the quintessential wraparound porch that every kid dreams of having," she says, smiling and swiping at her eyes. "I think everyone imagines having the perfect porch to rock on beside their person when they get older. Like it's a rite of passage into secure adulthood or something."

"You know, you might be right," I say, smiling wider. I never thought of it like that.

"I'm never wrong, Abs." She grabs another bite from the stack. "I mean, at least about other people's love lives." We laugh. "Now, I don't know what is going to happen next between you, but whatever happens, promise me one thing?"

"What?" I ask.

"Promise me you'll just enjoy this." She holds my hand across the gap of chairs. "You deserve every good moment he brings into your life. So just soak it up."

* * *

The next day, it's already time for Olivia to hop on a plane back to Hawaii. Starry has tucked a Tupperware of salted chocolate-chip cookies in her bag for Dom, along with a separate one for Liv to snack on along the way.

"Come visit soon. Bring Dax. Maybe once this deal is done? God knows you deserve one hell of a vacation after all this work. Plus, you already have all those new beach clothes. Just head west instead of east for a week."

"I'll let you know what happens here," I say, unsure of what a partner offer from Brett might entail, once The Nile deal concludes. That will be both exciting and horrible, since it means my time here will be done. "I might have to fly back for a few partnership meetings at the New York office right away or something. But I'll keep you posted."

"Okay," she says, wistfully, giving me a hug. "Just don't forget that little realization you had on the beach the other day, alright? About having a life outside the office? I'm going to hold you to that."

"I won't forget," I promise, hugging her tightly.

"You've worked your entire adult life for this, and I'm so proud of you. But just think long and hard before you accept it with this particular firm," she whispers into my ear. "I don't want you going back to that office with Brett yelling in your face, making you fall back into your old ways. You know how I feel about him. You deserve a hell of a lot better."

"I won't," I tell her, not completely trusting myself yet. "Once I'm a partner, I can explore other options. I just need the title first, and then I'll consider making the jump elsewhere."

She stares at me, but pulls me in for a second, final hug before heading out to the car where Starry and Charlie are waiting to give her a ride to LAX. It's about time for me to get back to work too after playing tourist with Dax while the owners of The Nile Group took a few days to mull everything over. We're reconvening this week for the start of what we all hope will be the final negotiations.

I watch them go down the long driveway, Liv waving out the back window at me, and remember how I felt just a few weeks ago, driving down that same path all alone with her on my phone, realizing how much has changed for me since that night.

CHAPTER 38

Dax

Trudy, a paralegal, sticks her head into my office, but her eyes only meet mine for a millisecond before she turns them on Silas, taking in every inch of him from head to toe.

"Oh, I'm sorry, I didn't mean to bother you both," she says in a voice as sweet as honey, which is very unlike her since Trudy usually sounds like she smokes four cigars on any given day and cusses like a sailor.

"I'm sure," I reply, shooting Silas a funny look.

She's the sixth female paralegal to find a reason to come in here this afternoon, ever since Silas' private jet finally landed back in L.A. today.

I lost track of where he was in the world after Spain. Frankfurt, I think? Maybe South Africa after that. Something about a once-in-a-lifetime chance to see the elephant migration over the plains there.

God knows.

"What is it, Trudy?" I ask.

"Oh, it's just that this was left on the printer," she says, holding up a few pages that I'm not even sure are printed on.

"I have a printer in here," I tell her. "Or did you forget?"

"Oh, gosh, that's right!" she exclaims, not even looking at me. She's studying Silas a bit closer, grinning. "My mistake."

Instead of leaving, she stands there, like maybe our billionaire client might ask her out or something. Silas is oblivious. He's picking out which scotch he wants to pour from the new collection his assistant sent over last week to replace the previous set of bottles he had sent, even though half of them weren't even open yet.

"Is that all, Trudy?" I ask.

"Unless you need me to do something? Take notes maybe?" she suggests.

"Take notes about Silas' experience with elephants?" I say, deadpan.

Trudy nods enthusiastically, then digs into her pocket for a pen.

"I can certainly do that," she says, shuffling over toward the couch, flipping the blank pages over.

"I was being sarcastic, Trudy," I say, gently. "I'll let you or any of the other five paralegals who have come in here today know if we need anything."

"Right," she says, then turns to Silas. "I'm Trudy, by the way. Did I mention that? Let me know if I can do anything for you. Coffee, snacks. Anything at all—"

"Thank you, Trudy," I interrupt, then nod toward the door.

She turns to go, just as Lila breezes in.

I groan.

Then I do a double— no, a triple — take at her. Lila, who's normally pretty drab at the office, has a full face of make-up on, including a fresh coat of hot-pink lipstick.

"Oh, Mr. Davenport!" she says, stopping in her tracks, like she's surprised to see him.

Mr. Davenport? Really?

Silas looks up from his stash of fresh scotch bottles on my overflowing bar cart.

"I'm Lila. Lila Lancaster," she says, batting her eyes. "I've been working with Dax on The Nile deal for you the last few months."

"Well, hello Lila Lancaster," Silas says, suddenly losing interest in the scotch.

I look at Lila, and sure, she's cute — she has legs up to her neck, and red hair that falls into a long mane when she lets it down like she has now — but she's certainly not the type of woman that I imagine would catch Silas' eye. He tends to go for the real supermodel types, as in, just off the runway.

"So glad you were finally able to join us," she says, sliding into my wide, corner couch.

Us? Did we invite her in?

I stare at her until she finally stops drooling over Silas long enough to catch my stare. She narrows her eyes and jerks her head to the side, like she wants me to stop making it obvious that this whole charade is mildly entertaining.

I crack a grin.

She shakes her head, nearly imperceptibly, but her eyes flick back to Silas when he speaks to her again.

"What can I pour you, Miss Lancaster?" he asks, his voice smooth as glass.

Christ.

"I'll have whatever you're having," she says, neatly. "I hear you have quite good taste."

"In most things," he says, winking.

I clear my throat.

"Okay, you two, uh, we have some things to discuss. The Nile Group hasn't been impressed with anything we've been throwing at them, so I'm glad you're in town now, Si. Lila and I have come up with a new strategy that involves you doing—"

"I don't think I want it anymore," Silas interrupts.

Lila chokes on the glass of whatever he's just handed her, then stares up at him. The hearts that were floating around her eyes a moment ago have disappeared.

"You don't want it anymore?" she repeats, as if she's just heard that a bomb might go off down the street and it's her job to verify the threat.

"The Nile Group?" I ask, clarifying along with her. "You've changed your mind about wanting it?" His face curls into a mischievous grin, and I close my eyes. "Fucking hell, Si," I mutter, setting my own glass down harder than I mean to.

"Nah, I don't think I want it anymore. Don't worry, I'll go in with you guys tomorrow to break the news. And pay you, I dunno, double whatever I owe you for taking all that time away from our other deals."

Lila shoots me a panicked look.

"You don't have to pay us double for the hours we've already put into this, Si," I tell him, slowly. "There will be other deals. But we should talk about this. We've publicly positioned Davenport Media for months, and have a hostile takeover plan sitting on a hair trigger right now, waiting for your command to start it. I have everything ready to implement, which is what I was going to suggest today, actually, before—"

"Sir," Lila interjects, blinking rapidly. "We've been working on this for months. An entire team of Harper and Associate partners in the M & A division. You're looking at losing a staggering amount of money here if you decide to—"

"Yeah, no worry, Li. Can I call you Li?"

She melts into the couch a little, seeming to forget what's happening here.

"If . . . if you'd like," she stammers, before turning her eyes on mine, looking helpless.

"I'm thinking we head over to grab dinner tonight, the three of us, before we go in for the last time tomorrow to clean up the mess I've made," he says. "Have you tried that new place over on Sunset? The one with that Iron Chef. I met him in Cambodia last year."

"Si, with all due respect, if you pull out now, after all that's been made public, after everything we've put into this, your reputation will have significantly less clout behind it for the next deal we go into. As your friend, not just lawyer—"

"Lila, can we have the room, please?" Silas interrupts me.

She stares at him for a beat before jumping to her feet, placing her tumbler of scotch on my desk.

"Uh, sure," she says, then walks briskly from the room, glaring at me once her back is turned to Silas.

Once the door shuts behind her, he turns to me.

"You enjoy having the last few weeks with Abby?" he asks, grinning like the Cheshire cat. He bites his bottom lip, trying to hold it in.

I blink a few times, and narrow my eyes at him, shifting back on my feet.

"Don't tell me . . ." I can't even get the words out. He starts nodding, grin growing wider. "You set this whole thing up to get me on the same deal as Abby?"

I can hear the anger in my voice, though I don't exactly know why. If Silas wants to waste hundreds of thousands of dollars on attorney bills, plus probably more when this hurts his reputation, that's on him, not me. To a billionaire, that's a small drop in the bucket, but it's still a stupid way to spend his money.

He laughs, then pours another splash of Macallan into his glass before adding a second splash for me — one I don't think I can stomach right now.

"You were shaking like a leaf about seeing her in New York again last year. It made me see how bad you still had feelings for her. We needed to see that unfold naturally here. Give you a few weeks to flush it out, see how you really felt without a whole country between you."

"*We?*" I ask, still stuck on the first half of that explanation. The one that makes no sense whatsoever. And yet, the whole scenario fits Silas to a tee, doesn't it? The guy's officially gone off the deep end. It might be worse than I thought. "Si, this is a multi-billion-dollar deal. The Nile is going to be the next

Amazon, for Christ's sake. It's a career maker for me. How could you not want it? Especially now that we're this close?"

"Eh," he says, shrugging. "Let her have it. Your career is already made. There will be other deals."

"*Let her have it?*" I repeat, crumbling inside at what I'm hearing. "You really mean to tell me that you never wanted this thing to begin with?"

"Nope," he says, picking up his favorite stack of darts, then drains the glass to set it down.

"Si, money doesn't grow on trees, man. Just because your dad left you a lot of it doesn't mean—"

"I don't want it," he says, pointing a dart squarely at my chest, suddenly serious.

I take a step back, defeated. Speechless.

"Just come to this last meeting tomorrow. Hear what Lila and I have planned out for the next steps."

"Is this a career maker for your girl on the other side?" he asks, studying me. "From what I hear, it is."

"What do you mean *from what you hear*?" I ask, feeling like I've entered the twilight zone.

"Let's go have you make her career tomorrow then, bro," he says, throwing the first dart. "She'll love you for it. Money can't do everything . . ." He pauses, grief flashing behind his eyes. "But if it can bring two knuckleheads back together, then it's money well spent."

"Abby would never want this handed to her," I say, feeling the need to argue with him over this.

Abby will be ecstatic to know The Nile Group is now free for her client to take, just like she planned all along. But, knowing my friend set this whole thing up with the hope of bringing us into each other's orbit again?

No.

If she ever found out that Silas basically feigned his interest in The Nile Group, just to get us in the same city for months on end, it would embarrass her horribly. Make her feel like this whole thing between us was engineered by forces she couldn't control, that I couldn't control but which had everything to do with me. I won't do that to her.

"Let's just go together tomorrow and see how you feel after hearing what Lila and I have ready to go for you," I tell him. "Just consider it, alright?"

He walks toward the board to pull all three darts out of the middle ring.

"I'll do whatever you want," he says, grinning. "Except change my mind."

CHAPTER 39

Bringing Silas was a bad idea.

I can tell immediately that this was a mistake.

Every woman we pass on our way into the conference room trips over herself when he walks past, and he grins widely at each one of them, lapping it up.

Even after yesterday's shocking news, Lila is still dressed in a cherry-red business suit, with a sultry new hairdo to match her equally new *I'm single* vibe. I've never seen her put so much effort into her appearance before, and she smacked my words away when I tried pointing it out.

"He's our *client*," I reminded her, when she showed up looking like that this morning.

"And I'll never have another client again, if I can bag a man like that," she'd said.

Having grown up with Silas I know that sure, he was always a good-looking guy, but it's amazing what public knowledge of an inheritance like his has done for his likability. Si could have any woman in this building with a snap of his fingers today, and probably half the men, too.

A few minutes after Abby walks in with Brett, my phone vibrates in my pocket with a text from her.

You didn't tell me Silas would be joining us today.

I shoot Abby a quick reply, keeping it short, before the current owner of The Nile Group stands in the middle of the room, asking for the meeting to start.

I couldn't. There's a work wall between us, remember? We don't know each other personally when we walk into this room, or regarding anything that happens re: this deal.

My phone vibrates again, just as the owner is thanking us all for being here, extending a special thanks to Silas, "who's been rather busy," she says, smirking before adding, "according to the media."

It's a final text from Abby:

You're right. Sorry. Yes, the work wall is back up.

She smiles at me, almost imperceptibly, from across the long table.

I couldn't have warned her that Silas was coming, and she knows that. It wouldn't be ethical for me to give her any leg up regarding this deal. Plus, telling her that Silas would be in the room today would have sent her and Brett into a frenzy last night, trying to figure out what his presence would mean for their client today.

I wish I could respond, *It'll all make sense soon, Abs,* but I can't.

Instead, Silas stands abruptly, telling the room he has an announcement to make.

A few murmurs break out, and I completely avoid Abby's face, knowing I won't be able to hide my feelings if I lay eyes on her right now. And that's the last thing she needs, with Brett sitting directly to her left. We've almost made it through two months of negotiations without Brett catching any whiff of something happening between us. Once we make it out of here today, we're in the clear.

Lila kicks me under the table when Silas clears his throat, then shoots me a look that says, *you've got to be fucking kidding me*.

I wish I could apologize for Silas being an idiot, but all I can do is nudge her back, hoping my apology is known through my foot hitting hers, instead of my words.

"Hey everyone, thanks for coming today," Silas starts, giving the room one of his best megawatt smiles.

I breathe through my teeth and tuck my hands into my lap, steeling myself for the show stopping moment he tells the room we aren't interested in the deal anymore.

Abby and I will be celebrating her induction into the New York firm's partnership by tomorrow with the news coming out today, I'm sure of it. Which keeps her in New York, and me here in L.A., licking my wounds as the laughing stock of the M & A world. Losing a multi-billion-dollar deal on account of an out-of-control client is not something I want to deal with, and the residual effects of this will surely follow Lila and I around for years to come. Especially as we get to work on Silas' next deal.

"I came here today to let you all know that while I appreciate allowing Davenport Media to join you in the endeavor to acquire The Nile Group, my company will be pulling out, effective today."

An audible gasp circulates the room.

Fucking hell.

I can feel Abby's eyes burn into me, but I force myself to keep my eyes on Silas. I won't even look over at Lila right now, who's likely just as stoic and controlled.

The owner of The Nile Group pushes her chair away from the table and nearly stands up, but thinks better of it and stays seated.

"So, Abs," Silas goes on, grinning right at Abby. "Hi, by the way. Good to see you again."

My stomach plummets to the floor. I avoid Abby's face at all costs.

Don't say anything stupid, Si, I'm mentally screaming at him, straight-faced, wishing I'd warned him not to earlier. But I couldn't risk warning him off, because I didn't even want to plant the seed of stupidity in his head. Bringing him here was like bringing a loaded gun to play Russian roulette with the group of people gathered, but all I can do is sit here, holding my breath, praying to God that he's not about to humiliate me or Abby with whatever comes out next.

"The Nile is all yours," he goes on while I nearly pass out from lack of oxygen. "And by yours, I mean your client's. You've won, Miss Torres. I'm out."

Brett turns to Abby, looking like a bulldog that's just smelled a new pile of shit.

"As you wish, Mr. Davenport," she says, in a measured voice. "Thank you for making us aware of your withdrawal in person here today."

I can tell she wants to look at me, but she won't let herself.

"Let's all grab a drink the next time I'm out in New York, eh?" he says, smiling, just as Lila scoffs audibly beside me. "Celebrate that new partnership offer of yours."

He winks at her.

Brett looks at Silas, then back at Abby, who looks like she might be sick.

Finally, Brett stands and holds out his hand to Silas. They shake hands over the table, and Silas holds his hand out to Abby next, waking her up from whatever stupor has glued her to her seat.

I feel nauseous.

She stands up next, which causes a ripple effect of people standing up around the table, some clapping, others shaking their heads.

Abby's client has won. They are the new owners of The Nile Group. This makes it official.

I finally steal a glance at her face, but she's white as a ghost.

The room clears out quickly. There are press calls to be made, and statements to go out. Lila herself is probably halfway back to the office right now, leading the charge on a fresh

PR campaign she was working half the night on, to try and save our reputation as a competent M & A division after this complete disaster of a final quarter fallout.

I've assured her that the media has always seen Silas as a loose cannon, and that this latest move will only be seen as on point for him, but she's desperate to not let this affect our other clients, or have them pull out of any of the ongoing deals we're working on.

A few colleagues are shaking hands with Silas and me, thanking him for being here today, saying whatever else they can think to say that isn't along the lines of, *you idiot*.

Finally, Brett takes us both aside, thanking us for relinquishing our position today. I can tell he's ecstatic about the deal, though a little intrigued about the other part of Silas' speech. The part he should have never said.

"Thank you again, Mr. Davenport," Brett says, stealing his attention.

Abby is standing beside Brett, but looks as if she wants to hide. I need to keep Silas moving before anything else comes out in front of her boss.

"I am curious, though, you mentioned celebrating Abby's — *Abs'* — partnership offer at our firm, and you seem to know her. If you're at all interested in moving your M & A business over to New York, I'd love to set up a meeting, led by our newest partner here, of course, if that's what you have in mind."

Brett's fishing for business. He assumes that Abby must have impressed Silas enough to catch his eye in a business sense, and was hinting at wanting to work with their firm when he made that comment about celebrating her promotion.

I see Abby let out a slight sigh of relief when she hears this too, then manages to give me a polite smile — smart enough to keep any familiar undertones out of it.

"Oh, yeah, sure, I appreciate that," Silas says, shaking Brett's hand harder. "But I'm very happy with my team here at Harper and Associates." He claps me loudly on the back.

"Just like our girl, Abs. She's pretty happy with them, too, I think. Or, at least this one here."

Silas beams at me, happily.

Fuck.

My stomach lurches. He has no idea what he's doing right now.

"I think we're going to head out for a celebratory round tonight," I try to steer the conversation off course.

"Happy with *you*?" Brett interrupts, shifting his eyes to me.

"But, I turned it down," Abby quickly spits out. "The job offer. With Harper and Associates. I turned it down, didn't I, um, Mr. Harper?"

She swallows, then digs her eyes into mine, silently begging me to catch on.

"Right, the *job offer* — yes, she turned it down," I say, trying to save face.

"They tried to poach you?" Brett asks, turning toward Abby.

"Dude, you didn't tell me you tried to give your girlfriend a job," Silas says, slapping me on the back again. "You cheeky little son of a gun."

I swallow.

Abby's jaw hinges open.

Brett jerks his face back to Silas, as if he's not sure he heard that correctly.

"Girlfriend?" Brett says, throwing silent daggers over at Abby.

"Yeah, they're pretty cute, right?" Silas folds his arms, grinning, eyes darting between us.

Abby's jaw won't close.

She blinks a few times, as if slapped across the face, stunned by Silas' words.

Brett turns to Silas. "Torres has been dating your attorney?" he asks, looking gobsmacked.

"Let's all go out to celebrate your new partnership offer, Abs — what do you say? My treat? I've been wanting to catch up with you ever since Dax mentioned you'd seen each other over in New York. I always thought there was more to you two than what you had back in law school."

"Silas, stop talking," I say under my breath, but it's too late.

Abby's whole face has gone white.

Brett's gone silent, but his face now resembles a big, angry tomato.

"*What?*" Silas asks, turning to me, genuinely unaware of the mess he's just unleashed into Abby's life.

Just as everything was finally sliding into place for her.

CHAPTER 40

Abby

I reach for another one of Starry's cookies. I've been here eight weeks now, and I'm pretty sure that means I've earned a few new curves from her cooking.

However, I think as I take another bite, *it's been worth every calorie.*

A shocking part of me felt relieved when Brett ended the meeting earlier today by threatening my job, instead of offering me the partnership promotion. And yeah, I felt just as surprised by that sense of relief as I felt when the words about Dax and my relationship came tumbling out of Silas' mouth.

"He has to approve my removal through the partners," I explain to Starry, who's pouring a few glasses of red wine to go with the cookies this time, including one for Charlie, who's sitting right beside me.

"I still can't believe that guy had such loose lips today," he says, frowning.

I pull a pink streamer off the lamp beside me. I came home to a kitchen decorated in streamers, balloons, and a cake Starry had made with *Congratulations to Our Newest Partner!* written across the top in frosting.

Something broke in me then and I started laughing, overcome by the irony of everything that had just unfolded. We'd finally won The Nile Group for our client, and somehow, I'd still be losing my job. A three-sixty turn of events where no one loses but me.

Dax has already texted that he's on his way over.

"It's really not Dax's fault that his friend is the gossip queen of the century," Starry reminds me, patting my hand, gently.

"Who's this guy again?" Charlie asks. "We try to keep out of all the celebrity gossip. Tends to help us treat everyone equally around here, not knowing the dirt on people when Selma and Quinton have friends from the industry over to the house."

I pull a paparazzi photo of Silas up on my phone. He's shirtless on a beach in Australia.

"Okay, almost the most handsome man in all the world, second to my Charles, perhaps, but still a gossip queen, if you ask me," Starry admits, taking my phone for a closer look.

"What are you going to do?" Charlie asks.

I shrug.

"A little soon to ask, dear." She hushes him. "She's only just lost her job. And not if the other partners don't agree."

"I'm sure the other partners will agree to let me go, once they hear that I've been having a relationship with one of our opposing counsel through the biggest deal of my entire career," I tell them. "It's my fault, really. I take full responsibility for what's happened. I knew better than to continue on with this relationship. I could have waited until the deal was over."

"Still, this Silas guy shouldn't have blurted all that out right in front of your boss," Starry says, handing me back my phone.

"Dax says he really doesn't think he did that on purpose. He's just kind of oblivious to the way the world works for those of us with ethical legal standards, as dumb as it sounds. I think he's fairly harmless."

Starry tsks, then wipes up a spot of something on the counter with her apron. "Poor excuse, if you ask me. And after you've worked so hard to get that promotion," she says.

The intercom screen in the corner of the kitchen rings like a doorbell, letting us know someone's at the gate. Starry shuffles over to see who it is.

An image of Dax in the driver's seat of his car pops up on the screen.

"Hey, it's me," he says into the camera. "Still okay to come up?"

Starry turns toward me, and I nod.

She presses the speaker button. "Come on in, sweetheart".

She hits another button that'll swing the gates open for him.

"Before he gets up here, I want to say something, if that's alright," Starry says, coming back over to the enormous island.

She turns to grab a few dessert plates and a knife from the cupboard, likely for the cake we still need to demolish since there's no reason to keep it around any longer. I feel guilty she went to all that trouble.

"Abby, the girl you were when you showed up here all those weeks ago is very different from the girl you are now," she says, sounding just like Olivia. "I don't know whether it's the fact that you've been living with Charlie and me, who've really grown fond of you, or because you've seen the sun a bit more than you have in years, or if it's because you've simply let yourself fall for someone. But I want you to take all that into consideration when you decide what to do next. You have a big nest egg saved up, I imagine, since you haven't spent all of that big money you make on vacations and entertainment, I'm guessing. And certainly not on clothes," she adds, under her breath, a sarcastic twinkle in her eye.

I chuckle at my own expense, but nod. She's right about everything.

"They might give me some type of severance, too," I add. "Maybe, maybe not. Either way, yes, there's time to figure something out for myself."

"Then you don't need to do anything rash just yet. You have time, hon. And time's a luxury, believe me. I think you have an opportunity to do something with your life that'll make your heart happy, and not everyone gets that chance. Only the really lucky ones do."

Somehow her words make my eyes sting. God knows I've shed more tears here over the last two months than I have in the last few years.

"How did you get so wise?" I ask, patting her hand.

There's a knock at the front door. My heart pounds.

"I think that's our cue to head out," Charlie says to Starry. "Give these two kids some privacy."

She nods in agreement. "We've got to go get some work done, too. Quinny and Selma are coming back next week."

I smile sadly. "And I'll be headed back to New York by then."

"Hope not," she says, winking. "I'll go let Dax in, and then we'll be off."

"I'll get him," I tell her.

"There's cake here for you two, or you guys can throw it off the cliff out back if that feels better," she says, pointing to the platter. "We're heading to their other beach house in Malibu to check on a few things in case Quinton and Selma plan to go there for a few days while they're in California, so we won't be back until tomorrow. There's dinner in the fridge. You just have to heat it up."

I already miss Starry terribly. Without letting her finish, I step in front of her to stop her from spinning through the kitchen, still pointing out things she's prepared for dinner.

She looks up at me. "Am I forgetting something?" she asks.

"Just this," I say, hugging her tightly. "Thank you. For everything."

CHAPTER 41

Abby

Dax walks into the kitchen with me. We're heading outside, but he pauses when he sees the cake sitting on the counter. He stares down at the frosting letters that spell out *Partner*.

"I feel like the worst person in the world," he says.

"I was going to just cut the *Partner* part off and congratulate myself anyway," I tell him.

He looks at me, confused.

"Maybe this will be a good thing in the long run?" I suggest, shrugging.

I feel like I'm having an out-of-body experience for even thinking this way, a far cry from how I'd have felt about this massive blow to my career a couple weeks ago.

"What happened to working in your office eighty hours a week, sleeping on your futon, and having a panic attack at the mere thought of spending a weekend away from the office?" he asks, looking at me as if I've been replaced by someone else entirely.

"You and I both know that type of life was burning me out," I say. "I think I've also come to the conclusion that the only reason I wanted to work with Brett was because he kind of became this weird, toxic father figure to me. Always scolding me and keeping me in line. Which is an entire can of worms I'm probably going to have to open at some point in counseling, but I'm going to table it for now."

He studies me closely.

"Daddy issues with Brett?" he repeats, cocking a brow.

"Yeah." I smile. "Liv suggested that years ago, but I brushed her off. After the last few weeks, I'm starting to see that she might have had a point."

He frowns.

"You're not upset about Silas opening his mouth about our relationship?" he asks, taking a small step toward me. "I came here expecting to grovel for a second chance. I already let Silas have it for blowing up your career in there."

"You yelled at him?" I ask, feeling a bit of guilt seep in.

"He had no right to say any of that in front of your boss."

"No, you're right. But, like you said right after, I really don't think he did it on purpose. He truly looked like he was happy for us, and wanted to take us out to celebrate." I laugh, thinking back to the way Silas was beaming at all three of us after letting our relationship status slip in front of Brett.

Dax looks like I've knocked the wind out of him. "I literally spent the entire car ride over here yelling at him about it," he says, cringing.

I wince.

"There's only one thing Silas said that upset me," I say, taking a step toward him.

"Only one?" he asks. "I can't imagine picking out just one thing."

I laugh.

"What was it?"

"It was the part about me being your girlfriend," I tell him.

He closes his eyes, defeat settling over his face.

"That's just Silas being Silas," he says, shaking his head. "Don't be mad about it. I swear he was just being an idiot regarding everything that came out of his mouth today."

"No, that's not why I'm mad about it," I say, closing the gap between us.

"Then why?" he asks.

"How come I had to find out that I'm your girlfriend from your friend, instead of you?" I ask, grinning widely and then kissing his lips.

Dax finally smiles, letting a long breath out, and I think it might be my most favorite grin I've ever seen on his face. Even better than the ones that tell me something extra fun is about to happen between us. This one looks utterly joy-filled and free.

"You want to be my girlfriend?" he asks, his grin suddenly lopsided.

"Are you officially asking?" I tilt my chin up for another kiss, loving the feeling of his arms sliding around my waist, pulling me closer to him.

He kisses me, his lips warm and wanting, telling me the answer without saying a word.

"Yes, Dax, I will be your girlfriend," I tell him, nearly kissing his teeth, he's smiling so wide.

I pull the cake closer and grab the knife Starry got out before leaving. Then I slice the word *Partner* out and toss the piece into the bin under the sink.

Dax laughs.

"I think *Congratulations Abby* is a better use of this cake compared to anything that has to do with Brett, or my job back in New York right now," I tell him. "And these will go perfectly with it." I pick up a little bowl of strawberries from the counter and hold one up for him to try.

He takes a bite, leaving only the stem pinched between my fingers.

I wait for a review while he chews. This is actually really important to me.

"That doesn't even taste like a strawberry from the store." He looks impressed, kissing me again at the end. "It's so much better."

"I grew it." I beam.

He looks surprised.

"You? Not your urban gardener?" he teases.

"Well, I had help from Charlie," I tell him. "I'm planning to take over from the gardener when I get back to New York. There'll probably be some trial and error, learning by myself, but Charlie promised to walk me through it. We're going to have a standing FaceTime call every Sunday until I get the hang of it myself."

His eyes shift away when I mention New York.

"I haven't been officially let go yet," I gently remind him. "I'm guessing I'll go through a formal review process regarding our relationship with the managing board, and who knows, maybe they'll keep me on? Or maybe I'll resign before they can put the black mark on my job history."

"You've worked your tail off for years over there. You deserve that partnership offer, regardless of what came out of Silas' mouth today. You earned it. No one can question that."

"We'll see if they think I've earned it or not. If they decide to let me go over us having a relationship, they'd be within their rights. I can admit that."

"If it does go south, what about a job here at my firm? I saw you in all the negotiations. You were the most talented attorney in there."

I swallow, imagining leaving everything behind in New York.

"I don't know if working together would be the best thing for us," I admit, pressing pause on the panic rising up in my chest. But this time, the racing heart doesn't stem from the idea of working with Dax or living in L.A. It comes from the idea of continuing to work the hours that were killing me back home. "Thank you, I really appreciate it but . . ." I try to find the right words.

"I get that," he says, nodding. I can see he understands, and probably even agrees.

"I want us to be together," I tell him firmly. "But we have time to figure something out. Maybe I'll switch things up for myself, professionally. Follow a new path, something that fulfills me more than the heady life of an M & A associate with impossible hours."

We smile at each other, and I know he gets it. Neither one of us is going anywhere when it comes to what we want from each other. Even if that means taking some time to try long distance.

He kisses me, deeply. Then pulls back to ask, "Say that first part again? Out loud?"

"The heady life of an M & A associate?" I say, smirking.

He throws his head back to laugh. "No, the other part."

"I want us to be together," I whisper into his smile, kissing him again.

"Okay, now continue," he says, opening his eyes back up, like I've just shone a light on his whole world.

"Is it too much, to try a new career path doing something that might fit me better? I've always had this idea of trying the social work side of the law. Maybe look into starting an adoption firm, or something geared more toward the kids having a positive experience during the process since I know firsthand how scary it can be. I don't know. Does all this sound too far out of the realm of possibilities?"

He tucks my hair back behind my ears.

"It actually sounds brilliant," he says, cradling my face with his hands. "You are brilliant. And don't let this scare you but . . ." He pauses and I wait to hear whatever is not supposed to scare me. "I'm falling in love with you, Abby Torres."

I wait for that familiar feeling of fight or flight to pull at my gut when the words come out of his mouth, bracing myself for the onslaught.

Sweaty hands. Racing pulse. The way my feet get itchy, wanting to walk away from the depth of emotion barreling my way.

But none of that happens.

Instead, I only feel . . . excited.

"I think—" I start to say.

"Shhh," he says, holding a finger up my parted lips. "Don't ruin this by scaring yourself any more than what I've just done."

I laugh, and he joins in.

"No, I want to say that I think you can finally stop chasing your tail," I tell him, holding up another strawberry for him to bite from my fingers.

He bites, but looks me square in the eyes.

"That's a start," he says, kissing me after.

My heart pounds in my chest.

I grab his hand to start leading him out of the kitchen and down the long hallway that leads back to my room.

CHAPTER 42

Dax

I turn back to swipe the bowl of strawberries off the counter, then start to follow my girlfriend down the hall.

My *girlfriend*.

It seems too good to be true.

She stops halfway down the hallway and turns around, pushing a hand against my chest so she can get back around me toward the kitchen.

My heart sinks. She's spooked. That was even shorter-lived than I thought. Maybe it was too soon to tell her how I've felt ever since we took that ride on the Ferris wheel.

"What is it?" I ask, bracing myself for that awful flight response of hers to take over.

"I forgot I got something to go with the strawberries," she says, rushing toward the fridge.

I wait in the hall, hoping she reappears with a bottle of chilled champagne under her arm or something, but instead, she's holding a can of whipped cream.

"It's a celebration, isn't it?" she asks, grinning wildly.

I laugh, beyond grateful she's not in flight to the airport.

She holds the spray can high over her shoulder as she closes the distance.

"Open," she says, tapping my chin with her finger.

I open my mouth and tilt my head back.

She sprays a mountain of whipped cream into my mouth, then kisses me once she can't fit in any more.

We laugh, pulling away from each other, a bit of white cream on her bottom lip. I nip it off, tugging her back in for another one of those sweet kisses.

"I've never tried this," she says, grinning. "I've only seen it in the movies. Maybe we'll have to take this into the shower to keep the mess at a minimum, or something."

"What types of movies are you watching?" I ask, laughing. She pushes the can against my chest, rolling her eyes. "You're trying a lot of things you haven't ever done before this trip," I add.

She takes a deep breath, then looks into my eyes, suddenly more serious than she was just a moment ago. "There's one more I want to try." She lifts her face up to mine.

"Anything," I tell her.

She blushes that deep shade of pink I love. Then rises onto her tiptoes. But instead of speaking, she rakes her fingers through my hair then drags her palm down my cheek, studying my eyes intently.

"What is it, Abs?" I ask more gently, praying that whatever she's about to say is nothing that's going to tear her away from me.

The amber pools of her eyes deepen beneath her lashes.

"I want to tell you that I think I love you, too," she whispers, so quietly that I'm not sure I've even heard her right.

"You think?" I ask, pushing her hair back from her eyes.

Her eyes crinkle at the sides, and she nods.

"No, I don't think, I know. I *know* that I love you," she whispers louder, then her eyes gaze into mine and she repeats it, more firmly this time. "I love you. And if I'm being really honest with myself, there's always been a part of me that has always known. I've never been able to forget about you. Or how safe you make me feel. All the way back to law school, as long as I can remember knowing you. No matter how many times I tried to fight it, or deny it, or just be stupid about it, the feeling of wanting you in my life has never left me. At least, not here." She taps her temple, grinning. "Or here," she adds, placing her hand over her heart. "There's a solid chance that I never admitted it to myself because I was afraid that once I did, it wouldn't work out."

She watches my eyes, looking so nervous that it nearly breaks me. But it's all there, filling her face so clearly that there's nothing left in me to question what she's saying.

"I don't plan to go anywhere," I tell her, pulling her hand away from her heart, and placing it over mine. "Can you feel that?"

"Of course. Your heart's pounding like a damn racehorse." She laughs, blinking up at me.

"No one else has ever made me feel the way you do," I tell her. "I've wanted you since the first time I laid eyes on you. Some people just feel *different*, the moment you meet them. That was you for me. Different, somehow. I think you're my bookend, babe."

She presses her forehead into my chest to laugh, but when her eyes land on mine, all the nerves and uncertainty have drained out of them. Instead, she just looks happy.

"There's another thing I've been dying to do," she says, lowering her voice, glancing down the hallway.

I don't wait to hear what it is. Instead, I pick her up and put her over my shoulder while she squeals.

"Tell me on the way," I growl, feeling like I might burst open if I have to wait one more minute to show this girl how much I love her. "Which door is yours?"

"Seventh one down on the left!" she shrieks.

"Seventh?" I repeat, groaning. "You didn't tell me you had to hike to your bedroom every night."

She giggles. "It'll be worth it, I swear."

The hallway may as well be a mile, but I race down it. I don't want to waste another second.

I don't even have to count the open doors to know which one is hers. It's like a miniature version of her apartment back home. There're potted plants everywhere. Tiny yellow sunflowers burst open near one of the windows, succulents and tiny strawberry plants are scattered across a ledge, and a tree that's taller than me sits in a big, black pot in the corner.

I slowly bring her feet back down to the floor, looking around.

She spins around, smiling.

"I was planning to take them all back with me," she says, sheepishly. "I hadn't figured that part out yet, or I was just going to leave them here as a thank you to Selma and Quinton for letting me stay the last couple months. I know Charlie would find a place here for all of them. I just wanted a chance to learn how to take care of everything in person while I had him here to show me. He's been amazing, teaching me everything he knows."

I walk around, fingering the waxy leaves from another tall tree. Everything in the room looks like it's thriving, including Abby.

"You did all this?"

"No urban gardener. Just me and Charlie, but he made me do most of it. I mean," — she laughs — "I *wanted* to do most of it."

I watch her walk around, touching each plant as if it's a living breathing part of her. The same girl I saw back in New York, surrounded by her own tiny jungle, but somehow, everything about her is different. She matches her surroundings now. Vibrant. Alive. Growing and expanding in every which way.

I take her face in my palms and kiss her gently.

"You're beautiful, you know that?" I tell her, hoping she can finally see how amazing she is. She leans back to look into my eyes. "Now more than ever."

She kisses me again, then pulls me down on the bed with her, leaning back into the mattress.

"For the love of God, make love to me, Dax," she says. Then her hands curl up around my shoulders, and she brings her face up to meet mine, raking her nails through my hair as I position myself above her. I feel her hips press off the bed beneath me.

There's a whole future between us rolling deep in her eyes — where one had never been able to exist before.

She pulls her shirt up over her head, then pulls mine off next, tossing them both off the bed. I pull a condom from my pants pocket before those go off next.

"Do you want me to grab the can?" I ask, pointing to the whipped cream I left near the door.

"I thought I might," she says, kissing my neck. Then she whispers into my ear, unraveling something held tight within me, "But, I think I just want you, and only you, right now. Is that okay?"

I grin.

"I never thought I'd turn down covering you in whipped cream, but yeah," I whisper, smiling down at her. "I think just the two of us sounds pretty perfect right now, actually."

I pull both our pants off next, then whatever's left beneath. Then shift the bed sheet up across my back, hoping it's enough to keep her warm.

She bends her knees around my hips, a slow invitation for me to push in, drinking my eyes in with hers as she does.

I kiss her gently, our lips lingering and soft, every move between us slowing everything down, making the feeling swirling between us more clear, as if everything is unfolding exactly as it should.

Nothing feels rushed.

I want to take my time loving her.

Because this time, she's not going anywhere.

I kiss her neck, then her lips, dragging my mouth across the smooth, softness of her skin, wanting to remember forever the way her hips rise to meet mine, the tiny gasps escaping her lips when I nip that sensitive spot beneath her ear, the scent of vanilla and cream on her tongue, and the hungry look in her eyes, saying more than any carefully chosen words ever could.

Our breath mingles, and she grabs on to one of my hands, pushing our palms together when I thrust inside her, gasping gently when our bodies melt into one.

She moans into my lips, then finds my eyes, intertwining my fingers in hers.

We move together, rocking gently beneath the sheet as she wraps her legs around my hips, her breath hot and wanting in my mouth, tiny moans escaping her.

"Dax," she whispers into my ear. "I want you."

She kisses my neck, but I don't take my eyes off her.

I tuck the dark hair back from her face, moving slowly inside her, pressing my forehead into hers, desperate for this moment to last until the end of time.

"And I love you," she repeats her words from earlier.

"I will *never* not love you," I answer, kissing her cheeks, each one at a time, before pressing my lips into hers, feeling her breath quickening with mine.

I try to make the moment last as long as I can, memorizing everything about her looking up at me the way she is, no fear left in those big amber pools as they begin to summit the mountain we've begun climbing together.

And I cover her mouth with mine, rendering her speechless, knowing, with everything in me, that I will never love anyone more.

EPILOGUE

Abby, nearly two years later

Olivia's face fills my phone screen. It's a familiar scene, her and I eating a meal together through a FaceTime call. Something we've done hundreds of times at this point, possibly more.

"You're positive you and Dax don't want to take the jet?" she asks. "You two could really make good use of that bedroom in the back . . ."

I look up, wondering if anyone can hear her talking through that wall of glass in front of me. Outside, the sidewalk looks crowded, but no one seems to be paying attention to the conversation happening in here. And besides, the person I'm waiting for hasn't arrived yet, though they're only a few minutes late so far.

"Yes, I'm positive. Dax and I are perfectly happy flying commercial." I grin. "You're already being nice enough to offer us your oceanfront villa to use for the ceremony, for crying out loud. We don't need to steal your collection of private jets, too."

"Then I'm upgrading you both to first class," she says, firmly. "Send me your confirmation number for the reservation so I can make the call now, since those seats tend to go pretty quick on long flights."

"Have you told Dom your news yet?" I ask, scrolling through my email. She's practically glowing through the screen.

Liv's face flushes, somehow looking even more happy than it did just a moment ago. "No," she says. "I want you here when I do that. Why else do you think I'm dying to get you over here as fast as possible?"

I sigh happily, feeling over the moon for her.

Just then, the bell dings above the door.

I look up.

A little girl walks in, holding tight to the hand of the woman beside her. They both look around at the office; it's their first time here. I've made it as warm and welcoming as I can, using Starry's help regarding how to do that. Floor lamps are scattered across the room instead of using the harsh fluorescent lights overhead, and there's a warm candle burning on my desk that smells like apple pie, along with big cushy chairs and couches for clients to sit on. There're at least a dozen plants scattered around the room as well, courtesy of Charlie.

My home away from home.

"I gotta run," I tell Liv.

I grab the freshly-baked plate of salted chocolate-chip cookies from the table behind me and a couple bottled milks from the fridge. Starry insists on dropping off a fresh batch of her secret recipe every other day for the kids that come in.

"A little feeling of home for everyone who walks in," she told me when she came by the day I opened my doors for the first time.

"Are you Miss Torres?" the woman asks, looking over her shoulder at the sign over the door. It reads *Miss Candi's House*, with *Abby Torres, Owner and Managing Partner* beneath it. I know it's an unconventional name for a law firm, but I think it makes the place a little less scary for the kids that come in with their guardians. Plus, Miss Candi absolutely loved it when I told her about the idea, giving her blessing at least fourteen times when I asked if I could use her name.

"I am!" I say, beaming down at the little girl. "And who do we have here?"

Although I'm still across the room from her, I kneel down to the girl's height so I can greet her at eye level. She's thin as a rail, which seems to make her big, brown eyes look even wider.

She hides her face behind the woman's leg. "Kayla," she says, shyly.

The girl's probably six or seven, though sometimes the kids that come in are far older than I'd guess, given how small they are.

"Kayla, it's nice to meet you. My name's Abby." She comes a few steps closer when I hold up the plate, eyeing the cookies. "I'm so glad you could come today. My friend dropped these off this morning." I glance up at her guardian, who in this case I know is her aunt. Then back down at Kayla. "Would it be alright for your aunt to have one of these?"

The girl smiles shyly but giggles, nodding up at her aunt, like I'm being silly to ask her permission.

Her aunt smiles at me, gratitude filling her eyes, and takes a cookie off the tray. Then she looks down at the girl, squeezing her hand.

"Now, I'll ask your aunt." I wink at Kayla before turning to her next. "Aunt Sarah, would it be alright for Kayla to have one, too?"

"Of course," Sarah says, nudging the girl forward.

The girl grabs two from the tray, and I smile at her, happy to see her shyness fading quicker than most.

"Do you want one, too?" Kayla asks, holding one of her two up to me.

"Oh, I always want one," I tell her, then take my own from the tray, "but you can keep both of those for yourself, if you'd like."

I spend the next hour talking with Sarah about how the adoption of her niece will work, while Kayla plays with a few toys in the corner and a mix of children's songs are piped in through the speakers Silas insisted on wiring in, even though I told him a simple Bluetooth setup would suffice. It keeps whatever Kayla hears to a minimum while we go over the details.

Silas had insisted on funding the building for *Miss Candi's House*, along with the children's corner of toys, which looked like FAO Schwarz had exploded every possible toy all over the room when Dax first gave him the green light to handle it. I had to scale the toy collection back, keeping over half of them in storage for the coming years, when the current toys get too worn and I need to swap some out.

Silas, who swears he's eternally sorry for the little snafu with Brett, also insisted on funding the wish portion of the firm himself indefinitely. *As in, forever.* The kids that come in here with their guardians are all granted a childhood wish — either something they tell me they'd like to do, or one they pick out from my Wall of Wishes across the room.

Kayla's been playing with a doll this whole time, mostly pretending to feed it cookies and fake foods from the little toy kitchen in the corner. I don't know the reason for sure, but I can imagine why.

"Kayla, I have a question for you," I say, calling her over when I'm finished finalizing the adoption plan with her aunt. "Two questions, actually."

Kayla skips across the room, the doll held tightly in her arms.

"Question number one," I say, sitting cross-legged on the floor. "Would you like to keep that doll for yourself?"

Her whole face lights up and she hugs it tighter.

"Yes!" she shouts, then quickly looks at her aunt for permission.

"What do you say?" Sarah asks, smiling.

Kayla turns pink, suddenly shy again. "Thank you," she says.

"Second question." I hold up a second finger. "If you could choose to do anything in this whole city, what would you do? What's one thing that you've always dreamed of doing?"

She raises her eyes to the ceiling, deep in thought, and I purse my lips, trying not to smile too wide or make her feel silly. I just love this part the most.

"There's a big wall of ideas over here, if you need a little inspiration," I tell her, pointing to the mural I painted across one side of the room. It's a big rainbow with at least a hundred different shades, each one adorned with a different wish a child might like, paired with a picture of each wish for the kids who can't read yet.

Most of them pick the bigger wishes like a day at Disneyland or the Santa Monica Pier with their guardian or new family. Others surprise me by picking smaller things, like a milkshake from wherever they choose, or a trip to the store for a new set of clothes. And then there's the ones who simply break my heart by asking for the tiniest things off the top of their mind instead of choosing one from the wall, like a heavier jacket, or a breakfast from McDonald's.

I never try to sway them to choose bigger wishes though, knowing how powerful and in-control the ability to choose something about their own destiny can help them to feel. I always wish I could grant each child a thousand wishes each.

Kayla points to the lightest blue portion of the rainbow — the one that shows a day at the beach.

Sarah bites her lip beside me, choking back a fresh set of tears.

"I've never been to the beach," Kayla says, eyeing another cookie from the tray. "I almost did once, but my mommy changed her mind."

I hand her the biggest cookie off the tray, first tucking it into a napkin.

"It's amazing," I tell her, remembering my first day at the beach with my best friend and my fiancé as one of the very best days of my life. "We're going to make that happen for you, sweetheart. Second chances are everything, aren't they?"

We come up with a plan and I send Kayla and her aunt off with a little tin of cookies for later. I'm waving them off when I see Dax walking down the sidewalk, passing them as he comes toward me.

He lights up when he sees Kayla with her little tin of sweets as she skips down the street, then he pulls me inside by the waist as he gets to the door.

"I don't know if I'll ever get over seeing how happy you make the people that come in here," he says, kissing me gently. "I'm not completely sure, but I think it might come close to how happy you make me."

I bite my lip, flipping the door sign over to read *Closed* from the sidewalk.

"That was my last appointment of the day," I tell him. "We're officially on vacation mode. Liv is insisting on upgrading us to first class for the flight tomorrow."

I laugh, and he pulls me into him for a long hug, the feel of which might never grow old. I close my eyes, breathing the spicy notes of this morning's cologne on his skin.

"Of course she is." He kisses my neck. "What else are sisters for? It's not every day you fly to Hawaii to get married." Then he moves his lips up my neck, finding that spot just beneath my ear. The one that always makes my knees feel weak. "Did you know that this might be our last chance to make love on a Friday afternoon in L.A. as two unmarried people?"

It sends goosebumps flying down my arms.

"Obviously, it would be a tragedy to not take advantage of that," I say, tilting my head back, granting him free access to my neck.

He drags his lips past my jaw. "Funny, I had the same thought," he says.

I pull the window shades down over the door and windows.

He takes both my hands and pulls me toward him, but stops for another kiss.

"I love you," Dax says, looking into my eyes. "Possibly more than I ever did."

"You tell me that every day," I whisper, kissing him back. "And every day, it's true."

He kisses me again, slower this time, until his words melt into actions and he shows me just how true it's always been.

THE END

ACKNOWLEDGMENTS

First, thank *you* for holding this book in your hands. Connecting with readers has always been at the forefront of my work, and I want to thank you for picking this book up. Although I can't, I would hug each and every one of you if I could.

This book was not in my original plan for the series. Instead, I wrote the third book in the Off-Limits series before I ever started on this one. But because Fate does not always go in a linear path, and because I always want to see my own girlfriends enjoying their very best lives, this story was created out of pure necessity. Not to mention, every single person who read *The Best Wrong Move* (before it officially came out) immediately asked if I was planning to write Abby's story next. Thank you, all of you, for letting me know that I wasn't the only one rooting for her. We *all* wanted to see Abby get the beautifully complicated happy ending she deserved, full of redemption and second chances, because that's just the type of girl she is.

That's the type of girl we *all* are.

A huge thanks to my very first editor of *The Best Wrong Move*, Emma Grundy Haigh, who was the first to suggest that Abby may need her own story next. And to my utterly brilliant editor of the Off-Limits series, Becky Slorach, who formally championed Abby's book as the follow-up to my debut. I don't know what I've done in life to put me in the path of such wonderful humans, but I feel incredibly lucky to be working with you on these tiny pieces of my heart. You've made each book so much better, and the experience of publishing with Joffe is a dream come true. Thank you to the entire team at Joffe and Choc Lit for believing in this series.

Abby and Olivia's books each have one secondary love story — the one between them. Two friends who became each other's sisters. Without experiencing that type of bond myself, I couldn't have written about it. To Gundi, Molly, Noelle, Steph, Danae, Laura, Sarah, and Jordan: thank you for being a part of my family. Whether you were born into it or not.

Thank you to my mom, who cried with me over my first major book deal, and to my dad, who couldn't stop smiling. Forever thanks to my kids, who make me so proud to be their mom. I hope you always linger at the dinner table to keep talking with your dad and me long after the food has been finished. I thought a lot about you while writing Abby's story, and about how lucky we are to have each other.

And last, but never least, to my husband. I can't think of a time you thought to say no, but instead have always been the one to whisper, *why not?* I'm convinced there's no better partner in the world.

THE CHOC LIT STORY

Established in 2009, Choc Lit is an independent, award-winning publisher dedicated to creating a delicious selection of quality women's fiction.

We have won 18 awards, including Publisher of the Year and the Romantic Novel of the Year, and have been shortlisted for countless others. In 2023, we were shortlisted for Publisher of the Year by the Romantic Novelists' Association.

All our novels are selected by genuine readers. We are proud to publish talented first-time authors, as well as established writers whose books we love introducing to a new generation of readers.

In 2023, we became a Joffe Books company. Best known for publishing a wide range of commercial fiction, Joffe Books has its roots in women's fiction. Today it is one of the largest independent publishers in the UK.

We love to hear from you, so please email us about absolutely anything bookish at choc-lit@joffebooks.com.

If you want to receive free books every Friday and hear about all our new releases, join our mailing list here: www.joffebooks.com/freebooks.